pretty much

perfect

OTHER BOOKS AND AUDIO BOOKS

BY SALLY JOHNSON

The Skeleton in My Closet Wears a Wedding Dress

Worth Waiting For

a novel

Sally Johnson

Covenant Communications, Inc.

Cover image: *Nature Has Music for Those Who Listen* © PeopleImages, courtesy of istock.com.

Cover design copyright © 2018 by Covenant Communications, Inc.

Published by Covenant Communications, Inc.
American Fork, Utah

Printed in the United States of America
First Printing: July 2018

22 21 20 19 18   10 9 8 7 6 5 4 3 2 1

ISBN: 978-1-52440-392-8

To Jon Bon Jovi, the rock star I have yet to meet
and
to Bradley James, the actor who plays Liam in my mind

Acknowledgments

STEVE AND MY KIDS DESERVE the biggest thanks of all. They are always understanding, supportive, and encouraging. I love you all.

Thank you (as always) to my editor, Samantha Millburn. I appreciate all you do for me, especially being calm when I'm stressed.

I have a great bunch of friends who have helped out immensely along the way: Missy Krueger, for all the help with the British; Trisha Luong, for being the other half of my brain; and Meghan Jacobsen, for being so willing to read and give me feedback. I appreciate my daughter, Esther, for always wanting to read and give suggestions. Thank you to Lori Parker for helping me with my plot holes that felt like sinkholes. And, of course, my mom. I knew the story was a good one after she finished reading it and told me a few days later she missed Liam.

Chapter One

"YOU REALIZE YOU DON'T HAVE any pants on?" I asked as I rolled the window down.

"Thank you, luv, for so kindly pointing that out." His British accent was unmistakable.

The morning had been a bit crazy, even before I'd come upon the guy walking on the side of the deserted road in just an odd-looking T-shirt. The sight of him had snapped me out of my autopilot, cruise-control haze. As I'd gotten closer, I'd realized the shirt was way too big for him and it had a stiff crease running diagonally down it from one shoulder blade and what looked like a tire mark on one sleeve. Was it a starch job gone awry? Something had to be wrong. No one went for a stroll without their pants and wearing a shirt that had been run over by a car.

"But I do have pants on," he continued. "They're shorts. Want to see?" He started to lift his shirt.

My hand shot up. "No. No. Don't show me. I believe you." Even so, I saw a hem of black fabric. At that length, I was suspicious they were more underwear than shorts. I definitely did not want to see anything I couldn't unsee.

He shifted from one foot to the other, looking in one direction, then the other. Was he waiting for someone? Looking for someone? His behavior was hard to decipher.

"Were you involved in an accident?" I asked. Or possibly escaped from a mental health hospital or a corrections facility? I wasn't aware of any remotely close by.

"No, darling, but I was involved in a bit of a disaster." He gave a half-hearted grin.

He looked about my age but older in some unidentifiable way. His good looks were hard to miss. He had short, blond hair that was just long enough on top to be stylishly messy, sky-blue eyes, cheekbones, full lips, the works. But still, was he a weirdo?

"What do you say, luv, are you willing to help me out?" His hand rested on the window frame.

I made a show of locking the door, although I wasn't sure what good it would do. If he wanted to unlock the door, he could just reach in the open window and release the lock. I could always roll the window up if he tried. Having his hand stuck between the window and the frame was bound to be unpleasant.

I had been taught to help those in need, which was why I'd stopped in the first place. And the voice in my head telling me I *needed* to stop. But was it worth the risk, picking up a stranger? He could be a rapist or a murderer or—

"I'm not going to do anything," he said, still leaning in the window.

"What?"

"You're worried, wrinkling your brow." He flipped his index finger in my direction.

"I'm not wrinkling my brow," I said. But when I thought about it, I realized I was.

"You're probably thinking I'm an escaped convict or something. I'm not going to touch you."

"How do I know you don't have a weapon?"

He retreated a few steps from my car and held his hands in the air. "Do you want to pat me down?"

"Thanks, but I'll pass. How about you pat your waist and turn around?"

It's not like he could be hiding a weapon in a pocket, since I didn't think he had any pockets. I mean, I guess he could have pockets, but from what little I had seen of his shorts, they looked like snug-fitting, unusually short shorts—or boxer briefs. Even if they were the latter, they were unlikely to have pockets big enough to hold much of anything.

He turned around in a circle. Then he repeated the motion while patting his waistline. "I just need a ride," he said.

I didn't see anything that looked suspicious. "And some pants," I added, not wanting him sitting beside me dressed the way he currently was. *He* didn't seem embarrassed, but I was.

"Look," he said, returning to the side of the car. He lifted his shirt, and I immediately shielded my eyes. "There's nothing."

I peeked out and could see that the car door covered everything and the waistband of his whatever-they-were was the same height as the window. He turned around again just to prove there was no weaponry there.

"You really need to get some pants."

"Yes, trousers, also. Don't want to get arrested for indecent exposure, walking around in my knickers. That's the last thing I need." He gave a sardonic grin.

Why did he find it funny? I wouldn't be making jokes if I were stuck on the side of the road half-dressed. And "knickers"? I had to give up the notion that he was wearing shorts. They were definitely just undies.

"What do you say, darling? Are you willing to help out a desperate bloke?"

"I suppose I could," I said, wondering if I was making a huge mistake. With a quick glance at the dashboard to check the clock, I did the math. I had to allow myself two hours to get home so I could be to work by 11:00 a.m. I didn't really have time to interview him and do a background check.

"May I get in?"

I nodded.

"I'm Liam," he said once he was sitting. "And you are?" He put out his hand to shake mine.

"Camille," I answered, taking his hand.

"Nice to meet you." He smiled as if he were pleased with himself.

"You should know, I know karate and have a black belt."

"I don't know karate, but I do have a black belt. Well, had one. With my pants." He gave me a helpless grin.

Despite his being half-dressed, he was incredibly charming.

But most liars were.

One minute later, I was questioning my decision.

Why did I agree to this? I looked over at the strange guy with the good looks, the amazing accent, and my hoodie splayed across his lap. He seemed more annoyed than grateful at my insistence that he cover up. He didn't seem bothered that he didn't have pants.

"I'm calling my dad to tell him I picked you up." I snapped a picture and started texting.

"Hey!" he yelled, surprising me. "What do you think you're doing?"

I swerved unexpectedly. Driving, texting, and being yelled at were a bad combination. "A picture sort of guarantees you won't think about trying anything funny." I hit send, hoping and praying there was enough signal to get the message to my dad. I was, after all, in the middle of Nowhere, Utah.

"I told you I wasn't going to touch you. I just need to . . ." He looked around. "Where am I, anyway?"

"You don't know where you are?" Alarm. Maybe I should be worried.

He shrugged. "Well, not exactly. I mean, I know I'm in the States. And last night, I was at the airport. And this morning, I was abandoned on the side of the road. It makes for a very bad day. Throw in a smashing headache, and I would say my luck has run out." He pressed his fingers against his temples.

"You're almost to Delta," I told him. "It's the closest town, and we should be able to get you some pants."

He scrunched his face up. "Delta where?"

"Utah."

"Utah?" he repeated, letting out a breath. "Like, where all the Amish people live?"

"You mean Mormon?" I corrected him.

"Mormon? Is that what they are? The religious people who don't use electricity?"

I laughed. "We use electricity."

He looked at me closely. "You're one of them?"

"Yes, I'm one of them. You could be too," I said.

He grinned. "Yeah, uh, you wouldn't have me."

"Oh, we take anyone." I tried to act blasé, as if nothing he said would shock me.

"Trust me, luv, you wouldn't have me."

He was so smug and yet so . . . I didn't know what. I couldn't figure him out. "You're sort of contradicting yourself. You tell me I don't need to worry about you attacking me, but then you say my religion wouldn't take you?"

"My lifestyle has never been"—he thought for a moment—"religious."

"Maybe you should try it. You might like it."

He snorted. "Or not."

"Watch out, I'm never one to back down from a challenge."

"And neither am I, luv; neither am I."

"Should we stop to buy you a pair of pants before I drop you . . . off?" There was a Walmart in Payson, but that was almost an hour and a half away. And by then, I was only fifteen minutes from where I lived in Springville. I preferred to have him dressed more quickly than that. I was unfamiliar with the area, this being only my second time on this particular road. The first time was yesterday when I drove to my job interview. If I had a better signal, my Google Maps would be working and I'd be able to locate a store sooner rather than later.

"That would be a lovely idea if I had a wallet."

"You don't have a wallet?"

He laughed. "If you haven't noticed, I don't have any pockets."

I blushed, trying not to think about his scantily clad situation.

"Right, so, what's your deal? You're walking along the road half-dressed, without your wallet. Where are you going?" I couldn't help asking. I was curious.

"I suppose the closest city."

"Okay . . . ?" I waited. There had to be more. He had to have had a destination.

He looked at me like he was the one waiting. "And that would be?"

He didn't know? "Like, big city? Salt Lake."

"Salt Lake." He nodded like he was processing the information. "I need to get to the airport. It can't be far, right?"

"Yeah, it is far, but it's not going to do any good for me to take you to the airport. You don't have any money. And if you don't have any pants, security might want to have a talk with you. And if you don't have any ID, you're definitely going nowhere. Looks like you're out of luck."

He rubbed his temple. "Apparently." Even with his face scrunched up in frustration, he was attractive.

"What are you going to do?"

"I'll be fine if I can just get to a phone and make a call."

"You don't have a phone?" This was getting worse.

"Oh, I have a phone. It's just not on me right now."

"That's right. I forgot—no pockets." I momentarily found some amusement in his predicament.

He snickered. "Yeah, no pockets, but that's not why I haven't got a phone."

"Why haven't you got a phone, then?" I was able to imitate his accent perfectly.

He looked at me intently, leaning closer. "The girl I was with last night probably has it right now."

"Ah. A girl. She's at the root of this whole situation, I'm guessing."

"You're guessing correctly." He pursed his lips.

"What exactly happened last night with this girl that landed you on the side of the highway in your underwear and no pockets to carry your money or cell phone?" I glanced over at him, waiting for his response.

He rubbed his forehead. "Honestly, it's all a bit of a blur."

"Were you drinking?" I wanted to know if my hunch was right.

"Actually, I only had two drinks. I'm not usually a lightweight."

"Did you take anything?" Like drugs?

"Allergy medicine."

"Which probably interacted with the drinks."

He pinched the bridge of his nose. "Probably."

"And that's why you have no idea how you ended up in this situation?" How could he be okay with it?

"Oh, I know how I ended up in this situation. It's a small thing called revenge."

I could feel my mouth gape open a little. It took me a second to respond. "Let me get this right: the girl left you here for revenge?"

"Yup." He seemed less bothered by it than I thought he should be.

"Did you just meet her?" That scenario seemed unlikely, considering the revenge angle, but I wanted to get my facts straight.

"Nope." He shook his head.

"So how did you know her?"

"She's my girlfriend. Well, ex-girlfriend now."

How could someone who supposedly loved him do this to him? "And you think that once you get to Salt Lake, you can clear all this up?"

He looked over at me, his expression soft. "I might need your help."

I raised an eyebrow. "You *might* need my help? What kind of help?" He needed a lot of favors. It made me a little nervous wondering what he was going to ask.

"For starters, if I could use your phone."

"Okay." That wasn't too much to ask. Unless he was calling England.

"Then maybe if you could spot me some money so I could buy some trousers."

Money. Maybe he was a con artist or a thief. I eyed him. "That's a little bit forward, don't you think?"

"I'll pay you back." He said it like it was a given. "But I've got to have trousers."

"But how will you pay me back when you have no money and no pockets?" I asked him.

"I didn't say I don't have money. I said I don't have any money on me. I'll pay you back and then some for your trouble."

"Pants and a phone call and all your troubles will be solved?" I was still very doubtful.

"Yeah. Pretty much." He nodded.

"All right, I can agree to that. But you're going to have to wait to make your call."

He looked confused. "Why?"

I motioned to the vast area of nothingness surrounded by mountains that we were driving through. "Don't have much of a signal out here." I hoped his headache made it too hard to think because I still didn't know if the text to my dad had gone through.

"Figures. I can't believe she dumped me in the middle of nowhere," he muttered, taking in the scenery. I wasn't sure if he was talking to me or himself.

We drove in silence for about ten minutes. I tried the radio once we were closer to a more populated area and was grateful when I was finally able to tune in to a radio station. Music could at least fill the silence.

Right as my favorite song came on, he started up a conversation. "So, uh—"

"Oh!" I said, cutting him off and turning up the radio. "I *love* this song."

"You love this song?" He seemed surprised.

"Yeah, it's my favorite," I answered, annoyed that he kept talking.

"Do you know who sings it?" he asked.

I shook my head. "I have no idea. I just really like it."

"It *is* pretty catchy," he agreed.

"Brazen, brazen, brazen," I enthusiastically sang along with the chorus. He did not join in. Either he was impressed with my singing voice, which wasn't too bad, or he didn't know the words. Maybe he was too shy to sing in front of a stranger. I didn't take him for the shy type though. Especially since he was sitting next to me in his underwear and didn't seem the least bit bothered by it.

"You really fancy that song," he commented when I turned the radio back down.

"I do. Sorry for cutting you off," I apologized. "I haven't had radio reception for a while . . ."

"No offense taken." He looked over at me for a second with obvious curiosity. "You honestly don't know who sings it?"

"No." I shook my head and shrugged. "Should I?"

"It's like the number-one song right now."

"Well, that makes sense why they play it all the time."

"The band has played on all the awards shows," he supplied more information.

I looked over at him, my expression blank. "I really don't know. I have been out of the country for the last year and a half."

"Where have you been?" He sounded intrigued.

"New Guinea."

"New Guinea? Why there? Fancy it quite a bit, do you? I'm guessing it wasn't just for holiday?"

I assumed by "holiday" he meant "vacation." "No. I was on a mission."

His eyes widened. "Oh yeah? What was your mission?"

I laughed at how he said it. "It wasn't like a mission on *Mission Impossible*. It was a mission for my church—you know, the Amish."

He cocked his head. "But you said you weren't Amish."

He was paying attention. "I know. I'm kidding. Making a joke. I'm Mormon, you know, LDS?"

"You were a Mormon missionary? Like those guys in the white shirts and name tags?"

"Yes. Except I was a girl in a skirt with a name tag." I loved any chance I got to talk about my mission and the Church. It was one conversation I felt comfortable having with any stranger.

"You did that for a year and a half?"

"Yes. I got home six weeks ago."

"How much do you get paid to do it?"

I shook my head and gave a little laugh. I was asked that many times. "Nothing. It was completely voluntary. I paid for it myself."

"You paid for it yourself?" He sounded incredulous.

"Sure did." I nodded.

"Are you going back? To New Guinea, I mean?"

"Nope. I'm done with my mission. Now I'm at home, working until I go back to school next semester."

"What school is that?" he asked.

"Brigham Young University. BYU."

"That a Mormon school?"

"That it is."

"What are you studying?"

"Marketing or public administration. How about you? Did you go to college?"

He grimaced. "Never went to any higher-level schools. I'm lucky I passed my final year."

"What do you do?"

"Sometimes I work. Sometimes I do a whole lot of nothing. Depends." He shrugged like it wasn't a big deal.

"On what?" I had no idea what he meant.

"It's complicated."

Again, I didn't know what he meant. His work was complicated?

"Are you in sales? Or . . ."

"I work in the music industry. Sales can be a part of it. You just never know. One day you can have a job, and the next day you don't."

Since I wasn't getting anywhere with the "what do you do for a living" questions, I changed tactics. "You're originally from England?"

"London."

"Very cool. I've never been there, but I want to go someday."

I expected him to say something about living there or about living here now versus living there, or even a "You should," but he said nothing. I tried again. "What brought you to the States?"

"Work."

I felt I had to extract every piece of information from him. He wasn't exactly forthcoming. Yet he had no problem asking questions about me. What were we going to talk about the rest of the way home?

"Where do you live?" I asked. He didn't seem familiar enough with Utah to be living here.

"I've lived in several places. New York City. LA."

"And you move a lot?" I fished.

He shrugged. "Gotta go where the work is."

Work again. Whatever that was. Maybe we needed to keep talking about me because he seemed much more comfortable with the conversation then.

Chapter Two

I STARED AT THE MEN'S section in the farm supply store. It wasn't much of a section, more like an area. How did I get roped into buying clothes for some half-dressed guy I met on the side of the road? He was probably outside hot-wiring my car. And guy jeans? I had never bought jeans for a guy and didn't know what to choose.

What size was he? I held up a pair to myself, hoping I could judge what his size might be from comparing it to me. It wasn't much help. I guessed thirty-two by thirty-four. But then, if I bought the wrong size, it would be a waste of time and money. I should just go ask him.

Much to my relief, my car was still there when I went back out.

I opened the door and stuck my head in. "What size do you wear?"

"Thirty-one by thirty-four," he said.

I had guessed almost right. "'Kay. Be right back." I went to shut the door.

"Wait. How about a couple of energy drinks and something for my killer headache?"

"Okay." I turned back to the store.

"How about a T-shirt too?" he called.

Says the man with no money. I faced him, confused. "What's wrong with the one you have?"

"It's not even mine. I found it in the ditch. I think some animal might've made its home on it. It's all stiff and smells a little funky."

I sniffed the air but didn't smell it. "Anything else?" I meant it as a joke because I felt like I was going to have to start writing things down. The list kept getting longer.

"A couple bottles of water?"

Mentally repeating the list, I returned to the store. I bought the first pair of jeans I found. They were not quite the right waist size, but all I could find was thirty-two. I picked up a large white T-shirt with the face of a cow on the front and that read "I herd that." It was on clearance for four bucks. I couldn't *not* buy it. It was funny too. I moved along to the refrigerated display case where the energy drinks were. Having no experience with that sort of drink, I had no opinion on or preference for one or another. I wondered if Liam did. Not that it mattered, because there was only one choice available. I chose two large cans of Rockstar, a packet of Advil, two bottles of water, and two chocolate bars I grabbed on impulse before I was rung up. I also took the opportunity to call my dad and was relieved when he answered.

"Camille?"

"Yeah, hey, Dad. You got my text?"

"I did. What's going on?" His voice had a slight edge of concern.

"This guy was on the side of the road. I thought he might have been in an accident."

"Had he?"

"No, it doesn't seem it. He said his girlfriend dumped him there."

"Are you safe?"

"I think I'll be fine. He just needs some clothes and to make a few phone calls."

"Clothes?"

That did sound weird. "Well, he has clothes, but he needs pants." That didn't sound any better.

There was a loud exhale from my dad. "Camille, what are you talking about?"

I sighed. "I know, I know, it sounds completely wrong. She took his pants to get revenge or to get him in trouble or something like that. I'm picking some things up so he'll be decent."

"So what's the plan? Are you dropping him off somewhere?"

"I haven't asked him, but I will. He says he needs to go to Salt Lake."

"You keep in touch. Call me every half hour to check in, even if you don't say anything."

"Okay, I will. Thanks." If my dad had told me to leave him in the parking lot, I would have.

"Be careful, Camille."

"See you soon." I felt loved as I hung up. It was reassuring when my dad got all Mother Hen.

My good humor was immediately extinguished when I handed Liam my purchases.

"You bought me old-man jeans?" Liam blurted out as he held up the jeans. "Didn't they have anything a little more . . . hip than these?"

"They're not old-man jeans," I replied defensively. "They're just . . . regular jeans."

"I could fit both legs in one side," he objected, inspecting them again.

I paused to maintain my composure. "I'm sorry you hate them, but you need pants. I'm uncomfortable with you in your underwear."

"You did this on purpose," he said. "You want me to look like a complete fool. Like I don't look enough like an idiot."

That was the first time he'd sounded even a little bit remorseful for his situation. He muttered under his breath as he pulled them on. I pretended to be interested in the people walking by in the parking lot. Once I heard the zipper, I figured it was safe to look. I still gave him a few seconds just in case.

I turned to him. "That's all they had." At least now, with pants on him, I could address him during the conversation. It had been very disconcerting before.

He peeled off the dirty shirt. I got a glimpse of a nicely toned abdomen. "You're right. I'm sorry. I appreciate that you bought me jeans. I'm just not real keen on the style." He did sound sincere and apologetic, then he froze. His eyes rested on the front of the shirt. "'I herd that'? Seriously?" he muttered, then pulled it on anyway.

I stifled a laugh.

His eyes moved to the energy drink, resulting in a smile.

Maybe my strange little hitchhiker would be more normal once he was hydrated.

"Rockstar, huh? You partial to that?" He raised his eyebrow.

I shrugged. "I've never tried any of them. That was all they had."

"Never?" He sounded incredulous.

"Nope."

"Why not?"

"They never appealed to me. And I heard stories about kids getting sick by drinking too many of them."

"You can get sick from too much of anything." His voice dropped, almost like he was being suggestive. About what, I had no idea.

He popped open the can and took a long gulp. "That is good. Now I should be able to think. Want some?" He offered me the drink.

"Um, no. But thanks." I was not about to share germs with a total stranger I knew nothing about. He could have some contagious disease or something.

He threw the Advil into his mouth and chased them down with another long drink. "Okay. I'll be feeling better soon."

"So what's next?" I'd be much less anxious once I knew where I was dropping him off.

"Next." He said it as if he were mulling it over.

"Yeah, you know, like, what are you going to do now? From what you've told me, you have nothing but the clothes on your back, and you don't even own those. You need to make some phone calls, get to an airport, and pay me back for all my favors." I ticked the list off on my fingers. "How are you going to do all that?" If I were in his position, I would be completely overwhelmed.

He looked directly at me and grinned. "I was thinking maybe you could take me back to your place."

* * *

"So, this is the young man who lost his pants?" My father greeted us as we walked in the front door.

My mom and dad had been waiting. They were sitting in the formal living room, the only room in the house with windows that overlooked the front of the house. The room we never sat in.

"Yes, sir." Liam stuck his hand out to shake my dad's hand. I could tell he was trying to make a favorable impression. "Although, I don't want to make a habit of that. It could get me in a bit of trouble quite quickly." He still sounded only mildly inconvenienced.

"I would think so," my mother chimed in.

"But Camille was kind enough to purchase me some clothes." He pointed in my direction.

"That he hates," I added.

"I don't hate them. I'm just not very keen on them," he said quickly.

"He said they're dad jeans."

My mom threw back her head and laughed. I'm not sure why she found it so funny.

"I didn't say 'dad jeans.' I said 'old-man jeans,'" he defended himself.

"I hope I don't look like I'm wearing either. Dad jeans or old-man jeans—neither one is very complimentary." Dad patted his own jeans, trying to view them from every angle.

Liam looked from my mom to my dad and gave a hesitant chuckle.

My mom ushered us into the kitchen. "Make yourself at home. Sounds like you have had a very rough day."

"And night," Liam said, but only I heard it.

"Are you hungry, dear?" My mom directed her question at Liam. She was in full-on mom mode.

I hadn't eaten anything other than the chocolate bar on the drive home because I hadn't had much of an appetite. And since Liam had added a disruption to my schedule, I never considered if he was hungry. The chocolate probably hadn't filled him up.

"I'm starving." He patted his stomach.

"What would you like? We can have a late breakfast or early lunch. Camille and her sister, Kaela, never seem to eat breakfast. They're always rushing out the door instead of enjoying a good, hearty breakfast. I think it's really that they're too concerned about their figures," Mom said.

I coughed. "Um, thanks, Mom." A blush crept across my cheeks, though I wasn't sure why. I wasn't trying to impress Liam. It was probably just the way he looked at me, taking in my 'figure,' after my mother said that.

"Bacon and eggs?" Mom suggested.

"Great. I haven't had a home-cooked meal in a very long time."

I took a moment to do a once-over. He didn't look like he was starving. He was thin. Thinner than I liked my guys to be, but it wasn't starving-student thin.

"Grab a seat, and I'll whip up some breakfast. Camille, how about you, honey?"

"No, thanks. I'm not especially hungry."

Mom gave me a sympathetic look. "Things didn't go very well?"

I glanced over at Liam, who was watching me, trying to decipher the conversation.

I tried to sound positive. "I'd rather not talk about it right now."

Mom realized my hesitation. "Of course, honey, later." Then she turned to my dad. "Charles, do you want bacon and eggs too?"

"Sounds delicious," he said.

She went to work cooking up all of it.

"How'd the job interview go?" Dad asked in a low voice.

"Probably time to explore other options," I whispered. I didn't want to share my interview-gone-wrong story in front of Liam. "It was a huge waste of time and a big disappointment."

"That good, huh?" Dad put his arm around my shoulder.

"I'll tell you all the gory details after we eat. I don't want to ruin your appetite."

He gave me a sympathetic look and a pat on the shoulder.

I joined my mom in the kitchen. "How about toast?" I suggested, taking the toaster out of the cupboard.

"Please." Liam nodded. "Thank you."

"So, Liam, tell us about yourself," my dad said. He loved to question any male who entered the house in the company of either of his daughters. He had less of an opportunity these days since I hadn't been on a date since I'd returned home, and Kaela was sixteen and just starting to date. But this situation with Liam was different. He was a stranger, not a guy dating his daughter. I think we all wanted to question him.

"I'm originally from London," he said, clearing his throat.

"I could listen to your accent all day; it's so melodious," my mother said in a dreamy voice.

"I have lived in the States for a couple of years, mostly in Los Angeles. It depends where the work is."

"What line of work are you in?"

"Music. Lately I've been trying my hand at producing."

Why was Liam so relaxed about telling my dad about himself? He'd barely given me any answers in the car.

Liam continued. "If that doesn't work out, I'll need to come up with a backup plan."

"A backup plan is very important," Dad said. "Camille's learning that hard lesson right now."

"Thanks, Dad," I muttered. I loved my dad, but sometimes, in the name of experience, he shared a little too much personal information. Mostly when he was trying to teach his children a lesson. Maybe he felt Liam needed a bit of fatherly advice.

"Oh yeah? What's up with Camille?" Liam's gazed rested on me.

I pursed my lips while choosing my words carefully. "Nothing more than plans not working out the way I thought they would."

"Sorry to hear that, luv. Life can be tough."

I nodded, accepting his sympathy. I wasn't about to explain my situation to a guy I had known for only a few hours.

My dad continued asking him all the typical questions he would ask his daughters' date. Chances of that happening were, like, zero.

"How did you end up on the side of the road?" Mom joined in the questioning, then popped a bite of food in her mouth. I think it was a question we were all wondering about.

"Well, my girlfriend, now my ex-girlfriend, and I were stranded at the airport. We had a layover in Las Vegas, but winds shut the airport down, causing us to land in Salt Lake. We couldn't get a flight out since there were all sorts of delays. We thought it'd be a brilliant idea to rent a car and drive home. But I had some drinks, and so had she, and we were tired and irritable, and that's never a good combination. Then we had a bit of a row, I broke up with her, and she dumped me on the side of the road."

"I see." Somehow, Mom was able to keep her expression neutral.

"We had taken a trip for my birthday—"

"When was your birthday?" my mom cut in.

"Actually, it's today," Liam said quietly.

"Today! And you've had such a terrible day! You poor thing," my mother exclaimed in true motherly concern.

"That must have been some fight," Dad said.

"Yeah, apparently she was still upset about the last fight we had, which led to the next fight we had, which made me break up with her. She's quite keen on revenge."

"Uh-huh." My dad processed the last comment but said nothing more.

"You didn't have much of a chance to celebrate your birthday, did you?" my mom was still in the concerned motherly mode.

"No, no, didn't get much birthday celebrating done today. It has greatly improved though, thanks to your kindness."

I rolled my eyes. He sure could be charming when he wanted to be. But why were my parents falling for it? Both of my parents. My dad was usually a pretty good judge of character.

"The day is not over. You shall have a birthday party before the day ends," my mother announced, a gleam in her eye.

I hesitated. "Mom, what are you thinking?"

"Everyone deserves a great birthday. We are going to do something nice for Liam." She turned to Liam. "What is your favorite meal?"

"Home cooked?"

"Absolutely," my mom confirmed with a nod.

His eyes lit up. "Shepherd's pie, without question," he answered immediately.

"Birthday cake? Any requests?"

"Trifle. But that's more a British thing," Liam added.

"I haven't ever made it, but if you don't mind me trying a recipe, trifle it will be."

"I appreciate it."

"Of course."

I was suspicious. In less than an hour, he had charmed the pants off my parents, pun intended, without so much as their knowing who he really was. For a guy I'd picked up off the side of the road in his underwear, he sure could come off as a pretty normal, very likeable guy.

Chapter Three

I CHECKED THE CLOCK ON the stove. I had less than a half hour to get to work at The Swirly Whirly frozen yogurt place. Generally, I liked my job and was very thankful to have it, except when I was scheduled to work with Harris. He was the owner's son, but he thought he was in charge because he normally did the scheduling. Working with someone who thought I was working for him made for a very long shift.

I had to work today because Harris wasn't willing to change my schedule and no one else was available to trade shifts. Sometimes I thought the guy was difficult just to annoy me. But because I couldn't get out of working, I had to get up at almost the crack of dawn so I could get home in time to open. If I had gotten the job I'd interviewed for, I could have left Harris and The Swirly Whirly behind.

Liam followed my gaze to the clock. "I should make that call now. You do have reception, right?" He looked around.

"And electricity," I joked for good measure, handing him my phone.

"Right," he said. He punched in the number and wandered into the dining room but was still within earshot. "Yeah, it's me. I'm in a bit of trouble." He listened for a minute. "No, I didn't get arrested." Now he sounded exasperated. "More like abandoned." Then, "Yeah, she has my bag with all my stuff in it. Or, I don't know, maybe she chucked it out of the car and it's somewhere on the side of the road."

"Is it okay if they call me back on your number, luv?" He looked at me, waiting.

Our eyes met briefly, and my stomach did a little flip. His calling me "luv" evoked the reaction. I silently nodded.

When he hung up, he sat at the kitchen table, set my phone on it, and rubbed his temple.

I leaned against the counter. "Is everything taken care of now?" I asked with caution, taking in his annoyed expression and possible remaining headache.

"I don't know. We'll see."

Less than five minutes later, the phone rang. Liam grabbed it before I had a chance to check caller ID. It was more than likely for him, but I still would've liked to check.

"I didn't expect her to answer. Call the monitoring company about my accounts. I need you to send me some money and then put a hold on all my cards." He waited, listening, running his hands through his hair and pacing back and forth in front of the sink. He let out a long puff of air. "She's got my wallet, my phone, my passport, my clothes, everything."

Wow. He and his girlfriend must have had some fight. I couldn't imagine being so vindictive.

"Can you try to locate her?" He listened for a minute. "I thought we had made up, but then she started arguing again. Obviously, she thought I needed to pay a little more." He laughed bitterly. "Nothing's changed; you should know that."

He hung up and looked at me. "I need to ask you for one more small favor."

I raised an eyebrow. "Okay, what?"

"Put me up in a hotel."

My mother was not to be slighted as a hostess. "Liam! Don't be silly. You can stay here. We have a guest room."

"Mom, we don't even know him," I said under my breath. "He could rob us in the middle of the night."

Liam did not miss my comment. "I'm not going to rob you. Your stuff isn't exactly my style." He winked.

"Style?" I asked, perplexed. "Do you have a preference?"

He lifted a shoulder. "Let's just say I'm into minimalism." He looked at my mother. "If it really isn't an inconvenience, I would appreciate it and would be happy to pay you back for all your trouble."

"Oh, nonsense; we don't mind. It never hurts to be a good Samaritan."

"Um, Mom, Dad? Elizabeth Smart?" I said, uncomfortable that they were so willing to take in this guy they barely knew. We had no idea who he really was or what he was capable of. When I picked him up, I wasn't committing to anything more than a ride.

I had to run to work, so I missed the final decision. I was against having Liam stay. Sure, I was responsible for this situation because I was the one who had stopped and picked him up, but I hadn't planned on bringing him home when I'd stopped.

* * *

"Hi, honey," Mom called from the kitchen as I came in through the garage. I hit the button on the garage door opener to close it.

"Hey, Mom," I said.

"How was work?"

"Tedious and sticky. Harris made me unload all the toppings and crush the boxes for the recycling bin. And he didn't help. He stayed out front the whole time, even though we weren't busy and he could have helped. It wouldn't have been that big of a deal, but one of the colored sprinkles bags got sliced into when someone opened the box. I didn't realize it, unloaded it, the bag spilled the sprinkles all over the floor I had just mopped, and it was a big, sticky mess."

"Sounds it." Her tone was sympathetic.

"So I'm tired." I sat on the bench in the mud room and kicked off my shoes. The house smelled of homemade cooking. Meat and sauce. My mom must be making pasta for dinner. "And then I went to BYU and UVU to put up more flyers for my fund-raiser on every bulletin board I could find." I sniffed the air. "What is that? It smells delicious." I padded into the kitchen, kissed my mom on the cheek, and dropped my purse and keys on the counter.

Liam was sitting at the island, looking like he had been hanging out with my mom all afternoon.

"Shepherd's pie," Liam announced, a wide smile spreading across his face. He had an incredible smile. His teeth were white and perfectly even. It was probably the most perfect smile I had ever seen. "I haven't had home-made shepherd's pie in years."

My mother beamed, proud of her culinary success. "It's your birthday. You deserve to be treated special."

"Have we ever had shepherd's pie?" I asked my mom. I had heard of it but never remembered actually eating it. I couldn't even think of what was in it.

"No, but now's as good as any to try it. And we have trifle for dessert. I had to call around to a few people before I got a recipe that I think will taste authentic."

"I could've looked it up on Pinterest for you," I said.

"Well, of course, but I knew someone around here had to have served a mission in England. I wanted the real deal."

"I hope I didn't put you through too much trouble." Liam dropped his head a little.

"Again, it's your birthday—no trouble at all."

He looked at me. "Do you know how amazing your parents are? My mum would've never done this for me."

I was sort of surprised my mom was doing it too. I mean, she was as charitable as anyone in the ward when it came to bringing in a meal to someone sick or offering to help out. In fact, I thought she was one of the most charitable people I knew. I was just surprised at the lengths she was going to for Liam, the stranger we knew nothing about. "Yeah, my mom is pretty great."

He sat up straight and became animated. "Pretty great? She's bl—amazing."

Mom didn't even pause to enjoy the compliment. "Would you set the table, Camille?" she asked, stacking dishes on the counter for me.

"Yeah, sure," I said, grabbing them and heading into the dining room. While I set out the dishes, complete with cloth napkins and crystal goblets, Liam wandered around the room, looking at the pictures on the wall. Eventually, he went into the living room and stopped at the fireplace.

He picked up a picture of me from the mantel, standing outside the Missionary Training Center. "Is that you?" He pointed to me.

"Yeah, right before I went to New Guinea."

"What happened to your hair?" He squinted at the picture as he brought it closer to his face.

My hand went up to my head. "I cut it all off." My hair had been long and thick before my mission. It was the color of honey and wasn't really wavy but wasn't exactly straight. It complemented the generous sprinkling of freckles across my nose and my brown eyes. I never really fit into that blonde-hair, blue-eyed-girl look.

He set the picture back on the mantel and turned to me. "Why would you do that? You've got beautiful hair."

The compliment made a wave of warmth wash over me. "I thought if I cut it really short, it'd be easier to take care of." It made perfect sense at the time.

"You just cut it all off?"

"Yup. Then I let it grow back." The decision had been more practical than preference. Thankfully, it was almost back to the length it had been before I'd cut it.

"I like it better long," Liam said.

"Thank you." I wondered why he had an opinion on my hair.

He pointed to a picture of my younger sister. "And who's that?"

"Kaela, my sister. She's sixteen." Her hair was blonder than mine, and she had blue eyes.

"She's not home?"

"No, she's at girls' camp until Saturday. It's a Church thing." I picked up a family picture. "This is my brother, Caleb. He's the oldest and is married with a baby."

He nodded but said nothing.

"What about you? Do you have any siblings?" I asked.

"A brother. Rhys. He's older than I am," Liam said, still looking at our photos.

"Does he live here? Are you close?"

Liam looked at me, shook his head no, and then went back to the photos.

I was slightly afraid to ask about his parents after that.

"Dinner's ready," Mom called, pulling us from our picture gazing in the front room. We went into the dining room.

"It smells delicious," Liam exclaimed, taking in the table. Only the rolls had made it to the table so far, but the aroma was amazing.

Staying with tradition, my mom set a basket on top of the buffet. It was labelled "Check Your Phone."

"'Check your phone'?" Liam read.

"Rules," I said, rolling my eyes. I pointed to a chair across from where I normally sat. "You can sit there."

He went to the chair and pulled it out. "Why no phone?" Liam was genuinely curious.

"My parents are really big on dinnertime being family time. We don't answer the phone, use cell phones, text, or check social media."

"Do they enforce it?"

"Absolutely. Kaela tried to sneak it once and lost her phone privileges for a week. A week without a phone for a teenager is like the worse curse ever."

"Not just teenagers," he said, smiling while managing to look bashful.

"Going through phone withdrawals?" I asked.

He nodded. "Just a bit."

"My parents' point is it's okay to not be instantly accessible all the time. That things can wait, and in a world of instant gratification, learning patience is a good thing."

Liam cocked his head. "It has been nice not having my phone ringing and buzzing all the time."

I pointed back to the basket. "And that's why there are no phones while eating."

"I already broke that rule this morning."

My mom walked into the room carrying a casserole dish with hot pads. "You're a guest. We can make an exception." She smiled.

"Thank you. It won't happen again." Liam pretended to be chastised.

I made a waving motion. "It's no big deal."

Right then, my phone rang. It felt like every head swiveled at the same time to look at it.

"Do you need to take that, Liam?" my mom asked.

"Maybe it's for me, Mom," I said.

"No one ever calls for you unless it's for work," she said.

"That's not true." I frowned.

My mom laughed. "That's not what I meant. Most of your friends know not to call during dinner."

"I always silence my phone when we eat," I said. I didn't want Liam to feel bad that he was breaking the family rule now that he was aware of it. But more importantly, I didn't want Liam thinking I had no social life. And I especially didn't know *why* I was caring what Liam was thinking.

"Camille told me about your rule of no phones at the table. I can respect that," he said as he looked longingly at the phone.

"Maybe it's important." Mom looked concerned.

Liam gave a dismissive wave. "It's always important. If it's for me, I'll ring them back after dinner."

The phone stopped ringing, then promptly started again.

"Go take it," my dad said. "We understand you have things to take care of."

"Maybe it's for me," I repeated.

My parents looked at me. All right, it was true. It was always Kaela who had the problem with her phone ringing during dinner. No one really called me, except, like Mom said, for work. So, okay, I didn't have much of a social life.

Liam pushed away from the table. "Perhaps I will check to see if that's for me."

"Of course you should," Mom said.

Liam grabbed the phone, looked at the display, and nodded at us. "Gwen? Yeah," he said into the phone, making his way toward the front room.

Gwen? Who was Gwen?

The conversation at the table petered out. We could hear most of Liam's part of the heated conversation from the other room. It was much more interesting trying to figure out what was going on with him than anything being said at the table.

"Is it okay if I get something FedExed here?" Liam asked my mom, holding the phone away from his mouth.

"Of course," she immediately agreed, telling him our address.

"Thank you," he mouthed to her.

Like what? I wondered. What was he having shipped here? And then there was his story with his now ex-girlfriend. What was it that didn't make sense with him? Why was I the only one suspicious of him?

Chapter Four

"SORRY ABOUT THAT," LIAM SAID when he returned. He sat and immediately started eating.

"Is Gwen . . . ?" I started asking, then stopped. She couldn't be his ex-girlfriend.

"Personal assistant," he said between bites.

"You have an assistant?" It seemed weird that he would have an assistant.

"I do." After he swallowed, he pointed with his fork to his plate. "This dinner is amazing," Liam said, changing the conversation. "This is one of the nicest things anyone has ever done for me, and not a small thing. This might have been the best birthday I've had."

He was laying on the compliments a little bit heavy. My mom ate it up though. I wondered if he was trying to pretend we hadn't all just heard his conversation.

"It's been our pleasure." Mom grinned. "Now, what's a birthday without presents?"

What could my mom have gotten him? We'd known him for barely nine hours. Seriously?

She placed a lumpy package in front of him.

"Gabbi, you really shouldn't have."

When did they get on a first-name basis?

"Oh, maybe not, but I did. It's not much." My mom waved her hand. "Go ahead and open it."

Liam ripped open the wrapping paper, then paused before lifting the gift.

She'd found him a shirt that had British flags printed all over it.

"This shirt made me think of you. I thought it would go with your dad jeans." She immediately broke into laughter.

"Wow. Thanks. It's absolutely—"

"Hideous," I cut in before busting out laughing.

Liam found it so funny he laughed until he cried. It was nice to see he had a sense of humor too. "You read my mind, Camille. Although I don't think I would've admitted it if you hadn't said it."

"Mom, you shouldn't tease our guest." I had to blot the tears in my own eyes.

"If only I had found this shirt on the side of the road this morning. I would've felt so . . . patriotic."

"Oh, c'mon. The shirt I got you is in definite competition with this one for being the cooler of the two." I motioned for Liam to hand me the shirt. I stood and held it against me. "If it were me, I don't know if finding a flag shirt would make me feel any better." I scrunched my face up with distaste.

My mom walked up to me and hugged me. "You could pull off anything. Even that shirt."

"Not everything," I murmured. "I'm pretty sure I didn't get the job." My shoulders slumped.

"Everything happens for a reason," she said, then kissed me on the top of my head.

I tried to believe her reassurance.

Out of the corner of my eye, I noticed Liam silently taking in the whole scene.

"Would it make you feel any better to know that you have dish duty tonight?" my mom said gently.

"No." I rolled my eyes. "Dish duty never makes me feel better."

"I know," my mom said in a fake, sugary voice. "But at least it's better than having to wear that shirt."

"Okay, dish duty it is," I announced as I turned abruptly.

Liam stood, following my lead. He looked around at the table and then back at me. I felt like he was looking to me for direction. I started stacking the dishes, and Liam picked up the casserole dish.

"Does your mum cook like this every night?" Liam asked as he followed me into the kitchen. I set the dishes next to the sink.

"Uh, yeah. Didn't your mom cook?" I took the dish from him and set it on the stove. Then I covered it with foil and put it in the fridge.

"We only had food you could microwave. I don't know if I ever saw her bake anything in the oven." He paused. "What job were you talking about?"

I realized we had been rude, having the conversation in front of Liam. "I had a job interview yesterday. It was just a temporary position that would end in August at a family reunion ranch. Before I got there, I was confident I would get the job, but now I'm pretty sure I didn't." We walked back into the dining room.

"You don't know that."

"I'm pretty sure." My laugh sounded more bitter than I'd intended. I was trying hard not to let it bother me. I gathered the glasses.

"Why do you think that?" His voice was soft.

I was surprised he even cared. Or was he just being polite?

"They said they would let me know by today."

"There's still time."

I paused before I smirked. "I think the girl who went in before me got the job. I wasn't even given a chance."

He cocked his head and looked at me. "Perhaps the other girl won't work out and they'll call."

"No," I said resolutely. "It's over and done with and wasn't meant to be." I headed back to the kitchen.

Liam was right on my heels, this time carrying the gallon of milk. "That's one way to look at it."

I leaned against the counter and shook my head. "I don't want to work for them now. If they run their business as impulsively as they do their hiring, I don't want to work for them."

"Great perspective."

"I try," I said, admitting my disappointment to myself momentarily. Then no more. I was moving forward, not looking back. "Something else will come along, and it will be great."

"So that's where you were driving home from?"

"Yes." I had stayed overnight with a friend from the mission who lived in Delta, which was sort of on the way home. It was about an hour's drive from the town where I'd interviewed. Along with work, I had a checklist of things I needed to get done before the fund-raiser I'd offered to do for a family in our ward who had a sick daughter. Otherwise, I would've visited with my old mission companion a little longer and also taken the opportunity to drive down to Las Vegas to see Sophia, my roommate from my freshman year at BYU.

"Isn't that a bit far to commute? Would you have moved there?"

I shook my head. "It is far. I would've stayed there for the rest of the summer." It would have been an easy job making good money. It seemed too easy not to have gotten it.

* * *

Against my better judgment, my parents invited Liam to stay the night. I might have muttered to hide the silver as I followed my mom into my brother's old room to help her make the bed.

"Are you sure about having Liam stay?" There was just something about him that made me hesitant.

"Dad and I visited with him today, and then we discussed it between us. We feel okay about it." Even though my mom said it calmly, I still felt like there was a gentle rebuke included.

I sighed. "Okay." I was going to trust my parents' judgment on this one.

When we were done, I said good night to everyone and gratefully went to my room. And I most definitely locked my door.

I took a couple minutes to update my social media posts with the countdown to my event on Saturday and sent a reminder email to those who had expressed interest in coming.

Once I shut down my computer, said my prayers, and climbed into bed, I finally allowed myself to cry. The sadness had been slowly pooling up inside of me, and I couldn't stop the tears from seeping out of me any longer. I had been sort of numb up until I'd run into Liam alongside the road. I knew there was still a small chance I had gotten the job, but I was pretty sure I hadn't. Disappointment enveloped me.

As I lay in my bed, spent from crying, I made my plans to move on. That was the only option. The fund-raiser was a first step for doing that. The next was returning to BYU next semester. I had plenty to keep me busy and look forward to instead of dwelling on a job I didn't get. At least I had a job, even if it was a frozen yogurt shop. If it had been meant to be, it would have worked out. Or at least it was easier to tell myself that than admit to myself how much it hurt.

Chapter Five

WHEN I CAME DOWNSTAIRS THE next morning, Liam was in the kitchen with my parents. He was wearing a pair of my dad's old pajamas and a flannel robe and had really bad bed head. His scruff from two days without shaving was a good look on him.

I raised an eyebrow and suppressed a smile. "For a guy who complained about my buying him dad jeans yesterday, you really look like a dad now."

"Lovely morning to you too." He tipped his head. "Hey," he whispered. "You guys got any coffee around here? I didn't see any this morning." He looked around conspiratorially.

I smiled despite myself. He really had no idea what he was in for in the middle of Mormonland. "Nope, no coffee. We don't drink it. Besides, it's kind of hard to brew it when there's no electricity to turn on the coffee pot." I put two slices of wheat bread in the toaster.

"I'll never live that down. Do you think you could take me out to get one? I'm getting a killer headache, and some Starbucks would be great. I'd even be happy with an energy drink, a loaded Mountain Dew, or anything heavily caffeinated."

Again, he didn't realize he wasn't going to find a Starbucks close by. "You could get some at 7-Eleven or McDonalds." I had to think where the closest Starbucks was.

Liam grimaced at his coffee choices. "Maybe I'll just stick with the energy drink."

"We could pick one up at 7-Eleven after breakfast if you want."

"Yes, let's."

My toast popped up. "Would you like some toast or anything?"

"Sure, toast would be great." He smiled.

"What are you kids up to today?" My mom, who was sitting at the table, stood and adjusted her workout clothes.

"Why, Mom? Do *you* have plans today?" I asked suspiciously.

"I am going to the gym. Then I have some errands and things to do."

Obviously, she had plans, and I was in charge of Liam. More like baby-sitting Liam. I wondered if she was hesitant to leave him in our house alone. I would be. But if she did have any reservations, it would have been the first smidgen of caution I was aware of.

"Haven't you got work?" Liam said.

I shook my head. "Nope. I'm not scheduled today. I'm working tomorrow and Friday, so I have today to get ready for my fund-raiser this Saturday." Phone calls to make and flyers to pick up was only the beginning of the list I was putting together in my mind.

"Fund-raiser?" Liam asked.

My mom looked at me and then Liam. "Camille didn't tell you about her fund-raiser?"

"No," Liam said, then turned to me. "Tell me about it."

I thought my mom would have told him yesterday. What did they talk about the whole time I was at work? "It's to raise money to pay for medical treatment for our neighbor's little girl, Amanda," I said. "She has acute myeloid leukemia."

"Wow. Poor thing."

"I used to babysit for the family way back when the kids were babies. Since nonprofit work is what I want to do for a job, I offered to put this together."

"It's going to be great," my mom announced.

I could feel the heat creeping up my neck. "Mom," I said, feeling self-conscious and worried. "I don't think we should brag about it yet. Let's see how it goes first."

"You're being too modest," she argued.

"No, I'm being realistic. I'm not going to brag about it. What if it's an epic failure?" Which was my biggest fear. I mean, really, what if absolutely nobody came?

"Honey, you need to have a little faith in yourself. You've planned as best you can. I'm sure it'll be really successful."

Even with her assurances, I wasn't so sure. "But I do have flyers and the banner to pick up and then some other supplies to get before the fund-raiser." I finished my toast. "I better get going."

"Mind if I join you?" Liam asked, setting down the piece of toast he was holding.

I forgot that he was jonesing for some coffee and that he was my charge today anyway. "I'm just running errands, but sure, you're welcome to join. I can't guarantee it's going to be that exciting."

"Sounds great." He stood up, seemingly ready to go right now.

"But first, we have got to find something for you to wear other than my father's pajamas."

He looked down at the pajamas like he'd forgotten he was wearing them. "Oh, right. I'll just go . . ." He trailed off.

"Put on your dad jeans?" I offered.

He gave a little laugh. "I guess I have to, huh?"

He turned and looked at my mother and then at me. "Would it be terribly offensive if I didn't wear that shirt you bought me? It's a bit hot out, and . . ."

"It's a bit ugly," I said and started laughing. I could tell by Liam's expression that he agreed with me. "I guess you'll have to wear the T-shirt I bought you."

"I put it in the wash," my mom said.

I looked at my mom and then at the stricken look on Liam's face. This was a rare moment of seeing him ill at ease. "I think there's still a couple of things in my brother's room where you slept. I'm pretty sure his clothes will fit you. We can check the closet."

"I thought you said he was married."

"I did. And he is. But I don't think he really ever cleared all his stuff out."

"Does he have your same sense of style in guys' clothes?"

Was he worried I'd lend him something ugly? "Don't worry." I laughed. "I promise I'll find you something"—I searched for the right word—"benign."

"Thank you. I appreciate it."

Liam and I went to the room he'd stayed in. The bed was made, and there was no trace that anyone had slept there. His story didn't add up, but he was seeming more and more to be a gracious houseguest and a perfectly normal person instead of the psychopath I'd been suspecting. I dug through my brother's drawers, but there wasn't much left in way of clothes. I had to resort to my dad's clothes, where I found a plain, light-blue T-shirt.

"Sorry, you're stuck wearing more dad clothes for a little bit. But I tried to find the least dad-looking shirt I could," I said as I walked back into my brother's room, where Liam was waiting. I'd been looking at the shirt as I'd walked, and when I looked up at Liam, he was wearing his dad jeans and nothing else. He looked very nice. And that was putting it mildly. Especially since I had a chance to really appreciate it. "Uh, here." I handed the shirt to him, unable to say anything more coherent than that. His six-pack was very . . . defined.

He inspected the shirt, then sighed. "I suppose this will do. I really must buy something more proper." He pulled the shirt on. "Do you have a baseball cap and some sunglasses?"

"It's not that sunny out," I said. In fact, it was a little bit overcast. I hoped it wouldn't rain for my fund-raiser. I didn't want people to have any excuse not to come.

He shrugged. "Habit."

I rooted around the hall closet and was able to find him one of my brother's old caps.

"You might have to do without the sunglasses," I said. "I think all we have around here are women's."

He seemed disappointed. "I need to pick me up some. And some clothes too. Is there a mall around?"

"Don't you need some money?"

"Yes. But FedEx is supposed to be here by ten. Maybe we can go after then. But first, caffeine."

He followed me out to our faded-white Honda Civic, which had gone through Caleb and me and looked like it had been owned primarily by teenagers.

I unlocked the car with the key fob, and Liam settled into the car and put his seat belt on.

"Let's get you a drink." I backed out of the driveway, and we rode in silence the few minutes it took to get to the convenience store and park.

Neither of us moved for about five seconds. Finally, Liam spoke. "I generally prefer Rockstar. Would you mind grabbing two?"

I blinked at him a few times, trying to understand where he was coming from. "Are you always this . . . bossy?" I couldn't think of a nice way to ask.

His mouth opened and then closed. "I'm just usually the one . . . Never mind. Sorry." He shook his head as if physically clearing his thoughts. After a moment or two, he reached for the door handle. "Want anything?"

"No, I'm good, thanks," I said.

He got out and walked to the entrance.

"Liam." I rolled down my window.

He looked back.

I held up some money. "Did you need some of this?"

The most beautiful smile crept across his face, almost bashful. He hurried and grabbed the money, mumbling a quick "Thanks."

He came back out a minute later wearing a pair of mirrored sunglasses and holding a large energy drink.

"You probably should have bought two, you know, one for tomorrow."

"Or I might have to have you chauffeur me again." He grinned as he popped open the drink and took a long sip. "Ah. That should help the headache."

"Do you regularly get headaches, or is it a withdrawal thing?" I put the car into reverse and backed out.

"Withdrawal, but I'm not ready to quit." After a few more sips, he spoke. "Tell me more about your fund-raiser."

"Well, it's this Saturday."

"I gathered that."

"I work at a frozen yogurt shop, and they did a fund-raiser for an elementary school last year; that's how I got the idea. So I talked to the family and then to my boss and asked if I could put together this fund-raiser. Since I got the go-ahead, I've been trying to tie it all together."

"You volunteered? This was all your idea?"

I nodded. "It was."

"How did you get into this?" Liam asked as I drove.

"What? The fund-raiser?"

"Yeah, and just that type of thing in general."

"I just like to do it. When I was in Girl Scouts, I always wanted to do the fund-raisers. I'd make posters and decorate them and tell everyone I knew. I was a little bit obnoxious about it."

"But passionate."

"I do love it. My first year at college, I got involved with BYUSA, and—"

"What's that?"

"The student association at BYU," I said.

"Okay." He nodded.

"I loved being involved in making something like that happen. It helped me not only figure out my major but what I wanted to do with my life career-wise."

"What is it about it that you love so much?"

"At school, it was being involved in something that helped others. On my mission, it was just serving people with no expectations of something in return and making a difference. It's kind of like getting this high because you did something nice for someone."

"Doing something that gives you a high isn't a bad thing." He had a grin on his face like he was suggesting something else.

"How about you? Do you like what you do?"

Liam let out a breath. I saw it out of the corner of my eye, but when I turned to look at him, he was back to himself again. "Yeah, I like what I do."

"What got you into music?"

"I'm good at it."

"And humble," I joked.

"Not always," he said, not joking.

I cleared my throat. "Do you enjoy it?"

"Usually."

"Because you like it and you're good at it."

He picked at a thread on his jeans. "Lately, it's been a bit of a struggle."

"Why's that?"

"I haven't been motivated."

"How come?"

He shrugged. "Life."

I didn't know what he meant by that, so I stopped my questions and waited, thinking he would say something next. Or supply a little more information than just a one-word answer. When he didn't, I started up again. But he cut me off.

"The thing I don't get about you going to New Guinea to fund-raise is why you had to stay so long."

I laughed. "I wasn't fund-raising."

"But I thought you said . . . Weren't you there volunteering?"

"In a different way. I was teaching people about the gospel of Jesus Christ. I volunteered to do it. How about you? Do you do any type of volunteer work?"

"Sometimes, but I just show up and do what I'm told. I'm never a part of the planning." He watched the scenery out the window as he said this.

"You should try it sometime. It makes the satisfaction that much deeper."

"I have one more question about New Guinea." This time he turned and looked at me as he spoke.

"What?"

"Was it hard to live there without electricity?"

I narrowed my eyes, confused that he still thought that. But then I caught the big smile on his face, and he started laughing. "You didn't believe I still thought that?"

I laughed with him. "I wasn't sure. It's hard to tell if you've been paying attention to all my explanations."

"I've been paying attention." He tapped his temple.

"I still feel like I'm talking about this weird alien life I've been living." I normally didn't have any problem sharing mission experiences. With Liam, though, I felt like he had no clue what it meant to be religious.

"I admire your passion."

"Thank you."

"You're welcome."

I turned on my blinker and made a right turn. "I need to pick up a banner I had made at this sign shop up there." I pointed to the store I was almost at. "Then I need to pick up the next batch of flyers from the printers."

"Okay. I'll just wait in the car, if you don't mind."

"Sure. Be out in a minute." As I picked up my order, I wondered why Liam had wanted to come with me. He had to be so bored, but he'd volunteered to join me. At the printers, he once again stayed in the car.

He agreed to join me in Target. I figured the boredom must have gotten to him. I bought the necessities to make and hang up signs: zip ties, black Sharpies, fluorescent poster boards, and duct tape.

Once I had everything I needed, we headed for the checkout. I looked behind me and recognized the lady next in line as someone from my ward. She also had fluorescent poster board and a black Sharpie. Liam hung back, looking at an endcap near the line I was in.

"Hey, Sister Billings. Would you like to go in front of me? I have a lot of stuff."

She looked surprised. "Really?" She glanced at what was in my cart.

"Yeah, sure. It'll be faster." I nodded.

"Thank you. I appreciate it."

I stepped aside, allowing her to stand in front of me. "You're welcome."

"I'm in a rush anyway. The kids are doing a lemonade stand this morning and needed more signs. It's been pretty slow so far. They begged and begged all morning until I finally caved."

"Maybe we'll try to stop by for a minute." I brightened up.

"That'd be great. I hope people come. Selling lemonade can be hit or miss, you know."

I nodded in agreement. "I have my fund-raiser in a couple days. I feel the same way."

"Your event is down on my calendar. We're planning on coming."

"Oh, good." I let out a sigh of relief. "I worry that no one will show up."

"You'll at least have the four of us." She smiled, then turned her attention to the cashier.

She thanked me again once she'd paid and was grabbing her bag.

I pushed my stuff forward on the conveyor belt and put the divider behind it. Liam still seemed engrossed in the new-release movies. I paid, then took my receipt and bag. I glanced up at Liam, who was walking toward me.

"Do you always do that?" he asked. He had cut through the empty checkout aisle next to the one I'd used. He seemed overly interested in the gossip magazines. He must've been much more bored than I'd realized.

"What?"

"Give people cuts in the queue."

I shrugged. "Well, I know her."

"What if you didn't? Would you still have done it?"

"Sometimes. I appreciate it when people do it for me." I wasn't sure why he was asking me. He didn't seem annoyed, and it wasn't like he had anyplace to go, so he certainly wasn't in a rush.

"Are you really going 'round to her sale?"

"Of course. I said I would. It's good to be neighborly. But I can't stop for very long. I have too many things to do."

"She might not even take notice if you don't." I was getting the impression he didn't want to go.

"I told her I would. I hate when people commit to something and then don't show. Besides, I have to buy some lemonade."

"You have to?" He seemed puzzled.

"Well, it's the nice thing to do. Maybe I should buy the kids donuts." We had reached the car by now. "I can go through the drive-through, drop them off on the way. I'll even buy you one if you'd like."

"Thanks, but no thanks. Not a fan."

"You don't like donuts? How can you not like donuts?"

"I just don't. Besides, they're not exactly healthy."

"But you drink heavily caffeinated drinks."

"It's my one vice. Everybody's got to have at least one." The way he looked at me made my heart flutter a little.

Chapter Six

"FedEx came for you, Liam," my mom said by way of greeting when we came home. I was dropping off the sign and the rest of the supplies. Liam was still shaking his head in disbelief that I actually went to the lemonade stand and dropped off donuts.

"Thank you," he said, picking up the cardboard envelope from the entry hall table.

I watched as he ripped it open and took out a wad of cash. Not twenties but hundreds. Maybe they weren't all hundreds, but if they were, from the look of the thickness, it was several thousand dollars.

Liam looked up, the money still in his hand. He caught my reaction and casually dropped the money back into the envelope and closed it.

Uneasiness tugged at my mind. "Did someone rob a bank to send you that?" I asked.

He managed a small laugh. "Nope, but now I can repay you."

"I guess you can."

"But I'm still in a bit of a bind."

I tried to check my reaction. His story was getting more and more questionable the longer I knew him. "Oh yeah, why's that?"

"I still don't have any ID or phone. My assistant is working on it, but she hasn't gotten it all taken care of yet."

I nodded. Although I doubted his story, I had some sympathy. What a mess his ex had created. "You can't just get another phone?"

"I want *my* phone. I don't want the hassle of a new one. I'm hoping I can still get it back."

"I can see that."

"So could I possibly borrow your phone again?"

"Sure," I said, handing it to him. He dialed a number and then went into the other room, I assumed for privacy.

"Hey, yeah, I got it. Looks like enough. Any word from her? No, her number's on my phone. Cybil might have it. Just keep ringing my phone, and eventually she'll pick up. I hope. It'd probably be better if you ring her." His voice dropped. "Not very keen about leaving too many numbers on redial."

I found that funny. Why did he think his numbers were too important for us to know what numbers he called? Did he think I would be calling him once he left?

"Just keep on it." His words were clipped. He hung up after that without a thank-you or a goodbye. He wouldn't be a fun person to work for. Too demanding.

He returned and handed me my phone. "What's the plan? Now that you have money? Planning on flying out of here?" I asked. This situation was so bizarre I couldn't help but be curious.

"Are you anxious to get rid of me? Don't you like me?"

"Sure, I like you," I said smoothly. After all, with his looks and his accent and his charm, what was not to like? That was exactly what made me not trust him. Something didn't add up. Throw in that wad of cash he'd gotten today and I knew there was something I was missing. "I just don't trust you."

I must have gotten a guarded look. He looked at *me* like he was trying to figure something out instead of it being the other way around.

"You don't need to be suspicious of my motives, luv. I want to get out of this situation as much as you want me out of here."

I dropped my head. I didn't mean to make him feel unwanted. I just wanted to know what it was he wasn't telling us. "Sorry," I said.

"Apology accepted," he said.

I silently scolded myself and committed to be less transparent. Maybe even get over my distrust of him. But I couldn't help but wonder if I ever could.

"Now that I have money, how about we go shopping? I don't want to get a reputation for wearing old-man jeans and ugly shirts."

What a strange thing to say. "You're worried about your reputation at a time like this?" I asked.

"I'm always worried about my reputation, luv. It's exhausting."

I laughed at his overly dramatic delivery of that statement.

* * *

Lucky for Liam, there was a Starbucks right by the mall. He said he could smell it before he even saw it. I guess he liked his coffee. As soon as we stepped through the door, the smell enveloped us. He ordered something large and complicated, and between his drink on the way here and what he was drinking now, he was definitely going to be well caffeinated.

He stared down at the display case. "And a slice of lemon pound cake, please," he said, then looked over at me. "Would you like a slice too?" I found it weird how he stared at the floor when he ordered. He was a model of politeness at our house and didn't seem to have any problems making eye contact.

"I've never had it, but sure." I nodded. "Sounds good."

"Whoever came up with the recipe was brilliant. It is the best."

He took his coffee and the baggy with our two slices of lemon cake, and we sat at a little table.

He took a deep breath after his first sip of coffee. "That is good." He took another long sip. "What do you think of the cake?"

It was amazing. Sweet-and-tart glaze over a moist cake. What was not to love? "Yum," I said. "I have just found a reason to go to Starbucks."

"Fancy another slice?" he asked.

"Are you going to have more?"

"Absolutely."

"Then, yes, I would fancy another slice."

"I like a girl who eats." He grinned at me before going back to the counter to get two more slices. Again, he stared at the floor when he ordered.

When we were done, we crossed the parking lot and headed into the mall to a clothing store I normally didn't shop at because I found the prices too expensive. The first thing he did was look for one of those knit caps people wore in the winter. I wore something like that only out of desperation on really cold days or really bad hair days. He must have been wearing it out of desperation because it was not a cold day. He had to forage through all the clearance items before he was victorious.

"Won't that make your head hot?" I asked. It was June, after all.

"Nah," he said. He seemed to dismiss my question and continued shopping. He picked out some jeans and some T-shirts, and a button-down shirt, then he insisted I come with him when he tried them on. "What do you think?" he asked as he came out of the dressing room.

What did I think? I thought it was something I shouldn't say out loud because I would embarrass myself and possibly him. He looked hot. Way hotter than he did in the jeans I'd bought him. Suddenly I understood what he meant by old-man jeans.

"Well?" he waited.

I swallowed. "They're not old-man jeans, but I think they work."

"You think they work? Like, they'll do, or they look good?"

Why did he need to ask my opinion about how good they looked? "I'd go with 'they look good.'" I tried to sound casual.

The next pair he tried on looked really good too. But I didn't like the back pockets.

"What's wrong with the pockets?" he argued.

"They're really big and really detailed. It's like they're screaming 'Look at me.'"

"Is there something wrong with that?"

"Not if you're a rock star, but I don't think most guys strutting around could pull off jeans like that."

He sighed heavily and dramatically. "If only I were a rock star."

"If only," I added for emphasis.

He smiled, which made me weak in the knees. "It's a no, then?"

"Just to the fancy pants."

"Would you seriously think I was wearing, as you say, fancy pants if I were wearing those jeans?"

"Yeah, I would think, 'There goes a guy who thinks he's hot stuff.'"

"Do I not qualify as hot stuff?" he asked, his words challenging. He held my gaze until I felt myself blushing. Then he bumped me with his elbow.

I didn't know how to answer that. Of course I thought he was hot, but from the way this conversation was going, so did he. I'm not sure if he was trying to get me to stroke his ego or if he really was just joking.

"Burning hot," I deadpanned.

"It's no fun shopping with you if you're just going to tell me what I want to hear. I hate when people do that. I want the truth."

"Okay, then, you are smoking hot, but those jeans scream you are trying to show off your swagger. You don't have to flaunt your assets; they do a fine job flaunting themselves."

"Well, thank you. That was quite . . . honest."

"You wanted honesty." I lifted my shoulder and gave him an extra wide smile.

"Yes, I guess I did. Thank you for that most proper and honest opinion."

"Let's shop some more. Maybe we could buy some deodorant. I could tell you my opinion about the scents, whether they are manly or too fresh or too musky." I hammed it up, grabbing his arm and playfully pulling him along.

"I like you, luv, but not enough to have you smell my underarms." He grinned.

"I like you too," I joked. "But not enough to get that close to your underarms. There's some things that you just have to say no to. A firm no."

"Armpits are one of those lines you will not cross?"

"That's right."

"Would you change your mind if it were, say, some famous person's armpits?"

I shook my head vehemently. "It doesn't matter. Armpits are armpits, and that will always be a big, fat no."

He looked at me and laughed. "How did we get on the subject of armpits anyway?"

I wagged my finger at him. "I'm pretty sure you were the one who brought it up."

"I think not."

"Oh, I think so." I was liking the fun banter.

Liam stopped in front of a bunch of brown leather flip-flops hanging on the wall. "What do you think of those?"

I looked down at his feet and saw the shoes he was wearing now. It was an old pair of my brother's loafers that my mom must have dug out of the basement. "They would be a huge improvement on what you're wearing now."

"I agree." He grabbed a pair and added it to the pile of stuff he was buying.

"We should throw those shoes out as soon as you pay for the other ones," I suggested.

"You don't fancy them?" he asked with feigned innocence. "Your brother won't want them back once he realizes he left them at his parents' house?" He slipped them off his feet. "Would you like to do the honor?"

I didn't move but looked down at the shoes. "Um, no, not really."

"I guess I'll take care of that after I pay."

I followed him up to the register and stood beside him. He took the cash out of his dad jeans and stared at the ground the whole time while he paid the cashier. Did he have social anxiety? I hadn't seen any other evidence of it, but who knew.

Once he got the receipt, he asked to borrow some scissors, then he cut off all the tags and went into the dressing room to change. When he came out in new clothes, he had everything else in the shopping bag except the shoes, which he ceremoniously threw away in the closest trash can. "Good riddance. I hope no one goes through the rubbish bin and pulls them out."

As we walked out of the store, Liam stopped and looked around. "Are there any eyeglass places here?"

I was confused. "You need glasses?" Was that why he was always looking down? He couldn't focus on the sales person? But he always looked at me. "How have you seen anything the last couple of days?"

"I don't need glasses. They just help . . ."

"Help? With seeing?" I couldn't resist being skeptical. This didn't make sense.

"The glare. I can get headaches from glare." He pointed up to the ceiling and the lights. I followed his lead and looked up too. It left me seeing weird spots in the shape of the lights. I had to blink a few times to get my vision back to normal.

"Wouldn't sunglasses be better?"

"I suppose, but not inside."

I still didn't quite get what he meant, but we stopped at the mall directory and found a one-hour place. Once we figured out where we were, we headed over to the eyeglass store.

He looked around for a second until he located the men's section. He tried a pair on, looked at his reflection, and then turned to me. "What do you think?"

It was like being back at the clothing store: he looked good. Very, very good.

"What look are you going for?" I asked carefully. "Any style in particular?"

"I don't know. Maybe—"

"These?" I asked, donning a pair of big, tortoise-shell-colored plastic frames. They looked like something a grandpa or an elderly film director would wear.

He grimaced. "Too much of a . . ."

"Statement?" I asked, laughing, checking out my reflection in the mirror.

"Precisely. I don't think I'm ready to make that kind of statement."

I followed him around, watching him trying on glasses. The whole process was sort of odd and beautiful at the same time. I could see his personality coming through just by the glasses he was trying. After a few pairs, he chose dark-rimmed, hipster frames.

"Good?" He turned and faced me with the glasses on.

Since I wasn't sure what style he was looking for, I based my opinion on his overall appearance. "I'd say they look good."

"Brilliant. These will do." He took them off and carried them up to a salesperson.

The girl working at the desk took a double-take as Liam walked up to her.

"Hello, I was wondering if you could help me," he said pleasantly. Gone was the British accent. He leaned one elbow on the glass case and gave her a smile as he set down the frames.

Why was he laying on the charm so thick?

"Absolutely. That's what I'm here for. I'm here to help . . . you." Her eyes darted at him quickly. I could tell she was aware of her word fumble.

"Can I buy these frames?" He picked them up and handed them to her.

"Do you have your prescription with you?" She straightened her own pair of glasses. The part of her neck above her neckline was turning pink, and it was creeping up her neck in a blotchy pattern.

"I don't need prescription lenses, just the frames."

"Like, just the frames?" she repeated.

"Just the frames, yes." He grinned, causing her eyes to widen and her cheeks to burn.

She pulled out an order form. "It would still take an hour to put in a . . ."

"I was hoping I could buy this pair." He seemed to be acting on the edge of flirting, if that was the right description. Like he was trying to get his way, which I totally didn't get because all he wanted was a sample pair of glasses. And where was the staring at the ground thing he had done at the other stores?

She looked around the store. "Well, technically, I'm not supposed to sell the floor samples."

"I wouldn't tell anyone. In fact, I'll write your manager a note about how helpful you were."

"Really, we could have them done in an hour." She pulled on her earlobe and cleared her throat.

"See, I don't have an hour. If I could just purchase this pair . . ."

She chewed on the corner of her lip, then looked around again. "Okay, just don't tell anyone I did this," she whispered.

"Great!" Liam exclaimed happily.

I wondered if the salesperson had been a male if Liam would have gotten his way so easily.

"Do you have insurance?" she asked.

"No insurance, just cash." He pulled out a few bills.

"Cash?" The girl seemed surprised.

"Yes. I can do that, right?" He paused.

"Of course, and you can get a discount for paying cash with no insurance."

"Even better," he exclaimed. He handed her the cash, put on the glasses, looked at his reflection in the mirror on the counter, and smiled. He seemed so . . . pleased.

"Now if you have a slip of paper and an envelope"—he pronounced it "onvelope," which was very cute—"I will write your recommendation."

"Yes, let me just . . ." The girl looked under the counter and sounded like she was digging through boxes. "Here." She gave him a pad of paper with the store logo on it and pushed a pen in his direction. All the while watching him.

Liam scratched something out on the paper, signed it, and slipped it in the envelope. He slid the envelope and pen back toward her. "Thanks for your help."

She kept her hand on the envelope for a second, curling the edge. She made a sound like she suddenly inflated and her whole body lurched. "Are you, by chance—?"

"Single?" Liam said unexpectedly. "No, sorry, I'm not."

She seemed confused, and Liam took it as an opportunity to escape, hurrying out of the store.

"Are you single?" I asked him, staring at him while I kept up the pace beside him. "Why do you think she would ask you if you are single?"

Liam shrugged. "I get asked out all the time. It's unbelievable."

"But how can you assume she wanted to ask you out?" It was surprising, and I was unable to stop questioning him about it.

Liam looked at me and blinked his eyes innocently. "It's the truth. I think it has something to do with the British accent."

Or maybe more to do with his incredible looks. I burst out laughing. "I'm sure it all has to do with the accent. But for some reason, you went into an American accent with her."

"I guess I did, huh?" he said, his tone dismissive.

I shook my head in disgust. I just couldn't make up my mind about him. Sometimes he seemed pretty cool; other times he was too vain. When I looked up, I recognized the curly-haired, stocky guy coming toward us. It was Harris. I inadvertently frowned.

Liam caught my expression, then followed my glance. "Who's that?" Liam leaned in and whispered.

I stopped walking and turned my back on Harris to face Liam. "That is Harris. I work with him."

"Are you friends or . . . ?"

"He's the one employee I hate being scheduled to work with. He always calls me Cami instead of Camille. I've given up correcting him. He flirts with every girl who comes into the shop, and he always says, 'That girl is into me,' every time a girl leaves." I had never been attracted to Harris. He wasn't bad-looking or especially good-looking. He was just average to me. It was more his annoying personality that made him unattractive.

I continued. "Then he proceeds to tell me about all the dates he's had since the last time we worked together. Then finishes it with, 'Gone on any dates lately?'" My answer was always no. I would reiterate that I had been home for only six weeks. Then he would tell me how he was on a date the first night he got home and how he had three more lined up even before he'd made it home. Like that was supposed to impress me.

"What you are saying is he has a bit of a competitive streak and you guys aren't mates?" Liam whispered back and nodded knowingly.

"Exactly. Did I mention he's annoying?"

"He sounds like a charming fellow."

"Incredibly," I muttered.

I was hoping Harris wouldn't see me, but of course he did. With Liam.

"Cami, Cami, fancy meeting you out like this. Are you on a . . . date?" he added the pause for emphasis.

To my surprise, Liam threw his left arm around my shoulder and stuck out his right hand. "Liam. Nice to meet you. And you are?" His accent was back. But it wasn't what he said but how he said it that amazed me. He had this air of confidence, not even arrogance, that shut Harris up. He continued holding his hand out, waiting for Harris to take it.

Harris hesitated before shaking Liam's hand. "I'm Harris. Cami and I work together, but you probably already know that."

Liam looked from Harris to me and then back to Harris. "Should I? Quite honestly, *Camille* hasn't said much about her coworkers."

Harris stopped smiling. "She hasn't mentioned anything about you either, come to think of it."

Liam grinned and leaned close. "I like to have her keep me a secret," he whispered.

Harris stepped back with a puzzled look on his face. I wasn't sure if he knew what to make of Liam's comment. He finally spoke. "Well, she has."

"Good. I like it that way. Great meeting you." Liam waved and pulled me along.

"Yeah, uh, bye, Harris," I said over my shoulder.

"Annoying bloke, that fellow," Liam muttered.

"Try working with him. It's even worse."

"I'm sorry you must endure him."

"Yeah, me too, but at least I have a job," I said, reminding myself too.

"That's right, Camille. Chin up and carry on." Liam gave me a squeeze but didn't take his arm off my shoulder. And I was not complaining.

Chapter Seven

WE MADE IT OUT OF the mall and back home without any more purchases, flirting with employees, or run-ins with Harris or anyone else I knew.

As I pulled into the driveway, my phone rang. I pulled it out of my purse and looked at the display. I could tell from the area code it was not for me, so I handed it to Liam. "It's for you."

He answered, then listened for a moment before getting out of the car and following me into the house, though he lingered in the entryway, probably for privacy. "You've gotten in touch, then? . . . Just her number? . . . She doesn't pick up when you ring? . . . I'll try her and see if she'll answer. I doubt she'll pick up if she doesn't recognize the number . . . If you do, tell her I want my stuff back and to quit being a miserable cow." He was quiet for a moment. "I almost think I ought to send the cops after her. Maybe a night in jail will make a point. Enough with the games." He marched into the kitchen and grabbed a napkin and a pen off the counter, then wrote down a number and shoved it in his back pocket before he went back to the entryway.

"What's up?" my mom whispered. She was standing next to the counter, sorting through the mail.

"He's talking to his assistant, I think." I grabbed two water bottles from the fridge and offered one to her. She shook her head, so I set it on the table to offer to Liam.

He handed me my phone when he came back into the kitchen.

"Good news?" I asked, even though it hadn't sounded like it from what I'd overheard. I held out the water, and he accepted.

"Nah, I'm not any closer to getting my stuff back." He twisted the top off and took a drink.

"That's got to be frustrating," I sympathized. I really didn't know what else to say. He was so confusing to me.

"It will happen," my mother reassured him.

But what if it didn't? Was he just going to hang around here forever? I wasn't necessarily complaining, but did he have some sort of plan? I had plans, but Liam being here made me feel like I needed to entertain him.

"Have you considered this is her way of getting your attention?" my mom asked.

He snorted, and his water bottle crackled under the pressure of his grip. "She's certainly got that." He paced between the sink and the fridge several times.

"Perhaps she needs you to hear her out and she's going about it the wrong way?"

It was cute listening to Mom's suggestions because she didn't know it was more about revenge and putting him in an awkward and humiliating situation than a communication problem. I'd let Liam tell my parents that part of the story if he wanted to.

My mom continued. "It's like a two-year-old having a tantrum. They are frustrated about something, and that's the only way they can get the message across."

Liam sighed. "Whatever it is, she's made her point. I'm ready to move on."

"Have you called her and tried to work things out?" My mom really did like to believe the best in everyone. I smiled again but hid it by taking a sip of water. That would be one phone call I would love to hear, even if it was just Liam's side of the conversation. It'd probably sound like something close to World War III.

"There's no working things out after this. We're through; she just doesn't realize that this time it's for real." He ran his finger along the rim of the bottle.

"Maybe she needs a second chance?" Mom suggested. "Everyone deserves that, right?"

I didn't know if I wanted my mother encouraging a reunion between Liam and his ex-girlfriend. Despite my doubts about him, he was kind of growing on me.

He leaned back in the chair and shook his head. "It's past repair."

"You can always go back and make things right," my mom said and patted his arm. She stood up and excused herself.

"Nah." He shook his head and pursed his lips. "I'm about done with Twick."

"Twick? Her name is Twick?" I asked, surprised. The only Twick I knew of was famous. "Was she lucky enough to get the last name Openshaw?"

"Would you consider that lucky?" Liam asked me, his voice flat, his expression blank.

"I, um," I stuttered. "I thought I did, but maybe I don't?" I said it like a question because, obviously, I was missing what Liam was insinuating.

"I wouldn't want to be Twick Openshaw," he declared.

For the sake of our fragile, blossoming friendship, I decided to second his opinion. "Well, then, neither would I." He had to have his reasons, right?

He leaned forward and held my gaze. "Can I ask your opinion?"

"Sure." I felt a little bewildered, wondering what he was going to ask.

"I'm thinking about having Twick arrested."

"You want to have your girlfriend arrested? That's what you want my opinion about?" My voice had become a little squeaky.

He nodded. "My ex-girlfriend, and yes."

"To get more revenge? What will she do to get you back for having her arrested? It's like you guys never stop getting back at each other."

Liam furrowed his brow. "What are you suggesting?"

I shrugged. "Be the bigger person. Take the higher road. Something other than getting her back."

He angled his head, looking out the window momentarily. "You're saying let it go?" He looked back at me.

"As best you can. It's one of those things that's easier said than done. It might make her even madder if you don't respond at all," I suggested.

"Maybe. I don't know. I'm still trying to decide what to do."

Even with my advice about letting it go and taking the high road, it was hard to really offer suggestions to Liam. I knew he wasn't telling me the whole story.

* * *

"I was thinking we'd have pizza and strawberry shortcake for dinner and maybe have movie night," my mom said. I had just finished some final phone calls for the fund-raiser, and asking/begging for money had made me hungry and slightly frustrated. I had found several local businesses willing to donate money. Some gave donations, no questions asked, and the biggest target donor agreed to a donation match once we'd raised a certain amount of money on our end.

I looked to Liam, although I didn't know why. It wasn't like he had plans or I had plans or we had plans. I shrugged. "Sure, that sounds great."

Liam remained silent.

Mom started on the pizza dough while my dad set up the movie projector outside.

Liam leaned in close. "This isn't just go-out-for-pizza-and-a-movie?"

I shook my head. "Nope. Family tradition."

"You do this every Wednesday night?" Liam asked.

I opened the fridge and pulled out some shredded mozzarella, pepperoni, and ham. "Usually we do it on Friday night. But things might get busy with the fund-raiser, so I guess my mom thought we should do it tonight."

Liam slowly nodded, processing the information. I continued to gather toppings for the pizza. I found a can of pineapple chunks, a can of olives, and a green pepper.

Once the pizza dough had been rolled out, I handed a jar of sauce to Liam. He took it but stood there. "I don't cook for myself. Unless I can microwave it."

"I see." He did seem a little lost in the kitchen, standing off in the perimeter, looking around. But I had just assumed it was because he was in someone else's kitchen.

Pizza seemed like a staple food for guys, especially bachelors. But maybe pizza delivery was more a staple. "So you just get takeout or delivery?"

He shrugged and held his hands up. "Something like that," Liam said. His helpless smile made him even more attractive.

"Pizza's pretty simple. The dough is the hardest part. Now all we have to do is spread the sauce and put on the cheese and toppings."

"You don't have to cook the dough first?"

"Nope."

"Well, then, I can do this," he said confidently.

Once the pizza was in, we set the picnic table on the back porch. It was the perfect summer night for eating outside. There was a slight breeze, and the temperature was nice and mild.

Less than a half hour later, we were sitting around the table, eating pizza, drinking pink lemonade, listening to my dad retell stories his coworkers had shared, and discussing the plans for the rest of the week. Liam was rather quiet, and I worried that he felt left out.

"Are you okay?" I whispered to him as my mom and dad cleared the table.

"Yeah. Why?"

"You haven't said much during dinner."

He turned toward me, swinging one leg over the bench seat so he was straddling it. "I've never sat down with my parents for dinner."

"Never?" I was a little shocked at his admission but tried hard not to have my mouth hang open.

He ran his hand across the table, possibly wiping off imaginary crumbs. "A couple of holidays with some distant relatives, but no, I've never sat down and actually eaten dinner with my immediate family."

The concept was completely foreign to me. Not that we were the perfect family who ate every dinner together. But my parents had always pushed for it when I was in high school. I, being a teenager and wanting to spend time with my friends, of course, fought against it. I learned quickly to not push my protest too much. If I argued, my mom would launch into her "decline of the family" lecture. I guess having never known anything different, I didn't know that someone else had never had a chance to eat with his family.

He continued before I could say anything. "It's nice to see. I'll admit, I'm a bit envious."

I laid my hand on his arm. "I'm sorry, Liam. I didn't realize—"

He stood abruptly. "It was years ago." He looked around. "So what's next? Do we go inside for a movie?"

I pointed to the lawn. "We usually drag those patio chairs over there." I walked over to a glider and sat. "My dad sets up a portable screen on the back of the garage, and that is our instant, outside theater."

Liam took in the setup. "I see. Very . . . creative."

I shrugged and patted the seat beside me, indicating Liam should sit. "It's fun. Something different." I looked over my shoulder to the kitchen window. My parents looked like they were still working on getting the strawberry shortcake together. "How come you never ate together as a family?"

I had thought of different ways to ask the question, not sure if it was a sensitive subject or not. Maybe his parents just worked opposite shifts from each other.

"My mum has always been a single mum. I never met my dad. She was always working, so it was usually just me and my brother. I didn't know it at the time, but she was an addict. I mean, I knew when she was drunk but not when she was high. When I was thirteen, she just stopped coming home. I didn't know where she went. Sometimes she'd be gone for days, sometimes longer. Then one day she just never came home. I don't remember how long she'd been gone, but eventually someone figured out it was just me and my brother living in the flat."

"What happened?" I had to swallow hard against the lump in my throat. My heart was breaking for him.

He looked out across the yard, then shrugged. "Eventually we got taken away by NSPCC— National Society for Prevention of Cruelty to Children. They sent us to live with our great aunt since our grandparents were dead and we didn't know who our father was."

"So it's like being a foster kid?"

He pursed his lips before speaking. "It's pretty tough to live with someone who doesn't want you around."

This time my mouth did fall open. "Did she actually tell you that?"

He shook his head. "No, but she didn't have to. She did all the parent-y things she was supposed to. She made sure we had clothes and that we ate, and she sent us to a really posh private school. But she never seemed to want to be around us. It was like she was tolerating us."

The whole thing blew my mind. I couldn't claim to understand how he must have felt.

"I met my best friend, Tread, at the school, and we started the band."

I interrupted. "The band? What band?"

"Just a band." He paused. "I moved out of my aunt's as soon as I could. I've been on my own ever since."

"Did you ever find your mom? Where's your brother? Are you guys close?"

Liam snorted quietly. "Nah. I've never looked for my mum. I assume she overdosed on heroin. My brother followed in Mum's footsteps and also got hooked on heroin. What's the point to—"

"Who's ready for dessert?" My mom was walking across the lawn, holding a tray of mini pie pans with bright-red strawberries. My dad followed behind her, holding a bowl with recently whipped cream. The whole scene was so *Better Homes and Gardens* it was surreal next to Liam's story.

Liam's face became a mask of cheerfulness. "It looks delicious, Gabbi. I can't wait to try it."

I wasn't able to shake off the somber truth Liam had just shared, nor was I able to understand how Liam had been able to. Maybe it was just a truth he had long ago accepted and he didn't spend time dwelling on the past.

It was my time to be quieter than usual. While my parents and Liam made comments about the movie we were watching, I was lost in thought. There was definitely more depth to Liam than I had given him credit for.

Chapter Eight

"I'D LIKE TO HAVE YOUR permission to take your daughter out," Liam said to my dad.

I had worked the eight-to-four shift, and Liam had spent the day with my mom, although I was not quite sure what they had done for the day. When I arrived home, Liam suggested the date, and I readily agreed—although I hadn't expected him to ask for my parents' permission, especially when I was a grown woman and was standing right there. It was a strange feeling, and I didn't take Liam as a guy who asked for permission.

My dad glanced over at my mom, and she nodded ever so slightly. "We have some conditions before we agree to it," he said.

I wanted to die from embarrassment. It was not like I couldn't tell him I wasn't going to jump in bed with him myself. Or that there'd be no drinking or doing illegal substances. I was a big girl, even if they didn't want to admit it.

"I understand," Liam acknowledged.

"Make sure you are respectful."

"Respectful?" Liam seemed puzzled.

My dad continued. "In our family, along with our beliefs, there are certain things we don't do. If Camille says she doesn't want to do something, we expect you to respect that."

"Right. I understand." He nodded humbly.

I wasn't sure if I should feel excited or nervous. After all, he was still a stranger. I didn't really know anything about him.

* * *

We went to The Melting Pot for fondue. The restaurant was dimly lit, and every place to sit was a booth that easily made me feel like we were tucked away in our own private world.

We looked over the whole menu, which was pretty much all expensive, before Liam set his down. "Are you allergic to seafood?"

"Nope," I said.

"Are you up for the steak and lobster, then?"

I hesitated. It had to be the most expensive thing on the menu. I thought about what little money I had in my wallet but didn't want to be tacky.

"It's my treat, of course. You have been so nice to me; consider this on me," Liam said, as if reading my mind.

I was more hoping he was considering this a date because he wanted to spend time with me instead of payback because he felt he owed me. I was treating it like a date. I'd taken extra time on my hair and makeup and way too long deciding what to wear. Maybe I had read his intentions wrong, because he wasn't dressed up, but I brushed it off because he really didn't have much to choose from. But he hadn't shaved either and was wearing a baseball cap and glasses. Maybe to him, this wasn't anything more than an obligation.

I tried to clear the doubt from my mind and focus on deciding what to eat. "Lobster sounds great. Is the broth okay with you?" I asked him, eyeing the *choices of cooking* menu.

"Not the white wine?"

"No, I don't drink."

Liam looked incredulous. "You don't drink? At all? You've never had a drink?"

"Nope, never."

"Don't you feel like you're missing out?"

"On getting drunk? No. You can't miss what you don't know. It doesn't seem like any good has come from you drinking the other night."

His eyebrows arched for a moment. "I met you."

He sounded serious, and it made me blush and my insides flip, but I dismissed it as part of his charming act.

"But if you hadn't been drinking," I pointed out, "you wouldn't be in this mess in the first place."

"Perhaps you're right." He looked like he was actually considering what I said. "Just so you know, the alcohol evaporates during cooking, but anyway, the seasoned broth sounds good."

I checked it out. It sounded spicy, with garlic. "I'm not a fan of a lot of garlic."

"Not keen on garlic?"

"I'm afraid it would give me bad breath, and I want you to want to be around me tonight."

"Okay, I'll take your word for it. Besides, I do want to be around you for the rest of the night, so we'll go with your choice."

My cheeks burned more. I hoped in the dimly lit restaurant he wouldn't notice.

The waiter came over and explained the whole process of fondue cooking, described the art of search and rescue (using the spoon to fish out lost food), and cautioned us that things got hot. He then took our order. Liam didn't skimp. He ordered the spinach-artichoke-cheese fondue, house salads, and surf & turf, which included filet mignon, scallops, shrimp, and lobster.

"Is the no-alcohol bit part of the 'standards' your dad was talking about?" He was leaning forward, the expression on his face sincere.

"Yes, exactly."

"When I asked to take you out, did your dad think I was going to take you to a hotel and sleep with you? Take you to a bar and get you drunk?"

I laughed. "No, I don't think my dad was worried you'd do that. It's just obvious you have a different lifestyle from us. I'm surprised you haven't gotten bored with us yet."

The waiter returned with our appetizer and got the food cooking. I dipped an apple slice into the cheese fondue.

"Bored? Why would I get bored? I find you guys refreshing." Liam immersed some cubes of bread.

I thought "refreshing" was an odd choice of description, but okay. "From what you've told me, we are way more conservative than you." I tried to word it delicately, without insulting him. I wasn't going to judge him for his lifestyle; it was his choice. "But we don't smoke or drink or do drugs." I thought for a second. "Not that I think you do drugs or anything." My apple had slipped off my skewer accidentally. He waited. I peered at the pot, trying to look enthralled, hoping for my apple to surface. "Heck, we don't even drink coffee." Maybe the cheese was too thick and I was going to have to fish it out.

"That is a very sad thing indeed." He gave a wry smile. He picked up the rescue spoon, dipped it in, and recovered my apple, then set it on my plate.

"Do you know anything at all about Mormons?" I asked.

The waiter delivered our salads, momentarily halting our conversation.

"Other than you don't believe in electricity, no." He picked up his skewer, stabbed an apple slice, and dipped it in. He offered it to me when he pulled it out, but I waved my hand no.

"As you can tell from our flat-screen TV and our surround-sound system, we don't believe in electricity." I munched on my apple. Although I'd never thought I would enjoy apples and cheese together, it was actually very good.

"Would you like to keep the cheese fondue?" the waiter asked.

Liam looked at me, and I looked at the waiter. "I think we're good."

"All right, then." The waiter took the pot from the table.

"Okay, enlighten me."

For the next hour, in between eating our salads and having the main course delivered, I told him what we did and did not do as members of the Church. I told him our beliefs and basically everything I'd taught on my mission, just without a baptismal commitment and placing a copy of the Book of Mormon. The conversation continued, as did adding and extracting bits of food from the fondue pot that had come with the main course.

"You don't sleep with your boyfriend?"

I suspected he would get hung up on that point. "Nope."

"Really?" His eyes narrowed, then relaxed. He rubbed his chin. "That's got to be tough."

"I'm not really missing out on anything. I've never had a boyfriend that I've wanted to sleep with." I sort of laughed and shifted in my seat. Suddenly, I was getting a little uncomfortable revealing how inexperienced I was when it came to dating.

His blue eyes met mine and held my gaze. "But what if you did?"

I looked at my plate, unable to maintain the intensity of his look. After a moment, I replied, "I would wait until I was married."

"I don't know if I believe that."

"I think it's important to have the commitment of marriage first." This time I was able to maintain eye contact. I didn't want him to think I was uncomfortable with my beliefs. It was his piercing, expectant stare that did me in.

"Just because you're not married doesn't mean you're not committed."

I snorted.

"What?"

"I'm taking relationship advice from a guy who serves revenge a la carte?"

"Hey, that's not exactly fair." He leaned back in the booth and chuckled.

"That's what it sounds like from what you've told me about your relationship with your girlfriend."

He sat up straight. "There's much more to it. She and I don't have what I would call a proper relationship." Then he fished a piece of lobster tail from the broth and offered it to me on the end of the skewer. I took it, allowing him to feed me. I mean, it was lobster tail.

"What's not proper about it?"

"What I mean to say is it isn't how it should be."

"Why?"

He looked like he was choosing his words carefully. "We fight a lot. We've never really sorted out our differences. Perhaps it's our egos."

That was the first I'd ever heard him admit he had an ego. "Now that you're broken up, you don't have to compete," I said, helping myself to another scallop.

He didn't say anything. Our eyes met during that brief silence. "Can I ask you something completely random?"

"Sure." I wondered what it was.

"What brand is your shirt?"

Wasn't expecting that. "I have no idea. Probably a brand from Target."

"How about your jeans? Are they a certain label?"

Tilting my head, I watched closely for his reaction to my question. "Do you have a clothes fetish?"

"No."

"Um, okay, I think I got them at Gap."

"Are you willing to indulge me with one more question?"

"Only if you're willing to indulge me with the reason for all these questions after."

"Deal. What kind of shoes are you wearing?"

I kicked my foot out from underneath the booth, and we both looked down at it. It was a cute sandal. "I don't know the brand or where I got them. So why does any of this matter?"

"Because every time I went out with my ex-girlfriend, she wanted to talk about her outfit or her shoes or her hair color or what brand of lipstick she had on. It was really important to her, and I was trying to judge how important it was to you."

"Was she, like, a fashion blogger?" Was that still even a thing? I didn't pay a ton of attention to fashion blogs.

"She just wanted to get noticed."

"And what do you think? Did I pass your fashion-importance test?"

"I think that it is not what matters most to you. And I mean that in the nicest, most sincere way possible."

I was going to take it that way. I was fine with not being a fashionista. Not that I didn't want to dress nice, but it wasn't my highest priority. "What about you? Is fashion your thing?" I knew it had to be at least a little. He'd been willing to spend a *lot* of money outfitting himself since we'd been here—more than I would pay for clothes. But shopping at the Provo Towne Center Mall was probably limited compared to what he might shop at in LA.

"I like nice things, but I can take it or leave it. My day is not ruined if I see a guy wearing the same T-shirt as me, you know?"

His comment was amusing. How would he react if he ran into a guy wearing his identical cow shirt?

"Now it's my turn to ask you something I've been wondering about. Don't you need to get home for work or . . . anything?" I was curious why he didn't have any place else to be.

"Are you tired of me hanging about?" he asked it slowly.

"No, just wondering."

"I set my own schedule. Right now, I'm between projects, so I'm not very busy. What about you? You work at a yogurt place and have a fundraiser coming up, and then what?"

"Since I don't want to work at a yogurt place forever, I will be going back to school to get my degree."

"University?"

"Yeah. I went for one year, then went on my mission, and I have three years left."

"Then you go into fund-raising," he guessed. "Are you thinking politics?"

"No, I'm thinking nonprofit." I stabbed at a shrimp. This meal was so good I was ignoring how full I was feeling.

"It's admirable."

"Thank you."

"You're a very impressive girl, you know that?"

"Impressive? How?"

"I haven't ever met someone with your passion to volunteer. You're very kind."

"Thank you."

"You're welcome." He stared at me with that intense look of his. "And your family. My family left a lot to be desired when compared to your family."

I laughed. "We're far from perfect. You've only known us for three days, and we've been on our best behavior. My sister isn't even home. She and I still fight like sisters. Especially because we share a bathroom. I argue with well-meaning parents giving parental advice." I thought about some of the heated discussions we'd had as a family.

"At least they are there for you."

He was right. Not that I'd ever doubted it. I just didn't know what to say to him because of his family situation.

"Yeah. I'm pretty thankful for my family. I missed them like crazy while I was gone, but it just made the reunion that much better when I came home."

"Couldn't you ring your parents?" he asked.

"On Mother's Day and Christmas. We tried to keep our focus on missionary work and serving the people."

"Huh." There was a note of surprise in his voice. "You were very dedicated."

"I knew it was going to be like that going into it."

"It doesn't make it any easier. Sometimes we know what we want, but when we finally get it, it's a lot different than what we imagined it to be," he said, now running his finger around the top of his glass. He almost sounded wistful.

"What do you mean?"

"What I thought successful was when I left home compared to now."

"I assume you're successful."

"Why is that?"

I smirked. "No one's mailing me a pile of cash like you have."

He laughed. "Yes, financially, I've been successful.

"Isn't that enough?"

He took a sip of water and swallowed it before answering. "Despite what I thought, money does not equal happiness."

"Are you not happy?"

"When you have a girlfriend who dumps you on the side of the road, it's sort of a wake-up call that you might need to change some things in your life." He gave a weak smile.

I nodded. "At least you realize it."

His eyes suddenly lit up. He pulled an extra napkin from the dispenser. "Do you have a pen I could borrow?"

I found it an odd request but dug through my purse instead of asking for an explanation. When I found one and handed it to him, he wrote something down on the napkin. "Taking notes?"

"I realized I probably should remember what I just said about having a girlfriend who dumps you on the side of the road." He slid the pen back to me, folded the napkin, and tucked it in his back pocket.

"Do you have a whole collection of notes written on scraps of paper and napkins?"

He ran his hand through his hair and nodded. "Actually, I do. Someday I'll put them all in one place and have a nice book." He gave a half grin and lifted his shoulder.

"I do that too. You know, write down funny things people say in class or at work. I keep them in a little notebook. Sometimes when I'm annoyed at work with Harris, I make up stupid limericks about him."

Liam's eyebrow went up. "Oh yeah? Let's hear something."

"One of my limericks?" I could feel myself blushing.

Liam flicked his hand. "Sure. Impress me."

"Um, okay." My head dropped a little while I scrambled to think of something. I cleared my throat while my cheeks burned on.

"There once was a guy named Harris
Who liked to me, embarrass."

I thought for a second, running rhymes through my head.

"He thought he was funny,
Implying I's his honey,
But I could never be his lass."

I waved my hands, flustered. "Wait, wait. That wasn't very good."

Liam started cracking up. "That's hilarious. Do you always just pop off with clever stuff like that?"

I shrugged. "I don't know. I've always liked rhyming. It's just something fun. But really, I have better mad skills than that. I just didn't realize you'd put me on the spot."

Liam held my gaze before looking intently into the pot. "I lost some premium filet mignon somewhere in there, and I am not doing a very good job of fishing it out discreetly."

I offered him the big spoon. "Time for a search-and-rescue mission?"

He became animated, slipping into his charming personality. "Yes, because it would be a shame to waste perfectly good steak like that."

"This has been very delicious. Thank you."

"You're not saying you're done, are you? Dessert looked quite appetizing."

I was pretty full, but he was right—dessert looked very yummy. "I'm not one to say no to dessert, despite what my mother might tell you."

"You mean about you slimming?"

I swear his eyes roamed my body. I felt a heat inside my belly that I worried would present itself as a hot, burning blush. I was thankful much of my body was hidden under a table in the booth. "Yeah," I said. "I'm not slimming."

"Good. I like a girl who eats."

He had mentioned that before.

"But I have eaten so much food I feel like I'm going to burst. I'm afraid if we order dessert, I won't have any room left for it. What about you? Do you want dessert?"

"I agree. I am way too full. Perhaps it's better we pass."

I glanced at the bill before he casually took out his wad of cash and asked the waiter for change. It was well over one hundred dollars. And that was without the gratuity that was automatically calculated in. He didn't even blink.

The waiter came back with change, but Liam waved it away.

"Um . . ." The waiter hung around for a second. "Can I ask you something?"

"Sure," Liam said slowly. "Maybe."

"The waitress over there thinks you're—"

Liam cut him off. "Tell her thanks, but no."

The waiter's eyebrows knit together in confusion. "But . . . you're not—"

"I'm not." Liam shook his head no and stood. "Are you ready?" he asked me, holding his hand out.

"Yes," I said, taking it. He let it go as soon as I had scooted out of the booth. I was disappointed. "What was that about?" I asked. It was the second time something like that had happened.

"I'm always being asked if I'm this guy. Apparently, we look alike, and he's also British. I think people hear the accent and automatically assume I must be him."

My thoughts went back to the eyeglass store. It was oddly similar. And it was a strange explanation and sort of presumptuous on Liam's part, but then again, hadn't everything about Liam been a little strange?

Liam took quick strides, seemingly in a hurry to get outside. Once we made it out and were greeted by the nighttime air, Liam paused.

"Anything else you want to do?" I asked. I was having a good time with him and enjoying his company more than I initially anticipated. It was nice to be away from it all and not be running around trying to get ready for the fund-raiser. But what to suggest? "Movie?" I offered.

"I'm afraid I'd be a bore. If I sit down and the lights go out, I might fall asleep."

"And what fun would that be?"

"Sounds like no fun at all."

"Until I mess with you while you're sleeping. Say, take a picture of you with your mouth hanging open and two gummi worms hanging out of your nose and post it on my social media accounts."

He looked alarmed and maybe a little angry.

"Or maybe not," I said, retracting my joke because of his reaction. Maybe he was not a person who found that kind of thing funny. "You're not a fan of social-media sites?"

He scowled. "Social media is not always my friend."

"I see," I said, even though I didn't really. "Has it caused problems in your relationship with your girlfriend?"

"That and a bit more," he answered vaguely. I took it as a hint that he didn't want to talk about it.

I looked across the top of the car at him and had an idea. "You up for a little Chuck E. Cheese's?"

Liam groaned and lolled his head. "You want to eat some more?"

"You don't go for the pizza; you go for the games."

"I am quite brilliant at air hockey." A smile crept across his face.

"Is that a challenge? Because I'm pretty good at it too." It came back to not backing down from a challenge. And so the competition started.

Once we were there and had bought credits, we went straight to the air-hockey table. We played until a mother cleared her throat to make a point that we were being table hogs. Liam climbed onto the racing horse but was quickly told by management that it was a kids-only ride. We took pictures at the machine that sketched out our images, but what Liam and I spent even more time on was the game where you had to stop a wheel on a certain number to win tickets. He was really good at it. We played until closing time.

"Where do we go to redeem these?" Liam held up the stack of tickets we had won. They spilled out of his hand and onto the floor.

I pointed to a machine. "The ticket counter is over there. It's been years since I've been here, but I've never turned in more than, like, two hundred tickets."

After he put the tickets through the machine, he looked at the receipt. "Tonight is your lucky night, because we have over one thousand. You can exchange it for something that will forever remind you of our night together."

"I don't need something to remind me." I held up the sketches. "I have these pictures and my memories. You should take one of these pictures so you won't forget."

He tapped his temple. "I won't forget either. Although I would love a picture. But you need to promise me these pictures won't end up online." He gently took one from my grasp.

"What's up with you and pictures? You seem anti-camera." I guided him toward the prize counter.

"Here in America you say a picture is worth a thousand words. To me, it's like a picture lasts a thousand years. Once it's posted on the internet, you can't get it back. I try to be very mindful of that. I'm very cautious about my privacy."

Okay, so he was a private person. Didn't I realize that by his less-than-forthcoming-with-information conversations?

At the counter, we were in line behind a mother who was waiting for her son to choose his prizes while her younger daughter was in tears because her brother had more tickets than she had.

"Sweetie, I'm sorry, but I can't do anything about it. Your brother played different games and won more tickets."

"But I just want enough to get some cotton candy!" the girl sobbed.

I looked at the cotton candy hanging off to the side. It was only two hundred points.

I leaned into Liam and whispered, "Do you mind if I give her our points?"

"I was thinking the same thing," he said.

"Excuse me," I said to the mom. "We were just leaving and wondered if we could give her our points?"

"Really? That would be very nice of you." The mom looked relieved. I'm sure trying to deal with her daughter being upset while she was probably tired had to be hard on her. She turned to her little girl. "Did you hear that? They are going to give you their points. What do you say?"

"Thank you," the girl said, hiding behind her mom a little.

"You're welcome, honey," I said.

"There you go, luv." Liam squatted down and handed the slip of paper to the little girl. "Get yourself some cotton candy."

The mom thanked us again as we left. "That was fun," I said as we walked out the door.

"You're a very nice person, you know that?" He put his arm around my shoulder. It made me quiver inside.

"Thank you, but I'm not any nicer than the next person."

"I don't think you realize it, but you are."

Almost everyone in Utah was nice. Maybe he just didn't hang around nice people.

"I'm wondering something," Liam asked.

"What?"

"I'm wondering if it would be bothersome if I stayed a little longer and helped you with your fund-raiser. You've sort of inspired me, and I'd like to help."

I stopped and turned to him. "Absolutely!" I readily agreed. "That would be great."

I just wished I could differentiate between what inspired him: me or my fund-raiser.

On Friday night, we went to a free concert in downtown Provo, although Liam was reluctant to go at first because of the number of people who would be there. We came to a happy medium by settling on a restaurant close to the music. We enjoyed the food, could still hear the music, and talked for a long time.

The only downside to the evening was when it ended. These last two dates had been the best dates I'd ever been on.

Chapter Nine

MY SISTER, KAELA, WAS HOME when we returned.

"Aren't you supposed to be coming home tomorrow?" I asked, hanging up the keys by the back door.

"Tori had to leave tonight, and since we were counselors this year . . ." She stopped talking as Liam appeared behind me. She took one look at him and held up a finger, then dragged me to the living room. "Um, sis? Why is the lead singer of Gear standing in our kitchen?"

I stepped backward from her grasp, stumbled over the backpack on the floor, and landed on the sleeping bag beside it. She had just returned from girls' camp and had yet to do anything more than drop her stuff, notice Liam immediately, and drag me out of the room. "What?" I must have heard her wrong. Gear? The band? Was she serious? I scrambled to stand up but was in a really awkward position. I finally had to get on my knees before I could stand.

"That guy"—she pointed her finger to the other room and said in a fierce whisper—"is William Jones, the lead singer for Gear."

"Gear?" I repeated stupidly, matching her tone. I had heard of Gear; they had become all the rage while I was on my mission, but since I'd returned, I hadn't caught up on the latest bands. I probably knew their songs but would never be able to point out a member of the band in a police lineup.

My sister's mouth gaped a bit, and her eyes widened. "Yeah, you know, they sing that song 'Brazen' that you like so much?"

"Brazen"? Gear sang "Brazen"? The song I had belted out in the car in front of the guy who sang it for real? No. A wave of heat washed over my body. *No!* How absolutely, horrifyingly embarrassing. But it really couldn't be him, could it? Stars didn't just hang out in Utah, did they?

I whipped my phone out of my back pocket, and my fingers couldn't type *Gear* fast enough on the Google search bar. Within seconds, up popped his picture, along with a screen full of links, one of them being images of the band members. I clicked on that. Sure enough, there was Liam posed right in front. *No way.* I knew it! I knew there was something he wasn't telling us! It felt like my heart was pounding in my throat, and a wave of realization flooded through me like adrenaline pricking at my skin. He was famous. I slowly sat on the edge of the couch cushion, transfixed. Picture after picture showed the guy I had come to know over the last few days—his smile, his eyes, his messy blond hair.

My sister sat down beside me. "Am I right?"

"Yes." My heart thudded as I admitted it, maintaining a slightly frantic pace.

"Seriously? How did you not realize . . . ?" Kaela trailed off, looking from me to the other room and back at me.

How did I not realize it? Shouldn't I have figured this out earlier? The British accent that came and went. The story that seemed too fantastic to be real. The arrogance. The lack of stress over his situation or the lackadaisical attitude about time being of the essence. People asking if he was someone else. How did I not know? But in my defense, I hadn't been back in the country for very long, and my time and energy had been consumed with moving forward with life and organizing the fund-raiser.

"Oh my gosh," I murmured, sinking back into the couch. "This is seriously surreal."

"How . . . did he get here?"

I turned to face her, forcing myself to break my concentration from Google Images. "I picked him up on the highway, driving home from my job interview. He and his girlfriend had a fight, he passed out, and she dumped him off on the side of the road."

Kaela's mouth became an *O.* "His girlfriend, Twick? Twick Openshaw?"

Twick Openshaw was his horrible, spiteful girlfriend?

Suddenly, this was all making so much more sense. Twick Openshaw, the daughter of a hotel-chain magnate, who would one day inherit a fortune. Even I knew who she was. Twick was known more for her partying and escapades than for her charity work and fund-raising.

"I . . ." I was speechless. I had no idea who Liam really was and who this girlfriend was who had gotten revenge. I had been hanging out with, running errands with, dating someone famous, and I'd had no clue.

"Wait until I tell Tori and Natalie!"

I grabbed her arm. "No. Wait, Kaela. You can't." I felt the urgency that Liam had instilled in me to protect his privacy. Only now, I understood why.

Kaela looked unconvinced. "Why not?"

"He will freak out. I'm pretty sure he doesn't want anyone to know he's here. Like, he was vague about who he was on purpose." Even though I now had a glimpse as to why, my next thought was that he'd deceived me.

"That doesn't mean I need to be." She swiped her phone screen and tapped on the texting app.

I grabbed it out of her hands. "Seriously, Kaela, can you just wait a little? I at least want to talk to him and ask him what the deal is before we go viral with his location."

Kaela's shoulders drooped. "I guess. But I get first dibs on—"

"Absolutely not! He's way too old for you and sooo not—"

She giggled. "I'm not talking about dating, although I wouldn't mind. I was talking about posting it."

"Hold your horses, you social-media butterfly." I didn't want to betray the trust Liam and I had built, but I really wanted some answers from him.

Kaela stuck her tongue out at me. "Sometimes you're no fun."

"You may have mentioned that a time or two." I mimicked her antics.

She dropped her voice. "Do you realize who we have in our kitchen? Only the hottest singer from the hottest band around right now!" She squealed.

I continued clicking picture after picture, loading page after page. There were a lot of pictures. Selfies, him with girls, him with fans, him with Twick Openshaw. No need for click bait in this situation; I continued without any prompting.

Scrolling down the list of links, I couldn't choose what to click on first. "William and Twick at the award party." "Who Betrayed Who?" "Are They Together?" "Twick Openshaw Sighted Snuggling with Mystery Man." "Reunited." "Bandmate in Turmoil." "Rehab for Tread." "Nigel Arrested on Drug Charges." "Twick and William Take Separate Vacations." The list went on and on. Liam's life seemed to be embroiled in drama.

I opened the first link, scanning my way through the short blurbs, then continued reading, closing, and opening the next offering. Fascinated, shocked, unable to gather information fast enough to fit all the pieces of the puzzle together to make this situation with Liam make sense, I continued binge-clicking. I wished I had more time to read everything, but I just didn't because there was so much. As the shock slowly settled into slightly less shock, a new feeling crept in, one a little more real. I had been scammed. Here I was having this great time with this charming guy only to find out he wasn't who I thought he was.

But another question was plaguing me. Now that I knew, what did I do with the information? Did it matter who he was and why he was still here? Wasn't this just a temporary situation until he got his life back once he had his identification and money and things FedExed to him? Wasn't this going to be a faint and quickly fading memory in his rock-star life? Would he even remember who we were in a week? Probably not.

I went back to the kitchen, a little nervous and unsure about confronting him. "So, Liam. Or should I call you William?"

He froze. The silence that followed seemed to fill the whole room. It seemed to last a long time, but it couldn't have been more than a few seconds. "You know who I am, then?" he said quietly, staring at me. There was almost an expression of pleading on his face.

"Yeah. My sister figured it out. I think you have a little explaining to do."

He didn't look regretful. "Not really."

Surprised by his response, I looked at him closer. "What do you mean 'not really'?" Maybe I mistook the pleading look. Maybe it was something else. "Don't you think you owe me and my parents an explanation?"

"Everything I told you and your parents was the truth."

I folded my arms across my chest, buying myself a few seconds to form a rebuttal. "But you conveniently left out some details. Some really big details. Maybe you want to start at the beginning?"

He shrugged. "Yes, I am William Jones. Yes, I am in the band Gear. I saw a chance to be anonymous for a couple of days, and I took it. Is that so bad?" He sat on the couch. "It's nice to be around people who think the best of you without expectations. Can you blame me for wanting to be around your family?"

"So you used us and lied to us."

He held out his hands with his palms toward me like he was trying to defuse the situation. "I didn't lie to you. I may not have told you everything, but I didn't lie to you. I just felt like it was better if you didn't know who I was."

I rolled my eyes. "Better for who? For you or for me?"

He pointed across the room to where Kaela was hanging around the doorway. "What happened when your sister came home? What was the first thing she wanted to do when she realized who I was?"

"Post it," I said.

"Exactly. That's my point. It's better for you and for me if I remain anonymous."

"I just feel . . ." It took me a moment to figure out the emotion I was feeling. "Deceived."

"I'm sorry. That wasn't my intention." This time his expression was pleading. He shook his head. "Really."

I rubbed my forehead. "It's late, and we have a busy day tomorrow. I can't deal with this right now, so I'm going to bed. Excuse me." I turned on my heel and retreated to my room.

Once I had my door shut, I sat on my bed, replaying the revelation in my mind. What was I so angry about? So he hadn't told me who he really was. Was that such a crime? Would it have mattered to me that he was famous? Probably not. I didn't really get caught up in being a fangirl. I didn't typically have a ton of time to devote to that. Could I trust him? I didn't know. He had offered many times to repay not only me but my parents too for the help we had given him. Not that we were doing it for reimbursement. I couldn't tamp down the anger stewing inside. He hadn't really lied to me. More like left stuff out. But if he was selective about what he told me, what else had he left out? And had he been telling the truth about how he felt about me?

Oh. My. Gosh.

I really liked him.

* * *

I descended the stairs first thing in the morning to hear Liam howling—full-on laughing—which led to him gasping for breath. He was sitting on a bar stool with his mouth open, waiting.

Whatever my sister had told him had made him break out in laughter that caused his eyes to water.

"Your sister," he said to me when he finally caught his breath, "is funny."

I eyed the situation carefully, trying to take in what was going on and decide whether Liam was charming them or really meant it. I had spent several hours last night cyber stalking and information gathering.

It didn't resolve any of my issues as to whether I could trust him now. I had decided I just needed to be aware and not be suckered in.

"Why didn't you tell me how funny she was?"

"It never came up," I said flatly.

He slid off the stool and came up next to me. "Look, Camille, can we go someplace to talk?" He put his hand on my elbow.

I flinched, avoiding his touch. "Fine." I agreed. "How about, I don't know, outside?" I gestured to the glider we had on the back porch.

"Yes," he said. He followed me out, and we stiffly sat on the bench seat.

"You know—" I said.

"Camille—" he said at the same time.

I clamped my lips shut to give him a chance to talk, in case I was jumping to conclusions.

"You have every right to be mad. I didn't tell you who I was, but I was protecting you. I was definitely protecting me. Things change when people know who I am. It's hard to understand if you're not in the situation."

"I get that," I said. "But I still feel like you were using us."

"How?" he angled his face toward me.

I shrugged. "I don't know. Taking advantage of our ignorance."

He took my hand. "I'm sorry, Camille. I wasn't trying to hurt you or lie to you or deceive you. I just thought it was better to leave my fame out of it."

I didn't fully understand his reasoning and possibly never would. But I would force myself to give him the benefit of the doubt. I took a deep breath, telling myself to calm down. Maybe I was making too big a deal about it.

He went back inside, and I stayed on the glider, gently rocking back and forth. I grappled with my feelings, completely overwhelmed by them. He was a good guy, and I liked him, but I didn't like what he did to us. How could I trust him again?

Mom knocked on the window and tapped on her watch. We were going to have to start getting ready to leave for the fund-raiser, and I still needed to shower and eat breakfast. If I continued to sit here dwelling on Liam, I was going to run out of time. I pulled myself up and willed myself to get going.

Chapter Ten

LIAM WAS RELUCTANTLY FOLLOWING ME, carrying my pink, flowery messenger bag. It was full of flyers, tape for hanging the flyers and signs, and zip ties. He handed me a flyer, and I hung it up. We had quite a system going.

"You are out to totally humiliate me, aren't you?" he muttered.

"You could use a little humility, don't you think?" I teased.

"I thought I was exercising humility by not announcing who I was," he offered as a weak excuse.

"Ha," I said, then wagged a finger at him. "You were just protecting yourself."

"Actually, I was protecting you." He held up a handful of zip ties and pointed them at me.

"Uh-huh. You keep telling yourself that," I said. There had been more of a light, teasing air between us since we'd sorted things out earlier this morning. After a shower filled with contemplation, and some prayer and scripture study, I decided I needed to be a nicer person and extend the olive branch. Almost immediately, the tension of the situation was defused, even though I still had some slightly unresolved conflict and confusion. But the fund-raiser was demanding most of my time and attention, so I had to put my conflicted confusion on the back burner for now.

"And just so you know, I usually just write a check as a donation. I don't show up."

I wasn't sure how to take that other than I was the exception to his rule. But then again, maybe he felt obligated since I'd picked him up when he was half-naked and he was staying with us. And since we were all going to the fund-raiser, wouldn't he come along too?

The fund-raiser was from 11:00 to 3:00 p.m. at The Swirly Whirly. Liam and I drove there a little early to make sure everything was in order. Amanda arrived with her parents, Tessa and Alexander, shortly after, and my parents and Kaela were right behind them. Introductions were made, a table was set up by the side door to greet people, and that was the official start of the fund-raiser.

After the initial surge of extended family members and ward members in the first half hour, not many people showed up. I was disappointed at the turnout but kept hoping more people would show; we still had time. Who could resist an ill little girl with such a cute face? All my hard work and good intentions would have to be rewarded, wouldn't they?

An hour into it, we weren't any better off. Traffic had not picked up. People had yet to come in throngs. We had topped off at twelve, with a few people straggling in and random customers who had happened in on the event, but nothing of consequence. At this rate, I hadn't even recouped my money for printing the flyers. And we would never make enough to get the pledge match. I wished that business owner had just given out of the goodness of his own heart.

"What do you think, luv? Are more people going to show up or are you maxed out?" Liam had voiced my fears.

"I don't know. I hope not. I had it planned so well. I advertised, asked radio stations to announce it, pretty much threatened friends and family that if they didn't come, I would hunt them down and make them sorry. And even then, most of those who committed to come haven't yet. And once they do, I might have what—twenty more donations? Wow. Whopping success."

"Don't be so tough on yourself. You still have time. At least you had a go at it."

"But that's just it. Why try if I'm going to have results like this? It's like I didn't do anything at all. We might have raised a hundred dollars."

He touched my shoulder. "I'm sure whatever they get out of this, no matter how small, will be appreciated."

"Thanks for trying to make me feel better. I'm just frustrated with myself for not doing more to make this successful."

His face brightened, and he leaned close to me. "I can pull a few strings if you're okay with it."

I appreciated his attempt at cheering me up. "And what would that be? Bribe people to come? Pay people to come? Buy out all the frozen yogurt we have here?"

"There's a downside."

"What? Could it be any worse than this?"

Liam's face was completely serious. "It becomes wildly successful."

I didn't see there being a downside to the event's success.

He leaned in close, close enough that I could feel his breath on my ear, which made it tingle. His voice was low. "If I drop my name, there will be fallout."

All of this made it seem like we were deciding to detonate a nuclear device. Was there a way to save my feeble attempt? I was pretty defeated at this point. I assumed he was calling his manager and maybe having him write a big, fat check for the cause or having him drum up some traffic somehow.

"I'll consider myself sufficiently warned." The only fallout I could see would be a lot of people showing up. That still didn't sound too bad to me.

"So you want me to make the call?" He rubbed his chin and waited.

I nodded.

"Can I borrow your phone?" He took it and stepped outside, returning a minute later. "Okay. Let's see if that helped."

"What'd you do?"

He leaned close to my ear. "I called my manager and Gwen." He said it in a conspiratorial kind of way.

I had guessed that much. "Okay. What are they going to do?"

"Just wait and see." A smile played at his lips.

"You think that will help?" I wondered out loud. If his 'pulling strings' did absolutely nothing, I'd rather be mentally prepared for the disappointment than hoping for a miracle. But he was William Jones; he was bound to have a few tricks up his sleeve, right?

A little over twenty-five minutes later, two men in dark suits and sunglasses came in and shook Liam's hand. They looked like missionaries but older and without the name tag and had bodies that looked like Thor. They talked for a minute, Liam pointed around the store, and they all nodded in agreement.

Then he walked over to my sister and had her take a picture of them on her phone before taking his place beside me at the table. "You ready, luv?"

I pointed to the two men. "What'd you do? Call Men in Black?"

"Bodyguards. You can never be too careful."

He must've been really expecting something great.

Fifteen minutes later, a van showed up with a huge antenna, advertising the local news channel across every side of the van. Next, a radio station pulled in. Then the girls began to appear. And then the girls began to gather.

"It's show time," Liam announced, a huge grin on his face.

Media? Why hadn't I thought of that? Well, I had, actually, but everyone I'd contacted had given me little commitment to the cause and little reassurance that it was worth their time or effort. Liam was obviously a bigger draw.

"You managed all this with one phone call?" I asked as I saw another news van heading our way.

"Fame has its perks," he said, sounding like an ad for a credit card membership.

"I thought you were just going to have them write a check."

"I had them make some calls. Then I had your sister send out our picture to all her little friends, and we'll see if that does the trick. There's a reason Instagram is called Instagram. Let's see how instant it actually is."

And it seemed like it did do the trick. Before the news people were even set up, the fans started arriving. Cars were pulling into the parking lot from every angle possible.

Kaela came and found me. "Liam wants you at the table."

I glanced in that direction, wondering what he needed. I had just fought the crowd to get where I was; the thought of pushing my way back through was a little tiring.

When I got to him, he leaned toward me. "You're going to get interviewed, you realize," he said as I pulled up a chair beside him. He pointed outside to where one of the vans with a large antenna had a girl primping her hair and holding a microphone in front of a camera man.

I had to tear my eyes away from the glass storefront. "What?" I looked at him in dread, thinking of my appearance. Sure, I had gotten ready this morning, but I hadn't dressed up nicely or done much for makeup other than swipe on some mascara and apply lip gloss. The lip gloss was long gone, having been chewed off with all my stress.

"You're the one in charge, the go-to person, the—"

"Yeah, yeah, I get it. But really, can't you do the speaking?"

"Sure, I'll do some and promote this whole thing, but it's not my show, luv." He clicked his tongue.

"Thanks," I said dryly. I really wanted to slink back into the background, overwhelmed with the response. But this was my gig; this was my future dream job. I was eventually going to have to own that I was in charge, and it looked like it was going to be sooner rather than later. I squared my shoulders as I mentally prepped myself.

"You're welcome," he replied, matching my tone.

It took a few minutes, but sure enough, a girl who looked to be maybe a few years older than me turned to the store, the camera man still beside her.

"This is like *Field of Dreams*," my mom said, coming up to me. She had to press herself against the wall to make it through the line that had formed and was now out the door.

"Like what?" I had to talk loudly. The chatter around us was like a big bundle of nervous energy, making the noise level inside unlike anything that had happened inside those four walls.

"It's a movie. I suppose it's too old for you. It's about a guy who keeps having a dream that he should build a baseball field in the middle of nowhere. And he keeps hearing the whispering that tells him if he builds it, they will come. So, risking everything, including losing his house, his farm, and his family, he builds a baseball field in the middle of his corn field. And in the end, all these spirits of dead baseball players and spectators come from miles around to watch the games be played. You could see the headlights lined up for miles as the cars drove into the field."

It did sort of look like that, even though I had never seen the movie. But it was like what I imagined the movie scene to look like. Cars were driving into the parking lot, girls were spilling out of the cars like bugs scurrying from a dislodged home.

"What happened?" my mom asked. Her eyes were wide as she took in the sudden crowd.

"Well, Liam made a phone call, and all these people suddenly came."

My mom looked puzzled. "Who did he call?"

"I don't think it was so much who he called as it is who he is. I found out a little more about Liam this morning."

"What?"

"He's the lead singer of a very popular band. Kaela recognized him instantly."

"He did tell your dad and me that he was in a band."

"You knew?" I turned and stared at her. He told them and not me?

She nodded. "Yes. He said he wanted to be up-front with us and not have to worry about him staying with us or stealing anything. He pulled up a picture of himself and his band on their website. I didn't realize he was so popular."

I blinked a few times in amazement. "You knew this whole time and didn't tell me?" Did he not trust me?

She glanced at me and then back at the crowd. "He asked us not to tell you, so I assumed he told you himself. Like I said, I didn't know he was so popular. I was just glad to have a name to a face and know a little more about him."

"Yes, apparently, he is very popular. And that's why he was vague when he was telling us—or at least me—about himself. He didn't want to be recognized. He said this was a chance to be anonymous and he took it."

"I can understand that. But now he's ready to be recognized?" My mom looked around at the crowd of giddy girls. "This is amazing."

"I guess he was willing to do it to help out the fund-raiser."

"How nice of him," she murmured. I think she was in awe. She was not alone.

Liam was sitting at the table at the back of the store, next to where the row of self-serve machines started. The body guards stood behind him, legs apart, arms clasped in front, looking intimidating. The line of people waiting to meet him had tripled in size in the last five minutes and snaked out the door and around the corner of the building. He was politely smiling, taking pictures, and pointing the fans in the direction of the yogurt. Kaela was collecting money before the girls took their picture with Liam. Apparently, he was selling himself, or more appropriately, selling his photo op.

I made my way with much difficulty to where Kaela was. "What's going on?" I asked.

She answered without even looking away from the line. "If they donate five dollars, they get a cup of yogurt, meet Liam, and have a picture taken with him. Toppings are extra. Looks like it's working," she explained.

I eased over to Liam's side. "This is amazing. You really know how to draw a crowd," I whispered.

I had to lean in so close to hear him that his lips brushed against my face. It didn't go unnoticed by me. "It's what I do best, luv. I'm selling my image. And girls will post their picture online and send it to their friends, who will come, and before you know it, there will be so many fans here, we might need to call the police for crowd control."

"We might need to do that now." I took in the gaggle of girls waiting patiently for their turn to meet their idol.

"I'll leave that up to you."

I looked around in awe, then wrestled my way over to my mom. "Do you think we should call the police?" I looked past the line out the window. There were cars backed up in the parking lot, the line took up most of the sidewalk in front of other stores in the strip mall, and things were pretty congested.

"Why? Aren't you happy about all these people?" She was still standing where I had left her minutes before.

"Yes, but Liam suggested it. He's afraid that at some point, it might get out of hand and turn into a mob."

"Okay. I'll put your dad on it." She sprang into action and left in search of my dad.

My phone buzzed in my back pocket. If it weren't for the vibration, I would've missed the ring. It was way too loud to hear much of anything. I checked the screen, and the number was the place I had interviewed with. No one would miss me if I took a couple of seconds to answer. I hurried into the back room and stepped out the rear door so I could hear. I held the handle of the door to keep it from closing. "Hello?"

"Camille Winston?"

"Weston. Yes."

"This is Kane Webber. I spoke to you Monday."

"Hi." My heart started beating faster. This was unexpected. Had I misread the guy's attitude and the girl's comment and completely misinterpreted how the interview had gone? I held my breath. Out of spite, I said I wouldn't want it, but was this a second chance? Divine intervention? Hope sprang into my thoughts as new possibilities suddenly seemed, well, possible. If I got the job, it could be goodbye Harris and The Swirly Whirly.

"I'm calling to let you know that we enjoyed meeting with you . . ."

"And?"

"And although we were impressed with you, we've decided it would be more advantageous to go with a different candidate."

All the air went out of my lungs in a huff. "I'm sorry, what?" I lifted my hand to my other ear to block out the noise. I wanted to be sure I'd heard correctly. The door shut behind me, and I realized I'd just locked myself out of work.

"We've hired someone else."

I tried the door quickly, but it really was locked. I gave up and slouched against it. "Can I ask who?" I had my suspicions, and I wanted to know if I was right.

"I'm sorry. I'm not at liberty to discuss that."

"All right." My voice reflected my dismay.

"Miss Winston," Kane added. "Thank you for applying."

"It's Miss Weston," I corrected him before hanging up. It was my last-ditch effort to save my dignity. I should've stuck with my gut instinct about the interview instead of hyping myself up for an unexpected job offer.

I put my phone in my back pocket and tried the door for good measure. It was still locked like the last time I'd tried it, forcing me to walk around and use the front entrance to get back in.

I hadn't anticipated the extent of the crowd that had gathered. The people seemed to be multiplying exponentially even from the last time I had seen it. It was an awesome sight but made it impossible to get through the front door. I had to almost push and shove my way through, claiming my right as event organizer to people who were reluctant to give an inch.

As I continued with the same level of difficulty through the crowd, I heard snippets of conversation from girls waiting for their turn to meet Liam.

"I can't believe he's here!"

"I'm so going to die! I can see him there!"

"He's hot! I'm so excited to meet him!"

He was definitely the draw for the fund-raiser.

By the time I managed to get through the unyielding group, I could see through the window that I had missed the TV interview. Amanda's mom was talking to the reporter, then shaking her hand. A tiny part of me was okay with not being on TV; I didn't want to be in the public eye that much.

Once the camera shut off, the news reporter relaxed out of her pose and turned to Liam. I couldn't hear what she said, but she looked gushy. She shook his hand way longer than necessary, putting her other hand over his. I was pretty sure she also slipped him what looked like her business card.

I watched her carefully, but out of the corner of my eye, I saw a cop car had pulled into the parking lot, lights flashing and siren chirping. Great. I wanted to hide, knowing I would be the one they would eventually seek out.

After making his way through the crowd, stopping to talk to adults along the way, the cop eventually found my mom in the store. I didn't know if I should follow him in or run and hide. Mom looked around and finally located me, still outside, and waved. I reluctantly waved back and watched as the cop came over.

"Are you the one in charge?" His voice was gruff.

I was almost afraid to admit it. Cops always made me nervous, even when I hadn't done anything wrong. Which was the case right now. "Yes," I said timidly.

"Next time you're planning on bringing in someone with this much draw, you might want to give us a heads-up first. I'm gonna have to call for backup for crowd control, just in case."

"Okay. Thank you. Sorry," I said. I wasn't sure what the appropriate response to his disgruntled chastisement should be. Just being in his presence made me feel guilty, even though I hadn't technically done anything wrong. I just felt that with one false move, he'd find some reason to arrest me. Cops had that effect on me.

I took a step back. "Am I free to go now?"

He glanced at me but was talking into the radio on his shoulder. With a tilt of his head, he motioned that I could go.

I once again used my line that I was the one in charge to push forward.

I returned my attention to my original mission of making it to where Liam was, but once I finally made it through the door, I wanted to stop to catch my breath. A hand on my arm stopped me as I was about to push forward. It was Tessa.

"We're going to leave now. I hope that's okay. This crowd is too much for Amanda, and she's tired."

"I totally understand. Thanks for coming," I said over the din of the crowd.

"Thank you for doing this. It was so great."

"You're welcome."

We hugged and said goodbye. It was so crowded I couldn't even see where Tessa headed off to or where Amanda and her dad were.

Once I sat down beside Liam, I saw a different perspective to the craziness of the situation. The fan attention was something I had never witnessed before.

"Oh my gosh! I love you!" one girl claimed, gripping her phone and jumping up and down.

"I can't believe I met you. Can I kiss you?" another begged.

Two girls who looked about high-school age exchanged an interesting conversation. "Will you sign my wrist? I'm going to get your signature tattooed."

"Your mother won't let you get a tattoo!" the second girl screeched at her friend.

"I don't care! It's William Jones!"

"I'm going to remember this day forever!" This girl was in actual tears.

"You are so gorgeous!" was another claim repeated over and over.

Although he declined any kisses, Liam's response was generally the same. "Thank you, luv. Shall we take a picture, then?"

Girls were falling all over him, some flirtatiously, some outright hitting on him. His responses, although always polite, were charming. The way he smiled when he greeted them, tilted his head as he listened to them, and encouraged them to be close to him for the photo, it was all terribly attractive and hard to resist. He knew how to make each and every person feel like they were special.

I finally had to put a time limit on when the pictures were going to end, even though there were still many waiting in line. We ended up having to close and lock the doors. We had already gone one hour longer than planned, and three television stations had covered the event. I was completely exhausted and couldn't imagine how Liam must feel since he was doing much of the promotion himself.

It took another hour to get through the fans who were already in line inside and a few more cops to keep the peace as some in line were denied access and late comers were turned away.

As everyone left, I thanked them for being involved and helping me put on a successful fund-raiser. Liam made sure he took time to take a picture with all the employees.

I sat in one of the booths once the table was packed up and the store was cleaned. From that angle, I could see there were still people everywhere outside, only kept far enough back by the presence of a police perimeter. My feet were killing me, and I propped them up on the bench across from me. Liam sat beside me. "What do you say? You're the only girl in a twenty-mile radius I haven't taken a picture with today."

"I haven't paid my five dollars."

"Consider this one on me."

He took my phone, held it up, snuggled close to me, and snapped a picture.

My insides melted like frozen yogurt in the hot summer sun.

* * *

When I'd counted the last of the donations, minus paying for the yogurt, the total came to over $12,000. Thousands of people had shown up. Not bad, thanks to Liam.

We were still behind the locked doors of the shop, but I took everything into the employee area, out of sight of the fans who were still pressed against the window.

"Do you feel like celebrating?" Liam asked.

I felt giddy. "Yes! But I don't know what to do." It was difficult to imagine how to top the exhilaration I was experiencing.

"Welcome to my world. Exactly the same feeling after a concert."

"What do you do to come down off the high? I feel like I want to go out and tell the world what we did and what we accomplished and how happy I am about it." There was a ridiculous grin on my face, but I couldn't stop smiling.

"Um, I'm not sure if you really want to know. You know"—he cocked his head sideways—"different lifestyle."

I caught his drift, and although I was curious about what he'd said, I wasn't sure I wanted to know. The Liam I had gotten to know the last few days seemed like a far cry from the person he was professionally.

"Hey, hey!" Kaela called out. "We're on the news." We gathered around her, watching her phone.

"I'm Chantelle Daymond with Action News. We are live at The Swirly Whirly, where there is a fund-raiser for Amanda Mason, who has acute myeloid leukemia.

"Right now, we're talking to Amanda's mom, Tessa. How do you feel about the turnout today?" Chantelle turned to Tessa with the microphone.

Tessa bent toward the microphone. "We're so grateful to the Weston family for making this happen."

"And there is a very special guest here today." Chantelle turned to Liam. "William Jones, lead singer of the band Gear, is also here supporting the cause."

Liam grinned at the camera.

Chantelle held the microphone in front of Liam. "How did you get involved in this?"

"When I found out about Amanda, I couldn't help but offer to help in any way I could." Liam didn't seem nervous during the brief interview.

Chantelle positioned the microphone back to herself. "It looks like it is working." She stepped closer to Liam.

"Hopefully this will help get Amanda the treatment she needs."

"What is your part in all of this?" She held the microphone in front of him once again.

"I get to meet a lot of fans. For a donation of five dollars, you get a photograph taken of or with me and an autograph. At the end of the event, I will match all the donations collected today."

"That is very generous of you." Chantelle batted her eyes at him.

"Thank you."

"And will the rest of the band be joining you in this surprise appearance?" She tilted her head.

She was totally flirting with him.

"I'm afraid it's just me, luv. I hope that's good enough." He grinned at her, and I swear I saw her swoon.

"From the looks of the fans, it seems that it is."

Chantelle pulled out a five-dollar bill from her pocket. "So, can I get a picture?"

"Absolutely," Liam said pleasantly and posed with her. He knew how to work an audience.

After a quick snap of her phone camera, she looked back at the TV camera. "Reporting live at The Swirly Whirly, with William Jones of Gear, I am Chantelle Daymond."

I whistled slowly. "Chantelle Daymond. Wow. Flirt much?"

"Who cares?" Kaela jumped up and down. "Your fund-raiser was on TV." She had a point.

The fund-raiser turned out way better than what I'd imagined, but I also knew if Liam hadn't stepped in, it wouldn't have done even 90 percent as well as it had with his help. "Thank you."

He shrugged. "It was nothing."

"No." I shook my head, arguing. "It was definitely not nothing. It was huge. And it had to be exhausting having all those people pawing at you and talking at you and . . ." I had caught a glimpse of what his life was like, what he had been trying to explain earlier, and now I understood.

"Do you get tired of that? All the people? Having to be so . . . charming with them?" Being so charming with them, even when they're crowding in on you? Pawing you?" I added mentally. The sheer mass of people today had been overwhelming to me.

"It's a coping mechanism. I'm selling an image. You catch more flies with honey than with vinegar, so you have to be appreciative of the fans. Without them, the band wouldn't be where it is."

"Seems exhausting."

"I was glad to do it," he said, looking straight ahead. "In fact, you've inspired me, and I feel I'm leaving here a changed man."

"Amanda will totally appreciate it. It took way more effort than just writing a check, so thank you." This was why I wanted to go into this field of work. I loved this feeling.

"I didn't do it for her," Liam answered softly.

"Yes, you did," I said, rejecting that it could be anything more than that.

"Well, of course I want her to get better. But I really didn't do it for her. I did it for you."

I swallowed, sure that it was loud enough for him to hear. But I couldn't think of anything to say. I could almost hear the seconds ticking away in silence and my heart pounding away with them. His face was inches from mine, and I could feel his breath on my cheek.

"Shall we go out to eat?" my dad suggested, interrupting the moment.

I stepped back, both relieved and disappointed.

Getting away from the store, into our cars, and on the road in safety was something I hadn't planned for, and I gained a deeper understanding of the need for bodyguards in Liam's presence. We all had to sit and actually map out an escape route, or "exit protocol," as the men in black called it. It was an elaborate plan to get not only Liam but all of us out safely without being ambushed or followed by fans. The security company provided several large, dark SUVs with "limousine tint" windows, and after a complicated procedure, which included a few "meet-up points," we all switched to another identical dark SUV and were on our way to dinner. The men in black would be joining us for dinner that evening.

We traveled to a restaurant in Nephi, complete with Liam and his glasses, baseball hat, and American accent, to celebrate. It was a dinner that would forever remain a snapshot in my mind. Everything was perfect: the food, the conversation, the time spent together as a family.

As we drove home, the excitement of the day and coming down from the high caught up to us, and the conversation in the car lulled. I became introspective. Now that the fund-raiser was over, I hadn't thought about what I was going to do the next day or the day after that. It was like returning home from my mission all over again. It was a familiar feeling of, *Now what?*

"You're quiet," Mom said, peeking into my bedroom awhile after we got home. Liam had said something similar after we'd gotten out of the car. I had excused my behavior away as being satiated to the point of sleepiness.

I had just climbed into bed. "Can you talk for a minute?"

"Of course," she said, stepping in and closing the door behind her. She sat on the end of my bed and folded her legs under her. "What's up?"

Sitting up, I propped my pillow against my headboard. "I'm trying to sort through my feelings."

"About what? Liam?"

"Yes and no, but not directly him. More like what he did."

Mom's head leaned to one side. "What do you mean?"

I inhaled deeply. "My fund-raiser was a success, but I was a failure." Now that the dust had settled and the adrenaline of the situation had diffused, I had come face-to-face with the truth.

She immediately reached out and rubbed my arm. "You weren't a failure."

"If Liam hadn't rescued my fund-raiser . . . They came out to see him, not to help my cause. I'm thankful for him, and yet I'm angry about it. This is what I want to do, it's my future career, and I wasn't successful. All he did was make one phone call and bam! Hordes of people." I made an explosion noise and gestured with my hands.

"Oh, honey, don't feel that way."

"But I do. I don't want to, but I wish I hadn't needed help." I sighed. "And then I feel bad because he was willing to give up his anonymity to help me. Can I be grateful and upset at the same time?"

She thought for a moment. "I realize it's a little bittersweet. Sometimes we all need a little help."

"Please don't tell me to get over it. I'm just disappointed with myself. I feel compared to him, and my contribution and effort were inadequate."

"That's not what I was going to say. You might feel inadequate in his shadow. Maybe he shines, but it didn't just happen. I'm sure he had to work for it. You'll work at it, and then you'll shine. There was no stealing your thunder going on. It was more sharing his thunder so you could be successful too."

When put that way, it made it easier to adjust my attitude to become gratitude.

Chapter Eleven

As we were sitting down for breakfast on Sunday, my mom invited Liam to go to church with them.

He squirmed in his seat. "I appreciate the invite, but I'm not really a churchgoing bloke."

"You can always start," she offered.

"I think with yesterday's fund-raiser, people now know I'm around, and it might cause of a bit of a ruckus. I don't want to disrupt the services."

Kaela frowned, making a deliberate show of disappointment. "I told all my friends you were coming."

"Sorry to disappoint you, luv, but you'll thank me. It gets a little crazy with fans, and we don't want a repeat of yesterday. You might even have people hanging about your house as we speak." He walked to the front of the house and peered out the window.

Kaela turned to me. "Can I come with you and him to your singles ward?"

"I think we need to let the two of them alone." Mom tried to direct her away from us by putting an arm around her shoulder.

"That's not fair that Camille gets to date him and I don't."

I scoffed. "It's not really dating, Kaela." I kept my voice low. "It's entertainment. I'm just the shiny new toy, the distraction. It'll be over as quickly as it began."

"You don't know that," Kaela countered.

But I did. How could it be anything more than that?

At that point, Liam returned, and the conversation quickly ended.

He and I ended up skipping church and going to Temple Square instead. I figured it would avoid causing a scene but still be spiritual.

"How is it you don't have a boyfriend?" Liam asked as we wandered around the Conference Center. His question made my insides feel like jelly.

I gulped. "I haven't had time. When I got home from my mission, I had to get my paperwork in to return to BYU in the fall, find a job for the summer, and plan this fund-raiser and find people to sponsor it."

"You didn't have a guy on your mission?"

"No. We don't date on our missions." I realized he wouldn't know that, but I was more curious about why he was asking.

"At all?"

He was watching me intensely, and it was making me nervous. "Nope, not for the whole year and a half I was there."

"What about before?"

"Sure, I dated in high school and my first year at college. But no one serious. Why?"

"I'm just surprised." He shrugged it off.

I didn't know why he was surprised. It wasn't like I was Twick Openshaw or anything. Twick was a wispy waif with corn-silk hair. I was sure she had no problems or issues with getting attention.

I cleared my throat. "So you and Twick Openshaw. What was that like?"

"We dated on and off for two years. I met her at a concert, and we had a very tumultuous relationship after that."

I sat on a bench, and he sat next to me.

"Twick is always looking for a good time, which was exactly what I was looking for when I met her. But then everything changed when Tread met Cybil."

"Who is Cybil?"

"Cybil is Tread's girlfriend."

I could kind of put the name to a face from my cyberstalking but not really. Liam seemed like he was open to just telling me whatever I was curious about.

"When he met her, everything changed. We had always been closer than brothers, and she seemed to be a wedge. Don't get me wrong—she's a great gal and really good for Tread. She seems to even out his bipolar."

"He's bipolar? Your best friend is bipolar?" Was this a known fact and I was just oblivious because I didn't follow their band?

"Yeah, and if you ever breathe a word of that, I will sue you for libel faster than you can say sorry."

That answered my question. "Back off, buddy. No one's calling the *National Enquirer*." I held up my hands.

"She kind of calmed down his wild side. Like, he even started talking about settling down with her."

"That's not so bad."

Liam looked down at his hands. "Except I sort of became jealous."

That was unexpected. "How so?" I kind of had this impression that he could have anything he wanted.

"At first it was just how much time they were spending together. Tread and I always hung out, and I felt replaced. But that was before I'd met her and seen how good they were for each other. Things get sort of distorted in our world. You don't know who truly cares about you because it's always about the fame or the money or what they can get from you. Cybil came on tour with us, and it just sort of happened. But more than just the time they spent together, I wanted someone like her. That's when Twick became more of a distraction."

"A distraction from what?"

"From what I didn't have."

"Wouldn't it have been better to break up with her so you could find what you wanted?"

"It seemed like everyone I met was the same: in love with the image and not the guy. So I figured it was better to stay with Twick than to be alone. I thought it would make me less jealous."

"Did it?"

"Yes and no." He shrugged. "I decided I had to just settle for what I had."

I didn't know what to tell him, so I changed the direction of the conversation. "So how did that leave you on the side of the road in your underwear?"

"Like I said, Twick and I have always had a tumultuous relationship. When we fight, it's not pretty. Last time we broke up—"

Some of the articles I had glanced over came to mind. There was more than one containing the word *fight* in the headlines. But since it had been mentioned so much, it seemed to me it was a pattern for them. "You left her stranded in the middle of nowhere?" I guessed. What could he have done that warranted such backlash from her?

"No. But I publicly humiliated her at an awards party. I came with her and left without her."

"Hmm. Had that happen to me on a small scale. Prom, my senior year in high school, in fact."

"So you can imagine it made her really mad." His eyes met mine.

"And this was her way of getting you back for humiliating her?"

"Yeah. I think she was hoping I would get arrested. Get some unwanted publicity, maybe cause some sort of scandal. Or maybe she was just going for really inconveniencing me. Really, really inconveniencing me. I'm not quite sure what all her motives were, but I know she was trying to get me back for humiliating her."

"Sounds like a great relationship. An eye for an eye."

"I don't know if I've ever known anything different in our relationship."

"Never?" I found that really hard to believe.

"I can't say I've been in a lot of relationships, Camille. I've had a lot of . . ." He trailed off, realizing he was painting a less-than-chaste picture of himself.

"A lot of . . . ?" I raised an eyebrow, waiting.

"A lot of fan attention. But no one who wants to be with *me*. It's always who they think I am. They want the superstar, William, not the regular guy, Liam."

"Who am I getting?" I asked.

He looked intently at me, then lifted one shoulder. "You're getting Liam, the regular guy who likes shepherd's pie and has had Starbucks withdrawals every morning since he's been here."

"Don't forget the slice of lemon pound cake," I added. He had bought me one every time I'd driven him to Starbucks. I'd probably be up five pounds by the time he left.

"And how about me, Camille? Who am I getting?"

I laughed. "What you see is what you get, Liam. I'm not trying to be someone else around you." Would I have felt differently had I known up front who I was picking up on the side of the road the other day? Keeping his identity from me made a little more sense now.

"Thank you," he said.

"For what?"

"For being you around me."

"Well, you're welcome. Anytime." I laughed.

For a moment, I thought he was going to kiss me. He looked briefly at my lips, and he slowly made his way closer.

My stomach tightened in anticipation. I put my hand on his arm. "Liam . . ."

He pulled me to him and leaned in. I was pretty sure he was going to kiss me, and my lips parted.

Then I broke away, flustered and slightly indignant. "Wait, wait. Do you kiss everyone you've just met or have only known for five days?" I shouldn't have almost given in.

He grinned, seemingly proud of himself for trying to kiss me. "No, not everyone. They have to be female, at least. And it's been six days; I've been counting."

I had been seduced by that smile way too much. "And I qualify because I am female?"

"No. You qualify because I like you." His eyes met mine, and a thrill went through me.

"And what makes you think I like you?" I had tried to hide my feelings, but I'd also almost kissed him just now. I wasn't doing a very good job, was I?

"You can't fake the click," he said.

"The click?" I repeated.

"The click, Camille. We have it. You know, when everything fits." He wagged his finger back and forth between the two of us.

Without warning, he started singing quietly.

"You know it, you feel it
When everything fits.
You know it, you feel it
When everything clicks.
You can't fake it,
You can't force it
You can't make it fit.
But you know it,
You feel it,
When everything clicks."

I wasn't sure how to react to being serenaded. I thought back to the other night: playing games at Chuck E. Cheese's like we were kids, the easy conversation during dinner. But he was so charming—how could he not, as he'd said, click with everyone? He knew how to play the game. He knew how to perform and entertain. That was his job; that was what he did. And he did it very well.

I looked away, reality burning my mind. I hated it. I hated the truth. "Liam, get real. This isn't real. Whatever this"—I motioned between the two of us—"is, you'll forget about it as soon as you leave."

He took my hand. "Why do you think that?"

I pulled it back. No need to prolong the inevitable. "Because it's the truth."

"No, Camille, it's not." His voice was so sincere. I wanted to believe what he was telling me, but I couldn't. It was just common sense.

I stepped back to put some space between us, hopefully minimalizing his urge to touch me. "You're a rock star, and I'm the girl next door. Really. What are the chances?"

"Why leave it up to chance?" he asked in a soft voice.

He could be so romantic. I hated myself for feeling like I could melt into his arms right then. I didn't want to think about it anymore. We should just have a good time today and enjoy each other's company because this could all eventually fade into a memory of a weird week. I had to be realistic and accept it.

Liam closed the space between us again, reaching out to play with a strand of my hair.

I wanted to look away, to break the intensity of his stare, but couldn't.

He glanced at my lips and then met my eyes. Slowly, he leaned in and kissed me.

My lips touched his, and my heart skipped a beat. I closed my eyes as my lips parted and I kissed him back. His lips were soft and gentle. His hand pressed against my back, and the other threaded through my hair. I felt a quiver of excitement as my heart pounded in my chest. Enjoying the moment was easier than listening to the voice of reality whispering in my head that this meant nothing to him.

And then my phone rang.

Chapter Twelve

"THAT'S PROBABLY FOR YOU," I joked, hurriedly putting some distance between us and reaching for my phone. We had just kissed! "No one calls me on my phone, just people for you." I looked at the number, and I could tell by the area code that it was for him. "See, I told you," I said as I handed the phone to him.

"Hello?"

He was quiet for literally only one second before he exploded. "Twick? It's about time!"

My heart stood still. I'd known this moment would come, when he'd finally talk with his now ex-girlfriend. Would they resolve this and get back together? Although he denied it, there was always a chance. And what did that make me? The convenient amusement while he was in exile?

"Where have you been?" He waited. "Vegas? You're in Vegas? Are you kidding me?" There was silence on his part for a moment, but that didn't stop him from pacing and running his hand through his hair and shaking his head. "You wanted to teach me a lesson? . . . You're ready to make up? Are you insane?" He made sort of a strangled laughing sound. "There's no making up for this."

Of course I was listening to the conversation, trying to pretend I wasn't. But what I was hearing definitely answered my questions.

He stood still for a moment. "You're sorry? You dumped me out in the middle of nowhere with nothing, and you're sorry? Sorry doesn't quite fix it, Twick." He shook his head. "I don't want to see you. I just want my stuff back." Another pause. "How do you propose I get there? . . . Oh, you didn't think about that?" He exhaled loudly, exasperated. "I'll meet you, but there's nothing to talk about. I'm through." He hung up, gripped the phone tightly, and groaned. "She is unbelievable."

I really wanted to know what she'd said. And I didn't even have to ask because he started telling me. "She wants to reconcile."

"But you don't." I knew I was repeating the obvious. I was hoping for some insight as to where that left me.

"It was over when she dumped me off on the side of the road. Do you realize how bad things could've been if you hadn't picked me up and if your parents hadn't let me stay? It could've been a lot worse than just bad press."

I didn't understand how bad it could be for him, but I was sure pictures of him standing on the side of the road being printed in the gossip magazines wouldn't have been good.

"What does that mean?" Was he really done with Twick Openshaw for good? I had to know. But why did I care?

"It means that as soon as I get my stuff from her, I'll make it clear again that we are over."

"What are you going to do with yourself if you're not dating Twick?"

He looked me straight in the eye. "I have some good ideas."

Twick's phone call sort of killed the romantic moment we were having. We couldn't exactly pick up from where we'd left off. I couldn't bring myself to shamelessly say, "Hey, so about that kiss we were sharing before we were so rudely interrupted." That would be very awkward, at least for me. So instead, I remained silent.

"I've got one more favor to ask of you," Liam said as we started back to the car. I felt an unspoken consensus that the date was ending.

"For a guy who just met us, you need a lot of favors." I was teasing, so I made sure I sounded playful and not rude.

"I know. I'm at your mercy." He pretended to plead. "But I will make it worth your while."

"You keep saying that. I'm not sure how you're going to do that. My parents aren't exactly going to let you pay them for your stay here."

"I'll figure something out." He grinned. When he said stuff like that, he was so charming I hated it.

"I'm sure you will." I smiled back. "What do you need?"

"You make it easy to feel like you don't mind my asking."

I blinked my eyes flirtatiously at him. "Anything for you."

"Anything?"

"Within limits, of course." I became serious pretty quickly.

"I need a ride to Las Vegas."

"That will cost you," I said with a straight face. I preferred this banter much more than acknowledging our fledgling feelings.

"I figured it would. Of course, I'll pay you for your time and petrol."

"My time and petrol?" I quirked an eyebrow.

"I don't really want Twick coming to get me."

"No? Don't want to spend quality time with her?"

"I'd rather spend the time with you." He stated it so matter-of-factly.

I stopped, feeling that jumpy feeling in my stomach, along with a surge of excitement. Was he just flirting to get me to agree? He was certainly charming and experienced enough to get away with it.

I straightened. "You don't have to butter me up."

"Butter you up?" His brows knitted together.

"Yeah, you know, be all charming so I'll agree to drive you there."

"I'm not buttering you up, luv. I'm telling you the truth. Six hours in the car with Twick might land me in jail."

"From what you've told me, it doesn't sound like Twick has figured out that it's over."

He chuckled. "Nope. There's not much going on between those ears of hers."

"I hope you never say that about me."

"You're not like that, Camille." He laughed but not from embarrassment of being put on the spot.

"Oh, no? How am I like?" I was curious what he thought of me. I hadn't been the most trusting person when I'd first met him; I hoped my character had proven better since then.

"Pretty much perfect."

My mouth gaped. How did I respond to that?

"I'm not," I finally managed. "Nowhere near perfect."

"Okay, then, you're a very focused girl who has a whole lot more going on in her head than Twick Openshaw will ever have."

"I'll take that as a compliment, I guess?" My heartbeat quickened, but I still considered his word choice. Hopefully, *focused* was a good thing.

"Yes."

"Thank you."

"You're quite welcome. Is that a yes, you'll drive me?" The way he said it made him irresistible.

I shrugged and hung my head. "If there's no other way to get rid of you."

He was watching me when I looked back at him. "Are you that anxious to get rid of me? I thought we were having an enjoyable time." He waited expectantly, his eyebrows raised.

"I was just kidding about getting rid of you. But have you really been having an enjoyable time? Despite everything that was going on with Twick?"

"I'm not talking about what's going on with Twick. I'm talking about meeting you and your family. I've never met a family like yours. It was rather lucky of me to have been picked up by you. Maybe even kismet."

Maybe it was luck, maybe it was coincidence, or maybe it was even divine intervention. Who knew? Maybe it was nothing more than my being a good Samaritan and helping out someone in need. Whatever it was, I was trying hard not to read anything more into it. I had probably already gotten more involved than I should have, going out with him the other night. He was too much of a charmer for me to fall for him. He just screamed heartbreak. He would be done with me as quickly as it had begun, and I didn't want to end up being inspiration for one of his songs.

Monday, I had to work the four-to-eight shift, so Tuesday was the day we decided I would drive Liam back to Las Vegas. The good thing about that was maybe I could stop in and see my roommate Sophia from my freshman year. The bad thing was that Liam would be gone forever, and we would be a fading memory as he crossed state lines.

Chapter Thirteen

"You know, Camille," Liam said, starting the conversation back up.

We were driving back from Salt Lake and were definitely *not* talking about the kiss we had shared. The kiss I couldn't stop thinking about. The kiss I kept telling myself really meant nothing. The kiss that had happened only because we were in the moment. Why was I allowing myself to be seduced by his charm?

"Yes?" I asked cautiously. I needed to step back from my emotions and think about this logically.

"I had a great time with you."

It sounded like he was making a follow-up call after a date. I cleared my throat, swallowing down my disappointment. Clearly, I was conflicted. I kept hoping he was going to say something that solidified this being more than a weekend fling. But at the same time, I was just too practical. I was not his type. He did not share my standards, and I definitely did not belong in his world. "I did too. I appreciate all your help with the fund-raiser. I couldn't have done it without you."

"Thank you for your honesty."

"I don't know if you should be thanking me. I think I shared a little too much of my opinion."

"Honesty is a rare thing for me to come by."

"Well, then, you're welcome."

"I'd like to see you again."

"Really?" I said too quickly, giving away my desire. I had just told myself there was no chance, and because of our different lifestyles, I shouldn't hope for a chance. It wasn't low self-esteem; it was reality.

"Yes, really," he sounded amused. "Is that so hard to believe?"

"Well, yes. I'm not exactly your speed." It almost felt good to say that out loud and get it out of my brain.

He cocked his head. "What is my speed?"

"You know, like Twick."

"Didn't we clear that up? Twick isn't the kind of girl I want to be dating."

"And I am?"

"Well, yeah."

"Yeah right!"

"Are you going to doubt everything I tell you?"

"I just find it hard to believe." Yes, I was skeptical. It was that thing called reality that I was trying to be in touch with.

"What's hard to believe?"

"Me. You. Our very different lifestyles."

He frowned. "You're hung up on the lifestyle thing."

"You should be too." Did he miss my explanation about the whole Word-of-Wisdom and law-of-chastity thing? Did I really have to come out and say it?

"I'm not looking for a lifetime commitment. I'm just saying I would like to see you again."

Was that my problem? I was looking to only date guys I could have a lifetime commitment from?

"What would it take to convince you? Would a tattoo convince you?"

I snorted. "I'm not a tattoo kind of girl."

"That's good because I hate tattoos," he said and let out a big whoosh.

I thought back. I didn't remember any tattoos. Not that I was looking that closely. "You don't have any tattoos?" Strange. It seemed like it was the thing to do these days, especially people in the music industry.

"I did start to get one but had a very nasty reaction that was quite rare and quite painful. It was red and oozing puss and disgusting. I ended up having the whole thing removed and have never been tempted since. And I really, really hate needles."

That made no sense to me at all. "If you really, really hate needles, why would you get a tattoo?"

He laughed and nodded. "Precisely why I had to be very drunk to even get me to consider it."

Yet another reality check. "And you would get a tattoo for me?" I didn't want him to, of course, but it was a curious comparison.

"If that's what it took to prove it to you."

I let out a small laugh. "So it's really lucky for you that I'm not a tattoo kind of girl."

"Yeah, I don't know if I'd survive another reaction like the first one."

"You don't feel like less of an artist not having any tattoos?"

"If I'm ever feeling that way, I take a pen and draw a heart on my bicep that says 'Mum.' Then I feel much cooler about myself."

"You said you don't even want to know what happened to your mom."

"Good thing I can wash it off, then," he said, neatly sidestepping my probe.

"Well, spare yourself from the pain and don't get a real tattoo for me."

He laughed his deep, rich laugh. "I'm very relieved." He made a show of placing his hand on his heart and exhaling loudly. "We have one more day together. Let's do something. What's there to do in Utah?" Liam asked.

He voiced what I was thinking. "You mean tomorrow morning? If it were winter, you could go skiing. Or to Park City and Sundance."

"You like the outdoors kind of stuff?"

I nodded. "I do. I grew up in a great state if you love outdoors. There's skiing and hiking and—"

"Do you rock climb?" Liam asked eagerly.

"Never tried it." I didn't take him for Mr. Outdoorsman but then thought back to his bare chest. There was nothing soft about his six-pack. "You climb too?"

He nodded. "Actually, I fancy it quite a bit. You?"

"Not really. But I like hiking. I'm more of an occasional athlete. You know, the occasional hike, the occasional ski trip a couple times during the season."

"Is tomorrow a good occasion to go on that one hike?" He watched me, waiting for my reply.

I took that as encouragement. "Sure." Hiking would take up the morning and seem less intense than just being alone in the house with him. Stewart Falls in Provo Canyon would be perfect because we could easily get it done in the morning.

"Are you up to the challenge?" His chin was lowered, but he looked up at me from under his eyelids. Saying no would have been a challenge.

"Yeah." Did he not think I could keep up with him? I gripped the steering wheel as I mentally chastised myself. I shouldn't be doing this. I shouldn't be giving in to the flirting. He was leaving Tuesday. I needed to remind myself of that. Hiking could be as strictly friends, right?

* * *

As we made our way down the street, I noticed our block had an unusual number of cars parked on it. "Someone must be having a missionary homecoming," I murmured. I took in all the cars as I drove past them.

Liam looked up, then put his hand on my forearm, gripping it tightly. "Wait, Camille. I think that's paparazzi. Can you turn about?"

I took a quick left, checking my rearview mirror to make sure no cars started following us. Then I pulled over. Through the neighbor's yard, we could see the corner of my house.

"Do you see that van?" He pointed to a dark van with tinted windows pulled over just before our driveway. The brake lights were on.

"Yeah. What about it?"

"It has driven up and down the street and then turned around. And there are two other cars parked across the street."

"Okay?" I still didn't understand. How had he noticed this? How did we know the neighbor wasn't having a luncheon or something?

"It seems suspicious to me."

"Do you think it's SWAT and they're going to attack our house?" Because our house was situated on the curve between two streets that forked, it was often hard for people to find and many drove right past it.

"And he drove all the way up from California to do it?" Liam looked at me expectantly.

"So? The car has California plates? Lots of cars have out-of-state plates. You know, students." I held my hands out and shrugged. "We live next to a college town."

"Does that look like a van a university student would drive?"

I looked at it again, watching it as it drove down our street. It was nice and shiny and new. It crept up, stopped, and then finally parked in front of our house.

"I thought so," Liam said. He craned his neck so he could get a better look out the car window.

"What?"

"It's paparazzi."

I still wasn't convinced. "How do you know?"

"Look." He pointed to the van again. "See how the driver and the passenger both got out and went to the back of the van? They're getting their equipment."

"Are you sure it's not just . . ." I sort of trailed off as the two men emerged from behind the van, one of them carrying a large camera at his side.

There was another man with him who had a full set of tattoo sleeves and looked more like a Harley dude than a college student.

An odd zippy noise came from the passenger side of the car, and when I looked over at Liam, his seat was reclined as far as it could go.

"What are you doing?" I asked, alarmed by both the unexpected noise and his odd behavior.

"Trust me, luv, you don't want them seeing me." Liam peeked above the window.

"Wonder how they knew where I lived?" The whole idea seemed crazy.

"They're resourceful. Would anyone at work have given it to them?"

"I don't think they'd give a total stranger my address."

"They can access it through public records online too."

I thought for a moment. "Or find it where I posted it online when I invited people to come to my homecoming open house."

Liam's eyes widened. "Your address was just out there in the open?"

"Well," I cringed, "yes. How did I know the paparazzi would be stalking me ever in my lifetime?"

Liam looked behind him and then around the neighborhood. "Can we get out of here?"

"You mean drive away?"

Liam nodded. "Yeah, 'cause otherwise, they will not leave you alone." I couldn't tell if it was desperation or exasperation I heard in his voice.

"But what if I go outside and talk to them? You know, tell them you can't come out and talk?"

He scowled and shook his head. "No. There's no talking to them. Respect and personal space isn't generally their concern." His expression brightened. "Maybe they don't even know I'm here and they're just hoping. I'm just sorry they're coming 'round your house."

"Well, at least they don't *really* know you're here yet."

"No, but if some have shown up, others can't be far behind." This time he looked over his shoulder. I also looked out the rear window, trying to see if I could pick any more out.

"How many more?" I said, feeling the weight of his words settle on my chest. I glanced around the neighborhood with a more suspicious eye.

"Hard to say. If those other cars across the street aren't already them. They're like cockroaches. If you see one, you'll see more."

I called home. I wasn't sure if anyone was there, but it was worth a try.

"Camille?" my mom answered. She sounded concerned. "Where are you?"

"Parked around the corner."

"Good. Don't come home. We are surrounded by reporters and . . . I don't even know what to call them. Dad called the police, but since they are not technically harassing us, there is nothing they can do."

"What happened?"

"When Kaela was coming home from church, the reporters wouldn't leave her alone with questions about Liam, and she finally said something to the gist of he's not here right now. When they asked her when he was coming back, she said, 'I don't know.' So I think they took it to mean he was coming back here. They got back in their cars, but they haven't left."

"I see," I murmured. "How long have they been here?"

"I don't know. Dad and I got home an hour ago, but we drove into the garage. Kaela stayed after church for a few minutes and walked home, and that's when they got out of their cars and started bombarding her with questions. She feels really bad about accidentally admitting he was here. She shut the door and started crying."

"I'm sorry. I had no idea anything like this would happen," I said.

"Well, it's not your fault, and it's not Liam's either. It is what it is." My mom paused, then started speaking again. "And Kaela found something online where a reporter for some gossip show was interviewing Harris from work."

"Oh no, not him." I had a sinking feeling in my stomach. Harris was the last person I wanted to be opening his mouth about me. Or Liam. Especially after that display at the mall the other day.

Liam looked at me with an expression of slight alarm. "What?" he asked.

I held up a finger, signaling *Just a minute.* "Okay." I hung up and took a deep breath.

"What's up?"

"Well, you were right. The paparazzi is camped out at our house. Kaela mistakenly told them you weren't home right now, and apparently, they somehow talked to Harris from work, and that's all over the internet."

"Brilliant," Liam muttered sarcastically.

"So we need to figure out what to do from here." I looked out the window, still in disbelief that this was even happening. "I should probably look online to see what sort of misinformation Harris fed them." I googled William Jones in Utah, and it didn't take any searching at all. Harris's 'interview' was the first one that popped up. I scanned through it. "Oh, listen to this. Harris says we are keeping our relationship a secret."

Liam didn't respond to what I had read. "You know you can't go to work tomorrow," he said, his voice serious.

"I can't?" I hadn't considered it. Would it be similar to what was happening outside my house right now?

"They'll be waiting there too. And it will be very disruptive."

"Are you saying I should call in sick? Or not sick but just unable to make it?" The craziness of the moment made my head feel like it was spinning.

"I would."

"I'll see what I can do." I grimaced at the reality of the situation.

"Welcome to the world of paparazzi. They will follow you everywhere and hound you until you are ready to resort to violence."

Suddenly, I regretted having never heavily tinted my windows. "It's like that all the time?" I was a little bit in awe. You see it on TV, but when it's right on your front lawn, it feels very different.

"Yeah, pretty much, and this is just the beginning. It gets worse. Another reason I didn't tell you who I was: I was hoping to avoid this."

"How can you stand it?" Were we going to have to call the bodyguards back?

Liam shrugged. "I don't know; it comes with the territory. You learn to ignore them. Sometimes if you are nice to them, they'll leave you alone. But not always. I lost my tolerance for them a long time ago."

"Won't they give up and leave? I mean, there is not much of a story."

"I'm not sure how long it will last, luv. But I don't think they will give up until they feel they've given it a proper go."

I glared back toward my house. "Well, I hope their 'proper go' ends soon."

"As long as they don't know I'm staying at your house, it will end sooner."

"What should we do?" I asked. At that moment, I felt bad. I didn't know how my 'saying goodbye moment' would be, but I didn't want it to be like this, all rushed and panicked. "I think I better take you back today. It only makes sense."

Liam reached for my phone. "I'll text Twick and let her know I'm coming today."

Chapter Fourteen

WE REMAINED PARKED WHERE WE were and called my parents back. "I'm going to drive Liam to Vegas right now." I put the phone on speaker and set it on the arm rest between the two front seats.

"What about his stuff?" Mom asked.

Liam shrugged. "Not really much stuff. Although I do need to get that FedEx envelope."

"Should I run over and grab it?" I asked.

Liam's eyes bulged as he quickly shook his head. "No. They will follow you."

"What should we do, then?" I asked.

"We'll come meet you," Mom said. "The gas station right by the high-way exit."

It wasn't far from our house and would make it easy to leave for Vegas. "Sounds good."

Liam leaned closer to the phone. "Take different routes. We don't want them following us."

"Okay. Give us a few minutes and then we'll leave. Hopefully they won't tail us, but it's better us than you," she said.

"Right," Liam said.

"Sounds like a plan," I said almost at the same time before hanging up.

Within a few minutes, the garage door opened, and my parents' car backed out. As soon as the car was off the driveway, the paparazzi crowded around them, cameras out and flashing. It didn't even look like they were taking a picture of anything, just holding their cameras up in hopes of catching a picture.

"That is insane," I said, watching the scene unfold. Did Liam seriously do this every time he went somewhere?

A couple of the people even hopped in their cars and started following my parents.

"We should wait at least five minutes and then make a U-turn and leave the street in the opposite direction. Is there another way to exit your neighborhood?"

"Yes," I murmured, my eyes glued to the activity at my house. The photographers and camera crews were still hanging around.

We gave it a couple of extra minutes before driving to the rendezvous spot. I found myself checking my rearview mirror much more often than normal. My dad, mom, and sister were waiting for us.

"That was crazy. We had to stop and get out at a store so those people would see Liam wasn't with us," Kaela exclaimed.

I noticed we all took the opportunity to look around us in case we had somehow been followed or were being photographed.

My family gathered around, saying goodbye to Liam and offering him well-wishes.

"Will you come back in the fall and be my homecoming date?" Kaela asked as she gave him a hug.

Liam chuckled. "Sorry, probably not. And don't even think about doing a YouTube invitation."

"You're coming back though, right?" Kaela asked. Her plea was probably a question on everyone's mind.

His eyes flicked to me, and then his attention returned to my sister. "How about I get you some passes for the next concert?"

"For me and my friends?"

"Absolutely," he confirmed.

"I'm going to expect it."

"I'll have my assistant contact you when the time comes 'round."

"That is so cool!" my sister gushed.

Liam stepped over to my mom. "Gabbi, thank you so much for your hospitality."

"Anytime, Liam. We loved having you."

"I appreciate it more than you know."

My mom gave him a hug.

"Thank you, Charles."

Dad shook his hand. "Of course."

"And thank you for letting me take your daughter out. She's a special girl." Liam pulled me into a side hug.

Okay, I really hated Liam saying I was a special girl. It made me feel like that was equivalent to him calling me a sweet spirit, and no one wanted to be a sweet spirit.

"We think so." My mom looked over at me.

"Maybe someday I can repay all your kindness somehow." Liam seemed genuine in his hope.

"Or just do something kind to someone else, and don't worry about repaying us. It was our pleasure," my mom said.

I still found it hard to believe my parents had fallen for his whole charm act. I still found it hard to believe I had fallen for it too. I was more than certain this would be the last we'd ever hear from him.

"Oh, I almost forgot. I packed you two some food. I was hoping to sit down for dinner tonight, but instead, you'll just have to enjoy some Uncrustables from the freezer." Mom returned to the car and came back with a bag.

"Thanks, Mom," I said. I was kind of hungry.

With one more round of hugs and goodbyes, my parents and sister left.

Liam went into the store to buy himself some energy drinks while I hurried to my car, anxious for the safety it provided. While I waited for Liam, I called Sophia to see if I could stay with her tonight. Then I sent a text off to Tammi, telling her I wouldn't be at work tomorrow and asking if she could cover my shift. She responded that she'd take care of it. My phone beeped at me, and I realized I had a low battery and no charger. I hoped it wouldn't be a problem as I put it into airplane mode and turned off the screen. Liam returned just as I was finishing. I put my hand on the steering wheel and turned the key in the ignition.

The reality of the paparazzi put me in hyperaware mode, and I continued checking the rearview mirror more than normal. What if they followed us? What if there was a high-speed chase like with Princess Diana, resulting in a deadly accident? It all sounded overly dramatic until I was the one experiencing it. The adrenaline made my heart pound so loudly I could hear it in my ears.

Once we were on the highway, Liam put his hand on mine as I was about to turn on the radio. "Are you okay?"

I wondered if he thought I was being quiet because of the paparazzi, but it wasn't that. "I'm fine." Or at least I wanted to be.

"I really wish we didn't have to rush off like this. It would've been nice to have been able to spend all day tomorrow with you. Or at least half the day."

"Sadly, the paparazzi and work has ruined any chance of that even being a possibility. Hopefully, work won't be too upset that I called in for tomorrow. I can't give them a reason to fire me. Part-time jobs become scarce when college students return for fall semester." My plan was to keep babbling on about inconsequential stuff so we wouldn't have to talk about the end of the visit. Anything to veer away from us and the inevitable goodbye happening in just a few hours. It would be the ultimate reality check for the whole crazy time I'd spent with Liam.

"You worry about becoming redundant?" He sounded surprised.

I couldn't stop myself from snorting. I worked at a frozen yogurt place. "Do you mean unnecessary? Yes, I do." They could easily fire me and replace me. Since I didn't get the other job, I needed my measly little work until I could find something else.

"I worry that I will become redundant," Liam said unexpectedly.

I blinked back my surprise. "Redundant? You? How could you ever become redundant?"

"Yeah. What if someday no one wants to listen to my music anymore because it's not . . . good? Or it's not worth listening to?"

"I don't know how that would feel." I had the urge to reach out to him but quickly stopped myself.

"I worry that the creativity will run out, and then I'll be nobody."

I wasn't in the same industry he was, but as I thought about it, I really could relate more than I realized. Wasn't that my exact fear for the fund-raiser? That nobody would come and I would fail? "I'm okay if I'm nobody, as long as I am able to make a difference in someone else's life."

"When Tread went through his depression, it just seemed like everything we had worked so hard for could be gone so easily. And yet, if Tread wasn't around, would it even matter? But if the creativity dries up, then what? I would just be someone who used to be famous."

"Not to Amanda you won't be. To Amanda, no matter what happens to your career, you will always be the guy who made her fund-raiser successful."

His head tilted, and he pursed his lips. "I've never considered it that way."

"But it's a good way to think of things, don't you think?" It was how I was trying to think of it since my mother had pointed it out to me.

"Perhaps."

"Perhaps nothing. You made a huge difference, and you should be proud of it. Your success made my fund-raiser a success, which helped Amanda. Thank you."

"You know you're welcome."

The conversation lulled, and I sank into my own thoughts.

After a while, Liam broke the silence. "You haven't said anything in almost twenty-five minutes. Anything in particular on your mind?"

I turned to him. "Did you really mean those things you said to my family? Are you really going to send my sister tickets to your next concert and all that stuff?"

"Absolutely."

I ran my fingers through my hair as I processed his response. "Because she's going to hold you to it, and so am I. I can understand that sometimes you have to be all charming and flirty, like at the fund-raiser. You say things people want to hear, but Kaela believes you."

"Is this really about me disappointing your family?" He waited. When I didn't reply, he said, "I'm not a bad guy, Camille. Why won't you give me a chance?"

"I feel that you're only doing this out of obligation. You think you owe us because we helped you out of a tight spot. That's why you helped with the fund-raiser too."

His brow knit together. "I helped you out with your fund-raiser because I wanted to. I didn't feel like I had to." He then cocked his head and gave me a penetrating look. "I thought we had a good time the last couple of days, and I thought I showed you who I really am."

"And then you're going to leave and never think about us again," I blurted out. The realization sort of took my breath away.

"Ah ha. The truth comes out. Is that what it is? You think I used you?"

Was that what it was? I didn't reply. I didn't know how.

"I'm sorry," I said quietly after a moment. "I wish these last couple of days actually meant something to you."

"Of course they meant something to me. You have a lovely family that makes me envious. You have parents who love you and would do anything in the world for you. You have parents who were willing to give me a chance. And best of all, I met you."

Was I expecting something? I knew the worst thing I could do was expect anything from him.

I didn't look at him. I couldn't look at him. I swallowed hard and concentrated on the road with more focus than necessary. "Maybe you'll write a cheesy song in dedication. You know, something like:

There once was a girl from Springville,

Whose chances with me were about . . . nil

We spent some time

Always on my dime

But when I was gone, it was through."

"Camille?" he asked quietly. "What do you want from me?"

I gripped the steering wheel. "You mean, with all your vast experience with girls, you don't know what a girl wants?"

"If I did, do you think Twick and I would have had the relationship we did?"

I shrugged. "Do you really want me to answer that?"

"Yes, I do."

"You might not like what I tell you." I peeked at him only to find him looking directly at me. I quickly looked away. I was driving, after all. It was probably safer to keep my eyes on the road. At least that was what I told myself.

"But the truth is the truth. No one ever tells me the truth."

"I don't think you and Twick loved each other. You were together for some other reason or reasons. Because people who love each other don't treat each other that way."

He looked out his window. "You're absolutely right," he said quietly. I thought the conversation was over, but Liam continued. "You never answered my question."

I mentally ran through the conversation. "Which was what?"

He was still quiet. "What do you want from me?"

"I want the same thing you want: for you to be honest with me. Please don't ever lie to me."

"Why would I do that?"

I couldn't answer. I was sure there were more reasons than I knew.

In the midst of the heated argument, I happened to look in my rearview mirror to see flashing red and blue lights. Dang! I'd been speeding. I blamed it on the adrenaline-filled escape from the paparazzi and the current topic of conversation.

"You want me to handle this?" Liam asked.

My shoulders sagged. "Handle what? I was speeding. There's not much I can do about that now." I rolled down the passenger side window as I watched the highway patrolman in my rearview mirror.

He came up to Liam's window. "License and registration, please."

I started digging through my glove box. This was always when I wished I had gone through and organized it and didn't have fifteen old insurance cards and years of past registrations but couldn't seem to find the current one to save my life.

"You look familiar." He squinted at Liam. "Have I seen you before?"

Liam's identity had resulted in a mob of girls on Saturday and the paparazzi this afternoon. It seemed I was the only one who had been oblivious to who he was. "He's Springville's most wanted," I joked.

The officer looked at me for a second and then back at Liam. "Do you have some ID, sir?" the officer asked.

"Thanks," Liam muttered, scowling at me before addressing the officer. "Uh, no, sir, I do not."

"Do you have any outstanding warrants?"

"Not that I'm aware of, sir, no." He shook his head.

"What is your name?" The cop squinted again.

"William Jones."

"And do you have an address, William?"

Liam rattled it off, and the officer wrote it down and went back to his car.

"You don't have any warrants for your arrest, do you?" I asked, dreading the answer. I felt bad for what I had started.

"Like I told the cop, not that I'm aware of."

"Let's hope not. For your sake," I said, staring straight ahead but surreptitiously stealing glances in the mirror to see what the cop was doing. I hoped there was no reason for Liam to get arrested. That was the last thing he needed right now.

After what seemed to take forever, the cop came back. He looked through the window and addressed Liam. "You're William Jones in that band?"

"Yes, sir." Liam nodded but kept his head down.

Suddenly, the cop loosened up. "My daughters love you. There are posters of you on one kid's wall, and the other has covered a bulletin board with your face. I knew I'd seen you somewhere."

I didn't know posters were still a thing.

"Too bad they aren't here with you." Liam smiled.

"Do you think I could get a picture with you and some autographs? My girls will never believe this, and they're going to think I am the best dad ever."

Surprised at the officer's behavior, I looked over at Liam. He was back in rock-star mode, with the smile plastered on his face, charm oozing from every pore.

"It never ends," I said to no one in particular, lolling my head on the headrest. By then Liam had gotten out and was obediently signing his name on something with the pen the cop had given him.

"Hey, Camille, could you come snap a photo for us?" Liam sounded nothing short of cheerful.

"Of course. Why not?" I said sarcastically to no one in particular. Everyone just fell all over Liam, and I was desperately trying not to be one of those people. I was suddenly in a worse mood than when the cop had first flicked on his lights. Why couldn't this be like a normal traffic stop where I could get my lecture, my ticket, and be on my way?

I took a couple pictures, then waited by the hood of the car while the cop wrote out an address on the back of his business card and Liam promised to send the daughters some T-shirts or some other bribe, I mean, memorabilia.

The cop thanked Liam profusely, then turned to me. "I'm going to let you off with a warning. But easy on the gas pedal. There's been a lot of construction, and the roads are uneven and could cause a hazard."

"Thank you, sir," I said, accepting my cards and biting my tongue. I knew the only reason I had gotten out of the ticket, which would have been a double fine because I was in a construction zone, was because Liam had been my passenger.

"You're welcome." Liam grinned at me as he climbed back in the car.

"I'm welcome? For what?" My emotions were somewhere between relieved and crying.

Liam motioned with his hand. "I just spared you from getting a ticket."

"I wasn't looking for you to save me. I was speeding."

"What is wrong with you? I just did you a huge favor." His mouth gaped a little, and his eyes narrowed.

"You did. You're right."

"I would've preferred if you hadn't dropped my name."

I chewed on my lip, deciding what to say next. I did start the whole who-was-he thing. "I'm sorry. I'm just a little rattled by how people react to who you are. And the paparazzi this afternoon. I feel very unsettled." My emotions included.

"I have that effect on people."

Chapter Fifteen

As we entered Las Vegas, I was nervous. Thinking about meeting Twick Openshaw, for some reason, was intimidating and left my stomach in knots. Since our time was coming to an end, I knew our conversation strike needed to end too.

"Liam, I'm sorry. I'm overwhelmed with so many emotions I'm dealing with. I'm sorry I'm taking it all out on you."

Liam gave me a nod but said nothing. Was it safe to assume I was forgiven?

As we got closer to the Las Vegas Strip, Liam started talking again, by way of giving me directions. Eventually, we drove into CityCenter, a group of high-rises. And like everything else on the Strip, it was flashy and over the top.

"This building, when they first built it, had a problem with glare in the summertime. The sun reflected off of it and got the reputation of having a death ray. I'm hoping the death ray from the Vdara might burn Twick to a crisp," he said as he eyed the high-rise through the window. "What do you think the chances are?"

"Maybe not the death ray," I said. "Maybe just a sunburn. A really bad sunburn. That might be hard with the sun down. But weren't you giving up the revenge thing? Remember? It didn't work out the first time."

"Revenge is Twick's game. Remember I was thinking game over?" Liam reminded me.

"Let's hope for the best, then." I suspected it was going to be uncomfortable witnessing this reunion.

They had agreed to meet in the far end of the top floor of a parking garage. "There she is." Liam pointed her out.

I shut the car off and looked over at Liam in the passenger seat. "Do you want me to come out with you?" It was lip service. I didn't really want to go out there with him.

"Sure, why not? The more, the merrier." Liam seemed a little sarcastic. He opened the door and got out.

I hesitated for a second, surprised to be called out on my offer, although I didn't feel like Liam was necessarily doing it for that reason. I felt more like it was reckless abandon on his part. So then I decided what the heck? Who cared what Twick Openshaw thought anyway?

Twick gave me an obvious once over. It was a little intimidating how she made me feel so small with one glance. "You're the girl du jour? Where'd he pick you up?"

I swallowed hard, determined not to cower. "Actually, I picked him up."

"Yeah right." Twick made a sound of disgust.

"Let her alone, Twick," Liam said in a tired voice.

I didn't know where my burst of bravado had come from because Twick was beautiful and very intimidating. I now understood what Liam meant when he said he liked a girl who ate. Twick was a stick. Like a twiggy, breakable stick—model thin. She was pretty dolled up, looking as if she were going out clubbing.

Her makeup was heavy but flawless, her eyeshadow smoky, her lips glossy and completely covered with glitter. I wasn't sure if the lip gloss came that way or if she kissed a pile of glitter to achieve that look. Either way, I guess it was a good thing for her that glitter was nontoxic. I got the impression that she wanted to look good to make him jealous or maybe to make him want her back.

"Where's my stuff?" Liam asked.

Twick got an overly surprised look on her face. "That's it? That's all you have to say to me?" Her mouth formed a perfect *O*, and her hand went to her chest. Was she always this theatrical?

"Stop being dramatic, Twick. Give me my stuff, and I'll be on my way." He held his hand out, waiting.

"Don't you think we should talk about this?" Twick gave a quick flutter of her eyelids.

Liam shook his head emphatically. "Phone, wallet, passport, keys, clothes. C'mon." He motioned with his fingers to hand everything over. His other hand was on his hip.

Twick turned to her bag, which was sitting on the hood of her car. "Fine, here." She pulled out a couple of things and handed them over to

Liam reluctantly. Liam stuffed his keys into his front pocket and his phone into his back pocket. He flipped open his passport, leafed through it, and then slipped it in with his phone. He examined his wallet in the same way. He probably wanted to make sure his ID was still in there.

A big, muscled guy with a neck the size of tree stump stepped out of the car. I assumed he was either Twick's new boyfriend or her bodyguard, but I was leaning more toward the latter. He went to the back of the car, opened the trunk, and pulled out a black duffel bag. He strolled over to Liam and dropped the bag at his feet.

Twick stuck a hip out and crossed her arms over her chest. "Now can we get going?" She made a pouty face.

Liam's brows shot up. "Get going? Get going? Get going where? I'm not going anywhere with you." He picked up his bag and hefted it over his shoulder.

"Then how are you getting home, William? Are you going to ask your little girlfriend to give you a ride?" She sounded like a condescending mother instead of a girlfriend.

"Are you stark-raving mad? I meant what I said on the phone. We're done." He made a cutting motion with his hand.

Twick took a step forward and rubbed a hand up his forearm. "But, William, I said I was sorry." She dropped her chin and poked out her lower lip. Her voice was dripping with sugar. "You know how much I want to make things right with us."

She was so . . . sultry.

Liam shook her hand from his arm. "Cut it out, Twick. That's not going to work."

She flicked her eyes at me, then stepped even closer and whispered something in his ear that was too quiet for me to hear. She ran her long, thin index finger, with its perfectly manicured nail, along his jawline.

Liam started laughing. "I'm not interested in hanging out with you in Vegas."

Twick seemed taken aback. Whatever she'd whispered in his ear was not enticing enough to take her back. Her expression hardened. "Fine," she said briskly, then pointed her finger at him and poked him in the chest. "But don't you dare accuse me of stranding you here. This was all *your* idea."

"Goodbye, Twick." Liam picked up his bag, turned on his heel, and walked back to my car. I followed after him, glancing quickly back at Twick. She glared at me, and suddenly I guessed what Lot's wife must have felt as she'd turned to salt. Twick's look was that deadly.

By the time I got in the car and shut the door, Liam was already on the phone. "Yeah, first flight out. Whatever you can get me on. Also, arrange a security escort in Vegas. Call me back with the info." He clicked the phone off. He got a call a minute later. "Great. Book it. Have a car waiting at the airport for me."

He gave me the now-familiar grin. "I need to ask one more thing."

"My intuition is telling me it's a ride to the airport."

"Yeah, but it's not far from here." He pointed east. "It's not even a mile that way. You can see the planes landing."

I looked where he was pointing but wasn't interested in the proximity of the airport. It had nothing to do with how far it was. Or that it was another favor, for that matter. It was that this was goodbye.

He directed me to the airport, which led me to believe he was quite familiar with Vegas. It was a silent ride, lasting only ten minutes.

"Are you turning around and heading directly back?" he said, breaking the silence as the airport came into view.

"No," I said. "It's been a long day, and I'm afraid I'd fall asleep driving back." It was around 9:00 p.m.

"Did you want to get a hotel room?"

"With you?" I couldn't read his expression to know if that was what he meant and whether he was serious or not.

He didn't clarify. "Just offering, luv."

I cleared my throat. "I, uh, actually have a roommate from my freshman year at college who lives here. I'm going to stay with her."

"As long as you're taken care of."

Why was it so easy for me to know he cared about my well-being and yet so easy to discount that there might be anything romantic to his feelings for me?

"You can drop me off at the passenger drop-off. Just stay in this lane." He pointed to a sign with an arrow.

I did as I was told, creeping along in the lane, looking for a spot to pull up to the curb and live park so I could let Liam out.

"There. That will do," Liam said. He motioned to a spot where a car was just pulling out. "Watch out, the taxi drivers are very aggressive and will cut you off."

"Thanks for the warning," I murmured, maneuvering my way in. I put the car in park, and my hands dropped from the steering wheel to my lap. After a few seconds of silence, I voiced all the thoughts running through my head. "So."

"So." The obvious loomed in the air. "This is it."

"We say goodbye," I said.

He pulled his wallet from his back pocket. "Can I give you some money for all your trouble?" He fished out a couple of bills and offered them to me. "Five hundred. Will that do? Is that enough?"

I looked at the hundred-dollar bills he was offering me. "Remember, we agreed, no money. It's fine." I gently pushed his hand back toward him.

"But I owe you something."

"No, Liam, really, it's fine. You don't owe me anything." I swallowed down the lump in my throat.

He hesitated. His hand hovered in the space between us. "At least take some for petrol, and that's it. It's not meant to pay you back for anything else."

"Let me just do this out of the kindness of my heart." Heaven knew I hadn't been feeling exactly kind, and I needed to do something nice for him.

I met his gaze. "It's been nice . . . knowing you." I wasn't sure what to call this last week. Meeting him? Hanging out with him? Getting to know him? Having him visit?

"Knowing you? What? Do you think I'm going to forget you?"

Yes. That was exactly what I thought.

"I'm starting to think you have trust issues. I was the one dumped off the side of the road, not you."

"I was stood up at prom," I countered.

"And this is where all these issues stem from?"

I pursed my lips, then shook my head. It came from him being famous and me being easily forgettable. Maybe I did have unresolved trust issues. Or low levels of self-esteem in this particular situation.

Liam didn't wait for me to answer. "I'll call you?" He said it like a question, as if he was unsure if he should.

"Will you?" To me, it sounded like what a guy said to escape a bad date.

"Yes, I will." He reached out and pulled me to him. "I will." His lips touched mine, softly at first and then with more purpose. My resolve instantly broke down, and I melted into him.

A tapping at the window broke us apart. It was a traffic cop. "Move along or go park."

I gave a weak wave. "Okay," I called to the cop, then cleared my throat. "The cop has spoken," I said to Liam. "We don't need two run-ins in one day."

He pulled on his baseball cap, put on his sunglasses, and opened the door. I followed his lead. We met at the trunk, where his bag was. He lifted it out and set it on the ground, pulling up the extendable handle. He pulled me in and kissed me again. "I'll call you," he whispered, his lips on my forehead.

With a final hug and one last kiss, he walked off, disappearing into the airport terminal.

I watched until I couldn't see him any longer, got in my car, and drove off, tears spilling down my cheeks. I brushed them away, forcing myself to think of anything to distract me from my emotion. I failed miserably and ended up coming up with a new rhyme.

There once was a guy named Liam
Whom I told I didn't want to see him
How stupid was I
Trying to deny
My feelings for him weren't a whim.

* * *

Driving to my friend Sophia's house gave me almost twenty-five minutes to dry my eyes and get my emotions back on the right emotional track. By the time I rang her doorbell, I was my former self. Or at least I tried to convince myself I was.

Sophia met Travis when we were roommates, and they had a whirl-wind romance; she was married by Thanksgiving. After that, we fell out of touch, and I went on my mission, and she got divorced and remarried. I had only recently been in touch with her when I thought I would have time to visit her when I went for that job interview.

"Camille!" she exclaimed, whipping open the door.

"Hi," I answered back. "You look great!" Sophia was basically gorgeous. She looked like a Barbie doll, and not much had changed since our freshman year.

After a hug, I followed her in the house. We immediately settled in on the couch, popped open a couple of Diet Cokes, and proceeded to catch up.

There was so much we had to talk about. She told me what it was like to be married and divorced at eighteen, and I told her about my mission. She updated me on her new marriage, and I updated her on why I was in Vegas.

"William Jones, as in the lead singer of Gear?" Sophia's mouth gaped.

"That would be the one," I admitted.

She pulled her long blonde hair into a bun on top of her head. "You seriously didn't recognize him?"

I ducked my head, embarrassed. "Yeah, my sister asked me the same thing."

"So, what, now you're friends? Acquaintances? His Uber driver?" She laughed at her own humor.

"Yeah, I don't know; it's confusing. We kissed."

"Oh, so you're way past the friend zone. Are you dating?"

"More like Uber driver with benefits."

"It doesn't sound like you're too happy about that."

"He's hard not to like. Gorgeous. Charming. Has an amazing accent. A genuinely nice guy. But . . ."

"You live with your buts," she said, looking at me intently.

"What do you mean?"

"However you finish that sentence, you have to decide if you can live with it."

"But nothing will ever come of it."

"So you're okay with that?"

"Well, no. I wish there were a way to make it okay. I have a whole list of reasons why I shouldn't date him ticking off in my head: we don't share the same religion, the same values, I won't sleep with him, and he's basically the embodiment of temptation. Then I tell myself I should just find myself a nice Mormon boy whom I can marry in the temple and we can settle down and have a family together."

"Is that what you want? You're not very convincing."

"I wish I could explore a relationship with him, but the end result will not be a temple marriage."

"Maybe not now, but maybe in the future. Who's to say that won't happen?"

"The only way I could see that happening is if he gave up being a musician, joined the Church, and was content with being a family man."

"Maybe he could be both."

"I don't ever see that happening."

"Why?"

"It would take a miracle."

"And who's to say you won't get that miracle? I once heard this talk at church where the speaker said disaster was God's course correction for her life. Travis leaving me seemed like a disaster at the time, but it ended up being a huge blessing because I met Luke."

"Honestly, I don't know if I'll really ever hear from him again. I think he just felt obligated to say we'd keep in touch."

She placed her hands on my shoulders and gave me a little shake. "Camille. Girl, have a little faith—in him, in you, in the Lord. If it's meant to be, it'll all work out."

"I think it's better for me to not hold my breath for his call."

"You have never been much of a romantic. I do remember that."

My mind rewound to when Sophia had first gotten engaged, after only a couple weeks of dating Travis. "I don't remember exactly what I said when you and Travis got engaged, but it might be cringe-worthy now."

"You didn't say anything different from what my brother and parents were saying. There was a consensus that I was rushing into it, but at the time, I thought it was worth rushing for. But if you learn anything from my mistake, it is to take your time in a relationship."

"It will never make it to a relationship."

She patted my knee. "We can keep talking boys, or we can put on a chick flick, eat junk food, and stay up half the night like we used to do when we were roommates."

"I don't know if I ever stayed up half the night when I was a freshman. I stuck to a pretty tight schedule that first semester. I was afraid of failure."

"It's true. I don't think you ever stayed up. It was mostly me and Gretchen, but that doesn't mean we can't start now. Luke is on a business trip, and we have the whole house to ourselves."

We did just that. Up until about midnight, when I couldn't keep my eyes open any longer. It had been a long day in the car, and all the stress caught up with me. I asked to borrow a charger, plugged my phone in, and went to bed.

The next morning, all the junk food I had eaten late into the night, especially the white-chocolate popcorn, caught up to me, and my stomach felt like it had stones in it, and my throat felt like I had swallowed sandpaper. I got up, showered, and then went to talk to Sophia.

"I wish you could stay and meet Luke. He'll be back tonight," she said.

"I would love to. He sounds like an amazing guy. I am so, so happy for you. After all you went through with Travis, you totally deserve someone—"

"Who loves me more than himself? Who can actually commit to something? Yeah, I completely agree."

"Well, obviously I'm looking for that and a little more, but hopefully I can meet someone at BYU and see how it goes. But if that doesn't happen, life will go on, and it will eventually happen."

"Camille, I hope it all works out. Now, do you want something for breakfast? I have brown sugar cinnamon PopTarts and some Diet Coke to wash it down."

Her saying that brought back fond memories. Sophia used to eat that all the time, no matter what time of day it was. I groaned and held my stomach. "I feel disgusting, and putting food in my stomach will probably just make matters worse. I think I'll pass for now."

"If you're sure."

That was one thing I was sure of.

* * *

I turned on my phone just before I left Sophia's. I had over twenty-five missed calls, most with numbers I didn't recognize, and a similar number of texts. Again, like the calls, it was a mixture of people I knew, asking about Liam, and then complete strangers, also asking about Liam. My phone rang as I was scrolling through the texts, but I declined it, as it was yet another unfamiliar number.

Because of all the activity on my phone, I decided I would text my parents to let them know I was on my way home. I also needed to make sure Tammi covered for me. There was no way I was going to make it home in time for my shift. I pushed the Bluetooth button and called work.

"Hey, Harris. It's Camille." It was a conversation I was dreading, one I was trying to avoid. I didn't have kind feelings toward Harris, especially since he had talked to reporters.

"You're not at work."

I frowned. "No, I'm not. I'm calling in."

"Why?"

"Extenuating circumstances. There were photographers camped outside our house yesterday, so I had to take Liam to Vegas. I called Tammi to let her know—" It always seemed better not to give Harris my number. "Did Tammi come in?"

"Yes, but she is not your boss," Harris said.

"And neither are you." Jerk. I could feel my blood pressure rising. I noticed the needle on the speedometer was reflecting my blood pressure. I took my foot off the gas, not wanting to get pulled over *again*.

"But you need approval—"

"She said she could cover me until you got there."

"I'm supposed to handle the whole shift?" Harris demanded.

"Harris, it's Monday. You're not going to get overrun with customers."

"But who will cover my breaks?"

I bit my tongue instead of laughing at him. That would definitely get me fired, if I didn't get fired for skipping my shift today. "You're kidding me, right?"

"Cami, watch how you speak to me. I am your superior."

"Oh, please. You've worked there two months longer than me. If anything, you might be my quasi-superior," I muttered. Normally, Harris just deserved an eye roll, but this time, I couldn't bite my tongue.

"I'm writing you up."

"You're writing me up?" I repeated in disbelief. He was really on a high horse today. "I called in. You do it all the time. But I guess it's okay because you're the boss's son."

"Cami, don't make this any worse—"

"What are you going to do?" I challenged him.

"Fire you."

"Fire me?" I choked on a laugh. "You can't fire me." I really wished I could've beat him to it and quit, but that wasn't a wise thing to do. Harris was an annoyance, but I'd get over it. Considering I had just gotten passed over for another job, I needed The Swirly Whirly, despite my little hang-ups with it. Life required employment, plain and simple. Not that I got paid a lot, but I needed that money for school. I had planned my classes around my work schedule.

"I just did. Effective immediately."

"Effective immediately," I muttered, hitting the End button. "Unbelievable," I said to no one in particular. I shook my head slowly. Apparently Harris thought being the boss's son gave him power, and it had gone to his head. I decided to call his dad, riding on my wave of anger. I went through my contacts until I found James's number.

He picked up immediately. "This is James."

"Hi. It's Camille Weston. I called in today, and Harris fired me."

"Why did you call in?"

There was really no good way to explain the situation. "Because of the paparazzi." It sounded way worse out loud than it did in my head. Who had ever heard of the paparazzi in Springville, Utah?

"Paparazzi?" I could hear the doubt in his voice.

"Yeah, they were at my house yesterday. I was afraid if I showed up for work, it would be too disruptive."

"Was there a mob there like Saturday?"

"More photographers than girls. If they followed me to work and caused a scene . . . I was worried they would hassle the customers coming into the shop. I was thinking of the welfare of the customers." The negative possibilities were endless.

There was silence on his end for a moment. "I see your point. I realize there were extenuating circumstances, so I'm not going to fire you. But I am going to give you a warning like I would any other employee for being a no-show."

That was one bright spot in my day. "Thank you. I appreciate your understanding."

* * *

"How'd it go?" Kaela asked the moment I opened the door from the garage into the kitchen.

"As well as could be expected." I hung up the keys, grabbed a water bottle from the fridge, and went to the family room, where I sank into a recliner.

Kaela followed me, hungry for details. "Did you meet Twick Openshaw? What was that like?"

Kaela's enthusiasm was so naive and misled I felt bad. My introduction to Twick was way less than glamorous and probably very different from my sister's vision. "Simply put, she was fab, I was drab, and it was all over pretty quickly."

"What do you mean you were drab? You look fine to me."

"I looked like a girl who wasn't planning on taking an unexpected trip to Vegas. And Twick looked like she was ready to go out for a night on the town."

"But what did you say to her? Did you guys talk?" Kaela was still very eager to hear the details.

"Twick wasn't interested in talking to me. She was all about Liam and was under the impression they were leaving together."

"But he chose you. Yes! I knew it."

"Actually, he chose the airport. After saying goodbye to Twick, I drove him to the airport."

"How did you leave it?" Kaela leaned forward, practically panting.

"That he would call me."

"Did he call yet?" Kaela asked immediately.

"Why would he? It hasn't even been one day."

She put her hand on her hip and gave me a look. "Maybe he misses you."

I gave an emphatic sigh. "No, he hasn't called me. I don't think he will."

"I can't believe you're dating William Jones." She squealed as if she hadn't heard me.

I held up my hand. "Wait. Stop. Again, I'm not dating him. He's a player, Kaela. I was an amusing distraction to him while he was here, but he'll forget about me as soon as he gets home." I looked at my phone to check the time. "In fact, I don't think I'll ever hear from him again." Would he just delete me from his call log and his life?

"What's your problem, Camille? He likes you."

"Did you see how he interacted with his fans? He made every one of them feel special. I'm guessing more than one of them left thinking, 'He singled me out; he liked me. I bet, given the chance, we'd start dating.' It's fangirl mentality. His attention gives you a false sense of hope that you're 'the one.'"

"But he promised us stuff. He thanked us. We mean something to him."

I wanted to wrap my arms around her and hug that delusion out of her. "I would hope so also, Kaela, but who's to say? He is inundated with people wanting to be a part of his life. We're not special."

"But you can't deny you like him."

"Yes, I like him. But it was doomed from the beginning."

"Why would you say that? You could be dating William Jones. Or even marry him. Could you imagine?" Her eyes shone with excitement.

I went to a kitchen cupboard, pulled out a package of Oreos, and returned. I picked up a cookie. "It's like this. If I eat one Oreo, I'm probably going to eat the whole row. They are that hard for me to resist. But if I don't have even one Oreo, I don't end up eating way too many. It's better to never start because I can't stop at one or two." I would just have to fight the attraction. Eventually, it'd go away.

"I'm pretty sure he likes you."

I let out a slow breath. "Like I said, he's a player. You probably don't fully understand how that would make you feel—"

"Don't patronize me," Kaela cut in.

I stared at my sister, my mouth slightly ajar. It took me a second to form words. "Good use of the word *patronize*." Her outburst had cut the tension, which I was thankful for.

We grinned at each other, and then my sister nodded knowingly. "I don't think he's going to disappoint you. I think he's going to call."

If only I could be as hopeful as my sister, but I really thought she was being naive because she was sixteen. Rock stars didn't settle down. There was no future between us.

"And I still think dating him would be pretty cool."

If there were a way I could reconcile his lifestyle with my beliefs and my standards for a relationship, there was hope. But I didn't see any way that would ever happen. I would never ask him to give up what he loved most in life just because I didn't love the same things.

"You could at least be friends, right?"

Just what I wanted: to be friends with an incredible guy I was very attracted to. Just like with the Oreos—it was better to never start. "I'm just the shiny new toy who serves as a distraction. He'll forget me soon enough."

* * *

"Hello?" I answered my phone, wondering if I should bother with a call that came up as "Private." I'd had a number of calls since the fund-raiser from girls trying to get ahold of Liam. I'd even gotten quite a few from gossip websites. I needed to change my number but lacked the motivation. I hadn't been my usual resolute self since Liam had left. I hadn't done much beyond go to work and binge-watch Netflix. But since I had nothing to do at the moment but take the call, I figured why not.

"Camille?"

Guess I needed to eat my words and a whole row of Oreos too. He called. Liam didn't have to identify himself for me to know it was him. I'd recognize the way he said my name anywhere.

I sat straight up. "Liam?" As usual, if I wasn't debating the unlikelihood of our relationship, I was left tongue-tied.

"How are you?"

I scooted over to the edge of my bed. "I'm fine. And you?"

"I'm doing well."

There was a short silence. "You called." Like I needed to state the obvious. I had been hoping he would call but had convinced myself not to expect it.

"It would hardly be polite if I didn't call to thank you. I wanted to get your address to send something to your mum to express my thanks."

I could picture a grand gesture of a large bouquet of flowers or some showy something totally over the top. My mother would eat it up. "I'm sure my mom would appreciate it." I realized I was holding my breath. What else was he going to say?

"I'm wondering what you would like."

I laughed, feeling nervous. "I'm like most girls. I like chocolate and flowers."

"Flowers die," Liam said immediately.

"And chocolate makes me fat, but that's life, and I should enjoy it while I can." I flopped backward on my bed.

"I was thinking maybe something a little more memorable." His voice was soft.

My breath caught in my throat, and my heart did a little fluttery pitter-patter. "Your visit with us wasn't memorable enough? I know I'll never forget it," I said it lightly, but I was sure he could read between the lines. His visit was not only memorable but also left me incredibly conflicted. I truly thought I'd never hear from him again. And here I was, hearing from him again, and I didn't know what to say.

"It's not anything I'll ever forget either. I have never met a girl like you."

I could only hope that was a good thing. "What does that mean?"

"You make me want to be better."

I'd consider that good. I returned to the original topic of conversation. "So what do you have in mind, Liam?" If flowers died and chocolate got eaten, what was he thinking?

"How about a plane ticket so you could come visit me?"

"What?" I gulped. My heart started racing. He didn't go home and immediately forget about me. He'd been thinking about me.

"Think about it, Camille. I'd like to see you again, but I'll leave it up to you."

Leave it up to me. Aagh! Of course I wanted to see him again. And now it was my move, and I hated that. It was destroying my resolution to get over him.

* * *

I hurried downstairs an hour later, after hearing the doorbell ring. Did he send flowers anyway? I had been contemplating Liam's invitation for most of that time, trying to make a decision. Maybe if I took the problem to my mother, she could help me figure it out. She was sitting at the kitchen table, admiring a huge edible-arrangement bouquet that had just arrived.

"Wow. That's huge," I said, momentarily distracted from my throes of confusion.

"Um, yeah. Fruit?" She pushed the huge thing toward me. "Liam sent it."

I pulled out a stick with a melon flower on it as I took in the size. "How much did this thing cost?" I pulled out my phone, curious.

"That's not all," Mom said. She pointed to a set of tiered boxes on the counter. "Those came earlier. The card with the fruit said he wasn't sure what we liked, so he sent both."

I inspected the boxes. "Godiva? Yum. Can I have some now?"

"Sure. Bring a box over."

I found the fruit arrangement price online. "So that's almost $300's worth of fruit." I joined my mother at the table.

"I'm sure the chocolate was a couple hundred dollars. I was looking for gift baskets for you last Christmas. They get expensive pretty quick."

"I don't remember getting a gift basket of food on my mission."

"Exactly. It was too expensive to send." She popped a chocolate-covered strawberry into her mouth. "So what's going on?"

"Well," I started slowly, "he called this morning and invited me to come visit." I watched for a reaction, waiting for her response.

"What did you tell him?" My mom's words were measured. I took that to mean she was undecided about how she felt about it too.

"I told him I'd get back to him. See, the thing is, I can't imagine, with all the girls at his disposal, that he'd really be interested in me." I fell forward and dramatically put my head in my hands. "I don't want to fall all over him. I don't want to be seduced by his charm."

"Maybe he's not looking for a disposable girl. He might want some-one a little more stable." She plucked out a melon flower and took a bite.

"*Stable* sounds like *sturdy*, and no girl wants to be described as sturdy. Shoes are sturdy."

She pushed the bouquet toward me. "I don't think that's the case at all. Stable is something that could be very attractive to someone like him."

"What do you mean?" I took a chocolate-covered strawberry. Liam had delicious taste in gifts.

"He seemed drawn to our family. Maybe it's for lack of his own, but he commented several times about how much he enjoyed spending time with our family. I think his life has been anything but stable, and that could be an attractive quality for him."

"I guess that could be it, but I don't know." I took another strawberry. They were pretty yummy.

"Camille, he seemed genuine. Maybe he has a very different lifestyle from ours, but that doesn't mean he's a bad person. As long as you are very clear with him about your boundaries, I would be okay with you seeing him again. But just remember, his lifestyle is not your lifestyle, and you don't have to be ashamed of your standards."

"I'm not ashamed of them, I just can't believe . . ." I didn't finish my thought. What I wanted to say was, "he was interested in me when I was nothing like Twick." I wasn't glamorous and beautiful and in that league of the rich and famous. But I also wasn't nasty and revengeful and only concerned about myself. He said he was done with Twick, and I wanted to believe him. And if he invited me to visit, I needed to stop doubting myself and believe him. If only I could figure out my own feelings.

* * *

Liam's invitation was the topic of conversation over dinner that night.

"Ha!" Kaela said and clapped her hands in the air. "I called that one, didn't I?" Victory was all over her face.

I sent her an annoyed glance across the table. I had been so sure I'd never hear from him again.

Dad poured himself a glass of milk. "What did you decide?"

"I'd like to go visit him." I tried to not sound too overly enthusiastic.

"Where would you stay?"

"At his house. Liam said he has a casita."

Dad shook his head. "Look, you can't stay there. Things happen. Not that you'll do something, but I really think you should get a hotel room."

"Nothing's going to happen," I said.

"I'm not comfortable with you sleeping at his house unsupervised. It's too easy for something to happen," Mom added.

"Nothing's going to happen." I repeated, looking from my mom to my dad. "Remember, you told him we have standards and he needs to respect them."

"Maybe, but—"

"That's why they're called unplanned pregnancies, Camille," Kaela broke in. "No one plans to mess up."

When had Kaela become so bold? "Kaela! I'm not going to sleep with him."

She shrugged. "I'm just pointing out that accidents happen."

"And," my mom circled her fork in the air, "even though I trust you to do the right thing, I don't want you to make any compromises. The law of chastity may be a part of your life, but it isn't a part of his life."

I was very much aware of that. "Mom, you were the one telling me he was a good person."

"Yes, I was. But I think what your dad and I are trying to say is we'd feel better if you had a hotel room."

"Better to avoid the appearance of evil than try to claim you'll fight temptation with willpower," Kaela said.

"Young Women has taught you well," I said pointedly at Kaela.

"Oh no, that wasn't Young Women. That was you. You know, with the whole Oreo thing and it's better to just avoid it than try to stop once you've started."

Not exactly what I was using the analogy for, but it worked.

Chapter Sixteen

I ALLOWED MYSELF TO INDULGE in my daydreams as I flew to California. What if this really worked out? Could it really work out? What were the chances? Really? And what would it be like dating one of the hottest men in the music scene today? But realistically, in all practicality, there was a big gap to bridge between his life and mine. And while it was fun to play "What if," I scolded myself for dreaming and reminded myself that I just needed to see how this visit went and then go from there.

Liam asked if I minded meeting him outside the airport in the parking garage because paparazzi tended to lurk at the airport. I had only a carry-on, and I could walk straight out there.

I texted Liam once I landed, and he texted me where he was parked. When he saw me coming, he climbed out and jogged over to greet me. He was wearing a knit cap and sunglasses, obviously in his low-profile mode. He hugged me tightly, enveloping me in his arms. "Hi, Camille. How are you?"

I inhaled, taking in his woodsy scent. "Good." I was a little tongue-tied. He looked good. Attractive.

"My car is over here." He took the handle of my carry-on and led me to a black Porsche Cayenne with black tinted windows parked at the back of the parking garage. The brake lights had dark covers over them, as did the headlights. The overall feel was almost sinister.

He opened the door.

"I told my parents I'd call when I got in. I should do that now so I don't forget."

"Definitely. Ring them." He turned his attention to driving.

My dad answered.

"Hey, Dad," I said. "I made it okay."

"And you'll be back Sunday?"

"Yup."

"Call and check in, okay?"

"Okay."

"And he really has a casita with a lock on the door?"

I laughed and looked over at Liam. "You really have a casita separate from the house that has a lock on the door?"

Liam nodded in affirmation.

"Yes."

"Just want to make sure," my dad said.

"No worries, Dad. I promise." I was all smiles, giddy to be there.

"Well then, have a good weekend."

"I will, thanks. I love you, and tell Mom I love her too."

"Okay. Bye."

"Bye." I hung up and laughed. "My dad."

"Everything okay?" Liam asked. He merged onto the freeway. I had no idea where we were or where we were going.

"Yup. Everything's good."

"Great. Are you hungry?"

Yeah, kind of. I hadn't eaten anything for breakfast because I was a bundle of nerves. I did manage to gnaw on a couple of the pretzels during the flight, but that was it. I nodded.

"How about sushi? Do you like sushi? We could grab some lunch."

I bit my lip. "I've never had it," I finally admitted.

"Never?" Liam looked at me in disbelief. "I love it. You want to try it?"

"I don't know if I would like it. And I'm too nervous."

"Nervous? You're nervous? About what?" He squeezed my knee.

Now I felt stupid for admitting it. "Seeing you, being on an official date, that kind of stuff."

"You weren't nervous when I was at your house."

I lifted a shoulder. "That was before I knew who you were."

"That shouldn't make a difference, Camille. I'm the same guy I was at your house."

"Can we maybe take a rain check on the sushi, just until I relax a little?" I held my breath, waiting for his answer. I knew he wasn't going to force me to eat sushi against my will, but I didn't know what to suggest instead.

"We could get a couples massage," Liam said as if it were no big deal.

A couples massage? Like, we were both in the same room, undressed under a sheet? I shifted in the seat and scratched at my neck, hoping to hide the awkwardness I felt.

Liam looked over at me. "Massage? Yes? No? I know a great place."

My cheeks burned. "Um, probably not. Are you regretting having me come visit? Am I your lamest date ever?"

"C'mon, Camille, I don't think that. How about a swim at my house?" He gave me an easy smile, which put me somewhat at ease.

"As long as you wear a suit," I said without thinking.

Liam started laughing.

"What's so funny?" Was it my obvious sense of modesty?

"You'll go swimming if I wear swimming trunks?"

"Yes."

"Maybe we should save that for later. Have you been to California much?"

"Not really. I went to Disneyland when I was twelve."

"I don't go to Disneyland very often. Too crowded."

I laughed. "It's an amusement park. They're always busy."

"I get recognized too much," he corrected.

"Oh." It hadn't been much of a problem in Utah until we'd announced he was there. But then again, we hadn't gone into huge crowds. "I'm up for pretty much anything." Except for a sushi lunch or a couples massage. Definitely not those.

"How about a boat tour around the harbor?"

"Sure," I said.

We drove for a while and finally exited the freeway. The traffic was stop and go, so it seemed really slow going. We drove on surface streets before turning onto a windy road that brought us to the top of a hilly area. We entered a gated community, complete with a guard house. Then we stopped at a driveway that had a large metal gate, and Liam punched a code into the keypad before the ominous gates opened. We drove up to a very large, modern house. Some of the exterior walls were concrete, some metal, and some glass. I had to make a conscious effort not to utter a "Wow" or leave my mouth gaping open.

As we pulled up to the front, I noticed a small house perpendicular to the garage. "Is that the casita?"

"No," Liam said and pushed his garage door opener. "The casita's in the back. That's security."

"Security? Like armed guards around the house?" I checked out the yard, looking for men in black suits and sunglasses patrolling the perimeter. I didn't see any.

We pulled forward into the garage, and Liam shut the car off. "I have some of them, but it's more my security system and monitoring cameras. Don't want any crazy fans or stalkers breaking in."

"Do you usually have bodyguards with you?"

"Sometimes. Depends on where I'm going and what I'm doing."

Liam and I got out, and I grabbed my carry-on from the back. Liam insisted on dragging it for me. "Will we have bodyguards with us?" What would that be like, always having a third wheel with you? Then again, what would it be like always having people swarm you? I'd opt for the third wheel.

"I don't think we're going anyplace too public that we'd have to."

I followed him through the four-car garage, although there wasn't anything in it other than the Porsche he had just parked. The interior of his house was vast, open, and had an all-glass wall of windows at the back, revealing a beautiful view of the ocean in the distance. The house was bare, definitely leaning toward a minimalist's decorating style. "You're staying in the casita, as we have already established, and it's back here by the pool." He took my hand and led me through the house to a set of french doors that led to a concrete patio. Sure enough, off to the left, at one end of the pool, was the casita. "Lupe cleaned it this morning."

I didn't know who Lupe was and didn't see or hear anyone else in the house with us. She might have been on her lunch break or something. I stared out at the pool in the backyard, which was crystal clear, shimmering in the sunlight, surrounded by a perfectly manicured yard.

"Do you want to go swimming right now?"

"No. Later is fine. I'm just admiring your pool, taking in the view, appreciating that there are no bikini-clad girls hanging around."

"Did you really expect me to have bikini-clad girls hanging around?"

I lifted a shoulder. "No, not really. But that's kind of how it is always portrayed in the movies, you know? And drugs lying around. A medicine cabinet full of prescriptions. Honestly, I wasn't expecting that, but I didn't know what to picture."

"I hope I didn't disappoint you."

"Actually, I'm relieved."

"What do you say we eat?" Liam said. He walked to an open kitchen area, and I followed.

"Sounds great," I said, grateful it wasn't the sushi.

"Help yourself. Just make yourself at home."

It felt a little strange actually doing what he suggested. "What do you have?" I opened his massive, sub-zero fridge. There wasn't a whole lot of anything in there. I picked up a bottle of thick, red juice. "Clamato? You drink Clamato? I have never heard of it."

He hoisted himself onto the countertop across from me. "Never heard of it? It was one of my most brilliant discoveries here. It is a perfect blend of tomato and clam juice."

I scowled. "Clam juice? Not my cup of tea."

"Or juice," he said, laughing at his own joke.

I scrunched up my face and inspected the bottle more closely. "You seriously like it?"

"Seriously. It's like a cocktail without the alcohol."

I shuddered for effect.

"Think of Manhattan clam chowder without all the chunky bits in it."

"Still not appealing. It's the clams."

"Not keen on clams?"

"Yeah. I think we need to agree to disagree on this one."

"I can do that." He grinned. "I have tea."

I shook my head. "I don't drink tea."

"Don't drink tea?" Liam looked alarmed. "That's like a crime against British culture."

"It goes with the not drinking coffee and alcohol, so you don't have to bother offering me them."

A smile crept across his face. "I'm not a complete idiot. I remember quite well that you don't drink alcohol."

"It's not that I think you're an idiot. I was just refreshing your memory. You know, in case you forgot." I smiled. The last thing I wanted to do was sound condescending.

"You don't think I'd forget our conversations so easily, do you?" He looked at me, holding my gaze longer than I could hold his.

Instead of answering, I yanked the freezer so hard the door swung open and threw me off balance a little. I straightened myself and looked deeply into his freezer. I was feeling hot and prickly, even though I was standing in front of an ice box. From the corner of my eye, I saw him slide off the countertop and make his way toward me.

"Uncrustables?" I said suddenly, announcing the first thing I focused on. "You have Uncrustables?" It was cute. I wondered if he had always liked them or had started liking them when he'd stayed with us.

I turned and almost banged into him. He was *right* behind me. "I love those. Ever since I tried them with you. Whoever came up with the idea was absolutely brilliant."

"I just didn't picture you as an Uncrustables kind of guy," I offered as an explanation.

"What were you expecting?"

"Um, alcohol, chips, and pizza." I cringed, hoping that admitting it would be enough for him to forgive my ignorance. "Bachelor kinds of food."

"Do you think I drink and party all day?"

"Sort of, yes." I hunched my shoulders. I was embarrassed to admit that was exactly what I thought. "Isn't that a typical rock-star stereotype?"

"I thought I showed you I was respectable when I was at your house."

"You did," I said quickly. I grabbed an Uncrustable. "Do you want one?" I offered him a package.

"Nah. I'll save my appetite for the harbor tour. They feed us on it, so don't eat too much."

"Um, okay." I looked around for a microwave to defrost my sandwich. Would the cruise ship be like the ferry I had been on during a family vacation once or something smaller?

"Here, let me do that for you." Liam took my sandwich, opened it, and put it on a plate. He put it in the microwave for a few seconds before pulling it back out and offering it to me.

"Thanks," I said, taking it from him. "You sure know how to show a girl a good time," I joked.

"Just wait," he said, then smiled and winked.

Butterflies filled my stomach.

* * *

"Shall we grab a snack for the movie?" Liam asked. We were back at his house after spending most of the day on a private yacht, boating around the harbors. It had been amazing. The food was delicious, the weather relaxing. I could get used to the weather here. The only bad thing was the number of times Liam was stopped for an autograph or a picture. It happened before and after the boating and further nailed the point home that this was a part of Liam's daily life.

And while we were gone, my suitcase had been moved from the floor to a stand in the corner of the casita, and the dishes in the sink had disappeared. I attributed it to the unseen Lupe.

143

Liam slid an arm around my waist, and I could feel his breath on my neck.

"Chips? Cookies? Popcorn?" I stepped aside quickly toward his pantry.

"There might be some biscuits in there," he said vaguely. "I'm not really interested in snacks." He closed the space between us.

"You can't watch a movie without junk food," I said, pulling out whatever I could find and piling it in Liam's arms. "There, that should do it," I said, facing him. I was satisfied to see Liam's hands full, his face barely peeking out from behind the bags.

"Are you starving, Camille?" Liam managed to get his chin over the top bag.

"No, just not sure what I'm in the mood for." I pulled a face of indecision.

He set all the snacks on the counter and leaned in close. "I know what I'm in the mood for."

Redirect! my mind screamed. That was so *not* what I was meaning. "Clamato?" I suggested. My heart was hammering in my chest. I was in way over my head.

His voice was low. "No."

I was avoiding the elephant in the room. All afternoon on the yacht, his affection had been mostly holding hands and a couple of pecks on the cheek. But now that we were alone, I worried that he might expect more. When he suggested watching a movie in his home theater, I jumped at the chance. I figured if we were doing something, it would leave less of a chance of the situation turning into a compromising one.

"Good. 'Cause it still seems disgusting." I grabbed one more bag, this one white-cheddar popcorn, and shut the cabinet. "Lead the way."

Just as we started the movie, Liam's phone rang. He looked at the screen and then at me. "I've got to take this." He handed me the remote, and I paused it.

"Okay," I said.

"Cybil," he said as he stood up and walked out of the room. I could hear bits and pieces of the conversation from outside, and I wondered if he was pacing. Sometimes it was much clearer than others.

"Let me speak to him . . . Tread . . . sponsor . . . hold on." The door opened, and he appeared in the doorframe. "I'm so sorry, luv. Tread is having a bit of a crisis. This might be a little bit. Start the movie without me."

I did as I was told and settled into the plush couch. By the time Liam returned, the movie was more than halfway done.

Chapter Seventeen

I WOKE UP THE NEXT morning with a start, completely disorientated. I was still on the couch but with a blanket over me, still in my clothes, even though they were a bit rumpled for the wear. I padded upstairs, looking for Liam. A woman with dark hair, wearing a gray dress that made her look like hotel staff, was silently sweeping the kitchen. My guess was she was Lupe.

She acknowledged me with a nod and went back to her task. I looked around and noticed the glass door leading to the patio was open.

Liam was swimming in the pool. "Good morning, gorgeous," he greeted me as I stepped onto the patio.

But before I could enjoy his compliment, I had to get one thing straight. "Did I fall asleep on you last night?"

"Yeah. I hope you don't mind I tucked you in." He winked.

I bent my knees, and I did a half turn, looking away in horror. When I looked back at him, he had an amused smile on his face.

"How embarrassing," I grimaced. "I am so sorry. I didn't mean to . . . I mean, it's not like I was bored or . . ." The afternoon sun on the water and the overabundance of nerves must have caught up with me.

"Camille," Liam broke in, "it's fine, luv. I rather fancy the way you curl up to me when you're tired."

"But—" I started.

"Fancy a swim? Or shall we go out for breakfast?"

How could he brush over it so easily? "Did anything . . . happen last night?"

Liam's face scrunched up in confusion before recognition dawned on him. "Oh, you mean between us?" He motioned with his index between us.

Then he laughed. "No. You fell asleep. I thought it would be rude to leave you alone on the couch, but I never take a girl to bed unless she consents. I don't want to be accused of anything."

So he'd left me on the couch. Thoughtful, I guess, but he could've just as easily carried me to the guest house.

"Is it a yes for breakfast?" he asked.

I nodded. "Breakfast would be great."

He pulled himself up on the side of the pool, then stood and walked over to a chaise. He grabbed a towel hung over the back of it and wrapped it around his waist. I watched as he leaned his head forward and shook the excess water from his hair. It was all very . . . sexy.

"Have you got your passport?"

His question stopped me. "Why?" I asked slowly. "Are you planning on taking me out of the country for breakfast?"

"Not for breakfast." He laughed. "I was thinking of something to do today. Perhaps Tijuana? Have you been?"

"No." I was wondering if he was serious. I mean, he could be completely serious.

"Or possibly Catalina Island? It's beautiful. Or possibly London?"

"London? What?" I could feel my mouth hanging open a bit, but I couldn't seem to get it shut.

"Just checking to see if you were paying attention." He seemed pleased with himself. He pulled a T-shirt over his head and came up beside me.

"I didn't bring my passport. I had no idea a visit could possibly mean a trip out of the country."

"I've gotta keep up my rock-star image by having an over-the-top date, haven't I?" He winked at me as he swung an arm casually around my shoulder.

"You mean since I fell asleep last night watching a movie?" I gave him a sheepish smile.

"Don't be too hard on yourself. Being out on a boat all afternoon makes you tired."

"So if the offer is still open, I'd like to try sushi."

"You fancy you'd like it?"

"I don't know, but I'd like to try. Just not for breakfast. And maybe surfing? I have never surfed and have always wanted to try."

"Brilliant. Let's give it a go."

"Do you know how to surf?" I asked, wanting to know if I'd be making a complete fool of myself in front of him or if we'd both look like fools.

He scratched behind his ear. "I do. But I sing better than I surf."

"That gives me nothing to gauge it by because you sing really well."

He tilted his head. "You think so?"

"Of course I do. Me and about a billion other people."

"Hearing it from you means more to me than the other billion people."

"I probably surf as well as I sing," I said.

"I thought you said you couldn't surf?"

I burst out laughing. "I can't sing either!" I bumped him with my shoulder.

Liam made a face like he was trying not to laugh. "You don't sing . . ." he trailed off.

"What could be more embarrassing than singing your song in front of you at the top of my lungs?"

"Okay, it wasn't great, but . . ." He bobbed his head like he was trying to think of a nice way to say what he was going to say.

"But it took all you had not to burst out laughing at me?" I supplied for him.

"No, it was kind of flattering that you liked it so much. But it was also then that I realized you had no idea who I was and that maybe I could be anonymous for a couple of days until I got everything sorted out."

I smiled. "It was nice that you stayed."

"It was nice, wasn't it?" He leaned in and kissed me. "It's going to be a good day."

* * *

We spent most of the afternoon at the beach, with Liam trying to teach me how to surf. I was getting used to having Maddox, the bodyguard, always on the perimeter of us. When I found out he was coming to the beach with us, I asked if he'd also be in swimwear. Liam scoffed at me and told me he couldn't hide a gun in a Speedo. When the bodyguard joined us, he was in shorts and a T-shirt and a pair of very dark sunglasses. I was both thankful and delighted that he was not in a Speedo. We had a repeat of yesterday with a couple of fans stopping Liam and asking for an autograph and a picture of him. We weren't inundated, but it seemed to happen at least one time everywhere we went. Once we returned to Liam's house, I showered and got ready to go out for dinner. It was a big night, as I was trying sushi for the first time.

Knowing Liam had dated a girl like Twick raised the bar pretty high for how nice I needed to look to go out with him. At least in my mind, it did. I was not as glamorous, well dressed, or pretty as Twick. And she was a stick, and I, who had never been worried about my weight in my life, suddenly felt self-conscious about it.

The black-sequined dress that was modest and complementary and perfect didn't seem enough. I felt like a little girl playing dress up and lacking sophistication.

Even though Liam complimented me when I entered the house from the casita, I still had doubts.

We took off, bodyguard in tow, and drove off to dinner. Liam pulled into a convenience store parking lot. I looked around. "Is this the restaurant?"

"No. But I have to give you a heads-up. The paparazzi will more than likely be there. They're always hanging about. It's your choice if they see you. You can either go in first while I bring the car to valet and I'll come in a few minutes behind you with Maddox, or I can go in first and you can follow a few minutes later. Kind of comes with the territory. You have to share me."

Flashbacks from when they were camped in front of our house came back, and I chose to go in first.

Like Liam predicted, the paparazzi was there and waiting. My fears returned when we walked into the restaurant. It was quiet, dim, and elegant. As I looked around, I felt out of place. I wanted to say "outclassed," but it wasn't that the girls were classy, just glamorous. And way too immodest. I did not belong here.

I left the ordering to Liam. He explained different items on the menu, but honestly, it all seemed as appealing as the next thing. I didn't know the difference between tuna, snapper, mackerel, and salmon, but I was willing to try a little of everything. I was here for the experience, right? I was really happy for the miso soup and the edamame. At least I knew what they were because I had tried them before.

"What do you think?" Liam asked after my first sampling.

I pointed to my favorites on the platter. "I like that one and these," I said, helping myself to another roll. Honestly, it was easier to try them not knowing what was in them.

"The California roll," he said, pointing to what I had just eaten. "And that's salmon." He pointed to the other one I liked.

"I wouldn't say I'm a connoisseur just yet, but this has been a good start. I didn't realize there were so many different varieties of sushi."

"It's an art."

"Apparently." I was amazed at how much I didn't know about it. It took awhile to have a little of everything.

"Dessert?" Liam asked.

"Here? They do desserts at sushi restaurants?" I wondered what they would serve.

"Sure. There's tempura ice cream, sorbet, and banana tempura."

"What is the tempura?"

"It means deep fried."

"I have always wanted to try deep-fried ice cream," I told him.

He signaled for the waiter. "All right, let's do it."

I stood. "I'm going to the restroom. I'll be right back."

When I exited the stall, I saw a familiar face: Twick Openshaw. What was she doing in the restroom of the same restaurant we were at? Seemed a little coincidental.

I wasn't sure what the social etiquette was for this situation. "Twick?" I asked. My stomach tightened, and my pulse quickened.

She was leaning against the wall, her arms folded across her chest. Obviously, she wasn't there to wash her hands. She raised an eyebrow, her voice full of contempt. "You think you're here with Liam? I seriously doubt that."

And what was I to do? Argue with her that I really was? "I'm not here with anyone else." A light sweat broke out on my brow.

She stood straight and leaned toward me. "You realize you're just an amusement."

I stared at her reflection in the mirror. Was she trying to intimidate me? As if I needed any help feeling completely out of place in this relationship.

"He'll eventually come back to me. He always does." She smiled, if it could be considered a smile. It was more like an evil smirk.

"What do you mean he always does?"

"He has told you we've broken up before, hasn't he?"

I wished I had pockets so I had something to do with my hands. "Yes."

She turned to the mirror and checked out her reflection. She pouted and touched the corner of her lips. Then she smoothed her hair. "He tries to date others, but he always comes back. Always."

There really wasn't any good comeback. "Um, I'm just going to go now." I turned on my heel and left. It was rude, but Twick wasn't exactly being polite.

I returned to the table, flustered and unsettled. Twick had done a great job stirring up all my insecurities. The sushi wasn't sitting so well in my stomach.

Liam put his hand on my arm. "Are you okay? You look upset."

I took a slow breath and shook my head quickly, trying to let him know it was nothing.

He leaned in closer, and his grip tightened. "What's going on?"

"I ran into Twick in the bathroom," I blurted out.

He looked over his shoulder and surveyed the restaurant. "Like my ex Twick?" he asked when he was looking at me again.

"Yeah. She's the only Twick I kind of know."

He scooted his chair back. "She keeps showing up."

"She's stalking you?"

"Technically, no." He shook his head and then looked over his shoulder in the direction of the bathrooms. "Is she still here?"

I started feeling shaky inside. I wasn't sure if it was a residual effect from the bathroom scene or if it was in anticipation of what Liam was going to do. "I don't know. But it doesn't matter." Maybe she was right. Maybe I was just an embarrassment to Liam. Was I fooling myself? Did I really think I could somehow be a part of his world? Be in his world but not of it? Like I could straddle the line of appropriate and inappropriate?

"What happened? She obviously said something to upset you."

"She glared; I stared. We had a moment."

"What did she say?" Liam's voice was forceful now.

Before I could respond, Twick sauntered up to the table. I was surprised she was so bold.

"Twick," Liam said, narrowing his eyes. There was a vein in his temple I could see throbbing. I hoped there wasn't going to be a big scene between the two of them. "What are you doing here?"

"You are so predictable, William."

He looked like he was waiting for what she was going to say next.

He leaned back in his chair. His hands slowly balled into fists and then immediately reopened. "You're stalking me now?"

"No, more like checking up. I had an inside tip you were coming here."

"Or you bribed that maître de that you're always flirting with." He motioned over to the front door. Twick didn't bother to look.

"No, not him. But I do have connections." She flipped her hair. "I was just stopping by to say hello."

"Now what're you going to do? Order some celery sticks to go?"

Twick glared at him for a moment before turning and marching off.

"Sorry about that," Liam said, turning his attention back to me. "I haven't seen Twick since I got my stuff back from her in Vegas. I don't know why she's suddenly popping up."

I had an idea. She wanted Liam back. Who knew how hard she had tried since Vegas. Or maybe her efforts had been dormant until Liam had shown up at the restaurant with a date. Whatever the truth was, it didn't matter. Twick had accomplished what she had set out to do: make me doubt myself.

* * *

The conversation during the car ride home was one-sided. I didn't mean to withdraw, but I couldn't get out of my own head. I was sure Liam was aware of it, and that was why he delivered a steady stream of talking.

Once home, he suggested we go for a swim. The hot tub sounded appealing because I certainly could use some unwinding.

He was already sitting in the hot tub when I joined him. He held his hand out to me. "C'mere."

I walked the two steps down into the hot tub and over to him. He stood and pulled me into a hug. "I'm sorry about Twick tonight. I hope it didn't ruin the evening for you. You've been kind of quiet since we left the restaurant."

I didn't want to talk about it. I was afraid it would open the floodgate of emotions, and tears would be inevitable. "I just wonder if all this was a mistake," I said into his shoulder.

He pushed back so he could look at me. "If all what?" His head tilted as if he were trying to understand.

I held my hands out, feeling helpless. "Twick made me realize I don't belong here. I don't belong with you. The sooner I admit the truth, the better. I keep fooling myself into thinking that maybe it could work, but I see now that it can't. I'm not your speed." I stared at me feet. The lights reflecting off the water made everything look wavy.

He leaned down to catch my eye. "You think I care what Twick thinks?"

"I know you don't." If only I didn't. Well, not so much what she thought but what she said.

He put his hands on my elbows. "Don't let her get to you. She plays mind games. She's just trying to mess with you."

I didn't answer.

"If you didn't think it could work, why did you come?" Liam asked gently. It seemed as though he was trying to reconfirm what he thought I thought, but I flip-flopped too much with my answer. I came because I liked him and hoped there was a way. I just didn't know what that way could be.

He pulled me close again and lifted my chin so our eyes met. "I'm glad you're here." He looked at my lips momentarily and then back at me. I could feel my heart start pounding as his hand slipped onto the back of my neck. His other hand played with a strand of my hair. He glanced down at my lips before looking back at me and holding my gaze. Once he did, he leaned in and let his lips touch mine.

It wasn't until the kisses were more intense and his hand wandered down past my waist that I realized what was going on. He thought I was going to spend the night with him. "No, Liam, stop." I pushed myself back, my hands on his chest.

He blinked, confused. "Is something the matter?"

"I, uh . . ." I stuttered, trying to get the words out. It was hard to back away in the water. "I should go. You know, call it a night." I walked toward the edge of the hot tub where the steps were. I stumbled and ended up sitting on the top stair.

"Go?" He was so sincere *I* was surprised.

"To bed. The casita. There." I pointed behind me with my thumb.

He cocked his head. "The casita?"

"Yeah, you know, um, where I was supposed to sleep last night."

"Why can't you stay with me?"

"Remember how I, um, said I would need a separate bedroom? You know, when we planned this visit? Like I told my dad?"

He brushed the air with his hand. "I thought that was a bit of rubbish you were saying just for the sake of your parents. You were serious?" His mouth was slightly ajar.

"I was serious. Very," I reiterated, nodding.

"But that's madness. Why can't you stay with me?" He shrugged, then laughed, probably in disbelief.

"I thought you realized . . ." I started to explain, wanting to retreat as soon as possible. I wasn't worried he was going to force me to do anything; it was just a really uncomfortable situation. I had this sick feeling in my stomach that I was in way over my head.

"No one will know, Camille," he cut me off. His voice was soft. He closed the distance between us and put his hands on my arms and slowly rubbed up and down.

"I'll know, Liam. It's not negotiable." I tried to pull my arms away from his touch, but he held on.

"You know there are hundreds of girls out there, willing, who would think you're mad to pass up this chance—"

"I'm not one of those girls, Liam." My throat got tight.

He gave me a hard stare. I wasn't sure if he was testing me or if he was angry.

I backed out, feeling foolish and naive. "I'm sorry. I really am. I—"

He climbed out of the hot tub and sat on a chaise lounge, resting his elbows on his knees. "Just go," he said. His voice was cold, and he didn't look at me.

I walked away, feeling the weight of his anger as I did. I didn't look back or turn around in an attempt to make things better. I didn't want him seeing my eyes tear up and my chin quiver as the hot tears spilled over.

I couldn't believe how stupid I had been. I had convinced myself that maybe it would be okay. That maybe he could understand and respect my values. Please. He could get any girl he wanted; why would he wait for me?

* * *

My first impulse the next morning was to leave; acknowledge we had made a mistake, call a spade a spade, and take a morning flight out. But that wouldn't solve anything. All it would do was leave things unresolved, and I'd rather not leave like that. I'd have to deal with the situation eventually.

I took my time showering, not in any hurry to go to breakfast. Liam was already in the kitchen with a Starbucks bag on the table when I walked in.

He was dressed in a T-shirt and a pair of shorts and sat slouched in the chair, his legs stretched out under the table. He was talking to a woman who was probably in her late fifties, with silver hair, wearing a business suit. She was carrying a legal pad of paper. "Gwen made a Starbucks run this morning." He motioned to her.

"Nice to meet you." I stepped forward and shook her hand.

"Camille," she answered.

"That's it for now, Gwen. Thanks."

Gwen nodded and walked off without another word.

He pushed the bag toward me. "I know you don't drink coffee, but I had her get you some lemon pound cake."

"Thanks," I said, slowly sitting in a chair opposite him. I sat up straight, resting my elbows on the table. I needed the support, and maybe it would hide the fact that I was shaking.

"Camille, about last night, I'm sorry. I didn't realize you were serious."
He reached out and touched my fingertips. Although he sounded sincere,
I didn't answer. I was weighing my options for a response. "I crossed a
line," he continued, then cleared his throat. "It's just that I've never met
anyone like you. I don't know how to be around you."

"Isn't that why you like me? Because you can be yourself around me?
What do you mean you don't know how to be around me?"

"You're good and sincere and . . . I like you, Camille."

I slid my fingertips out from under his hands and ran them through
my hair. I leaned back in the chair and broke a piece off my lemon loaf. I
debated if I should eat it or say what I was thinking. The words won. "I like
you too, Liam, but let's be real. This will never work. I feel like it's more the
thrill of the chase, the challenge of the conquest, and then you'll move on."

He leaned forward and wrapped his hand around his cup of coffee. He
took a sip before he responded. "Or maybe not. It just might work. Aren't
you willing to give it a go?"

I swallowed hard. "You realize I will never sleep with you while we're
dating. You could sleep with any girl, anywhere, anytime. Let's just be honest
here. I can't give you what you want. So why pretend? That will only make
it harder later on." I hated the truth.

He squinted at me. "So that's it? It's a no? It doesn't just have to be
about that."

"Are you going to take a vow of abstinence just so you can date me?"

"You don't think I could?"

"Liam, I would love nothing more than to find a way to make it work."
He was gorgeous, rich, fun to be with, easy to talk to . . . but a rock star.
With that came a lifestyle I had no desire to be a part of. I shook my head.
"But we both know that's not possible."

"Why?"

"How do you picture your life? Probably not how I picture mine. My
life plans and goals aren't necessarily glamorous. I want to get my degree,
meet my husband, settle down, and have a family. I've always imagined he'd
be a member of my Church and we'd get married in the temple. There'd be
kids, maybe a dog. We'd buy a house and drive a minivan. You know, the
whole white-picket-fence dream. I can't picture you wanting that."

"Okay." His face was expressionless.

"Your life is full of exotic things—fans throwing themselves at you,
traveling, touring, red-carpet events, parties, paparazzi. You're recognized

everywhere you go and have to fight to maintain your privacy. Dinner the other night was over $500. I don't live in that kind of world. I assume settling down would be boring to you. I'm afraid you'd get bored of me or be unhappy. And I would never ask you to give up everything you love just for me. That is why I feel like there is no future with us. It is doomed from the beginning, so why try?"

"We get along so well."

"That was before I knew who you were."

He gave me a sideways glance before shaking his head. "That's not true, and you know it. We had a great time in Salt Lake." His words were clipped.

He was right. We did get along as long as it was just him and me. But throw the real world, or just his world, into it and everything changed. If we could live in the middle of nowhere, where no one had ever heard of Gear, maybe it would work.

Then there was still a difference of standards. And religious beliefs. I had to admit our differences on those topics might never be reconciled.

"I can't see the benefit of indulging a little bit." My throat felt tight as I said it. I leaned away from him. It would be romantic if he did give up everything because he loved me more than any of those other things. Unfortunately, that was Hollywood and not real life.

His thumb rubbed over mine. "No one has to give up anything. I just want to get to know you better. Can't we at least try it?"

"Liam, my heart says yes, but my head says no." Right now, I hated that voice in my head, but it was right. Indulging my heart would only get me into trouble. And maybe in more ways than one. "It's better this way."

"Better for who? For you? Shouldn't I be in on this decision before you completely shut me out?" His voice rose steadily.

"Don't make this harder than it already is."

"Is it religion? Say the word, and I'll give up electricity."

His joke caught me off guard, and I blinked a few times. It was nice to have some comic relief in this conversation. It gave me a breather and time to gather my thoughts.

"What I'm saying, Camille, is I'd give up much to have the chance to get to know you better."

My throat burned, and my eyes filled with tears. "You don't know how I wish it was possible. I just don't think that with the way things are right now, we can be together."

"Camille . . ." Liam's brow furrowed.

The truth was a little too sobering at the moment. "I'm sorry."

"I'm not ready to give up."

That just made it hurt even more. "That's very sweet, but I can't promise you anything."

"Are you willing to give it some time and try again? Will you think about it?"

My heart said, *I want that too.* My head said, *Get real, Camille.* My mouth said, "Okay."

"Here is my private number." He took my phone and added "LJPrivate" as a contact. "No one has it except my PA, my manager, and Tread and Cybil. I think it goes without saying that you cannot give it to anyone, including your sister. After you've thought about it, call me."

I thought about it all day. I thought about it as we kissed goodbye. I thought about it on the airplane and as I drove silently home from the airport. But no matter how much I thought about it, I couldn't come up with any way to make it work. My mind went blank. How *could* it work? I finally had to settle on the idea that it was better for me to give up on the idea of "us" rather than him giving up his whole life. I was letting him go because I loved him enough not to ask that much of him. That was what was best for everyone, right?

Chapter Eighteen

NEVER. WORKED. OUT. NEVER. WORKED. Out. I repeated the words in my head each time my foot hit the ground. Never. Worked. Out. I headed north on Ninth East toward the Provo Temple. Even though I was listening to the radio on my iPod, I chanted my mantra in my head as I ran.

I took up running to force myself to forget about Liam. One mile became three, which turned into four or five miles a day. Days blurred into weeks and eventually months. I ran, and I ran hard. At first, the rhythm of the running and the pounding of my sneakers on the ground was therapeutic. It helped me clear my head as I repeated and reminded myself over and over again that things with Liam would have never worked out. Never. Worked. Out. Never. Worked. Out. I talked myself out of him one run at a time until, finally, the day came that he wasn't the first thing to cross my mind when I woke up in the morning and the last thing I thought of as I fell asleep. Although there were some times while I was running that I had to stop to catch my breath because my throat felt too tight to breathe. And it wasn't from the running.

I was trying to forget him. I was trying to move on and not hang on to the hope. I had decided this was the best way to handle it. I knew his world would never be my world. As much as I wanted it to be possible. As much as I hoped, dreamed, and schemed, I knew I was only fooling myself. There was no way Liam and I could have a relationship that would be any different from the visit. He was worldly, and I was not, and what did he see or want in me that he couldn't find out in that big world that was at his disposal?

I had yet to delete his private number from my contacts but knew that when I did, it would mean I was finally over him.

School had been in session for three weeks. Returning to BYU had felt like a fresh start. I could leave Liam and the past in the past. I lucked out on roommates, who were very cool, and I liked most of my classes, except the general education required classes. Biology and physical science just didn't excite me. Human development was okay. Working with frozen desserts seemed to be my destiny, as I had to quit The Swirly Whirly because of my class schedule but found a part-time job at the Creamery. And there was running and extracurricular activities, like BYUSA, ward activities, and visits to the Y-Serve Center, which provided more than enough opportunities to serve. And, of course, boys. And even though I thought I had completely run away from Liam, there always seemed to be a lingering thought of him in the very corner of my mind.

"Here is the first release from the long-awaited album from Gear," the DJ announced, breaking my inner chant.

I stopped dead in my tracks. Should I listen to the song or shut it off?

"It's called 'Not a Tattoo Kind of Girl.' Here it is."

No, I thought. *It couldn't be.*

But it was. It was all about me. All about us.

I can't quite get it right
Where do I draw the line?
You said we could never
Bridge the gap
Between your world
And mine.
What do I have to do?
To show my heart to you?
To show you what I say
Is really what I mean?
I would get a tattoo
If it would prove to you
How genuine and true
My feelings are for you.
But you say you're not a tattoo kind of girl.

Without warning, a lump formed in my throat. Even though I wouldn't want him to get a tattoo to prove anything to me, knowing he'd be willing to made me miss him just a little. I gave up on the jog and started walking home, suddenly out of energy or motivation or willpower. Being reminded of Liam took the joy out of my run.

I thought about him the whole way home, trying to find a way to put him back in that little corner of my mind again until he was gone completely. I wasn't sure if he would ever be completely gone because of who he was.

Eventually, the feelings would fade, and someday, I would have a great story to tell. Once the hurt was no longer so fresh.

There was one other small hiccup in my attempt to forget Liam: my roommate Esther. Gear was a favorite on her playlist. She shared her passion for Gear by listening to them often. I counted my blessings that she was not a total fangirl but just a regular fan who liked their music but didn't cyberstalk their every move. I had always been able to avoid talk of the fund-raiser at The Swirly Whirly because Esther had been home in Illinois when it had happened. Since Liam was a can of worms, I was afraid to open up with her. I never confessed my secret of knowing him. Besides, it was in the past and not a part of my life anymore.

Esther had obviously heard the new release from Gear too. I could hear "Not a Tattoo Kind of Girl" blaring from our apartment before I even opened the front door. There was no way to escape it. And I hated to admit it, but it was kind of a catchy song.

I followed the music to her bedroom.

"This is the new song from Gear," she yelled over the music as I walked in. "I just downloaded it." She was jumping on her bed, her long, straight, auburn hair flailing behind her. Her blue eyes were bright with happiness and her expression joyful.

"So I hear," I yelled back.

"Don't you just *love* it?"

"It's great," I muttered, taking off my sneakers. Would a shower drown out the music? The shower insulated me from the song temporarily, but as soon as I shut the water off, the music was back, just as loud as before.

I quickly got dressed but took extra long drying my hair. The hairdryer worked as well as the shower for blocking out the music, and when I turned it off, miraculously, the music was off too.

"I heard William is meeting with the missionaries." Esther announced as she joined me at the vanity, holding a container of yogurt. She leaned back against the wall, a dreamy look on her face.

"Oh yeah?" I asked while I put makeup on. I tried not to get into discussions about Gear. But this time, I was more than just mildly curious about what she had to say. "Where'd you hear that?"

"You know how Mormon gossip is." She hoisted herself up on the counter. "A friend of a friend, whose brother is on a mission, knows another missionary who served in the same area with another missionary who claims he taught William."

"Hmmm." I made an appropriate noise but really didn't know what to say. Could it be true? I doubted it, but you never knew. Liam had listened intently when I'd told him about the Church, but it didn't mean he was going to go seek out the missionaries. Somehow, I couldn't imagine missionaries walking up that hill he lived on, getting through the first gate, ringing the doorbell on his front gate, and security letting him in. The whole scenario seemed a little farfetched to me.

"William is yum," she said wistfully, opening the yogurt and taking a bite.

"Yum or not, our standards wouldn't mesh with his lifestyle," I said, voicing my own personal worries. But my roommate didn't know just how personal it was.

"People change," Esther said, licking her spoon clean.

"Speaking of yum," our roommate Audrey said as she joined us in the back, still carrying her backpack, "I was thinking we should find some guys who are up for some cheap pizza and a movie night at our apartment. Maybe do ice-cream sundaes after? You girls up for it?"

"Haven't heard from your missionary lately?" I asked. Audrey became very social when there were long dry spells of communication from him.

Audrey shrugged. "It's not like we're exclusive. And he has a lot of growing up to do. He will probably be a completely different guy when he gets home, but just in case my predictions don't come true, I can still see what's out there."

I didn't understand Audrey's philosophy completely, but it wasn't my business either. She had a boyfriend she dated her freshman year here and promised to write him while he was on his mission. He'd been out just over a year. It didn't stop Audrey from flirting or socializing one bit. It didn't hurt that she was pretty. With her long brown hair and big brown eyes, along with her vivacious personality, she didn't seem to struggle socially.

"I'm up for it," Esther said. "Do you have any guys in mind?" Obviously Esther wasn't holding out until her "yum" fantasy happened.

"That apartment over there." She looked out the window and stabbed her finger against the glass. She was pointing to an apartment across the street and one building over from our apartment.

"Those apartments aren't in our ward," I said.

"I know." Audrey turned around, excited. "But I saw a couple of guys going in there, and they looked very attractive. It never hurts to make new friends."

That was exactly how Audrey was—always wanting to push the boundaries, always willing to take a dare or put herself out there. Me, I was more levelheaded than that and didn't enjoy the thrill of the unknown like my roommate.

"Are you just going to walk up to their front door and introduce yourself and invite them?" Esther asked.

"Yes, I was thinking about it. Maybe a plate of cookies or brownies would break the ice."

"I can start looking for a movie to stream," Esther volunteered. "What do you think, a romantic comedy?" She was grinning when she said it because it was a total joke among us about the difference in movie choices between the sexes. When we had invited guys over before and asked them to bring the movie, it had inevitably ended up being some shoot-'em-up action film. Not that there was anything wrong with that, but we as roommates tended toward the romance.

"I think there's an action movie out with What's-His-Name—that actor you like," I said. "So even if we don't care to watch the action, we can watch the actor."

Audrey laughed. "The whole point of inviting boys over is to find guys who are actually available to date and are not movie stars." She looked at me, then at Esther. "Or rock stars. Remember, girls, there are perfectly eligible bachelors right in our midst. We just need to find them."

"Well, if William joins the Church, I need to be available," Esther said.

I snorted. That would be the day. "You're going to have to hold out for a very long time."

"You don't believe me, but you just wait," Esther said, defending her claim on Liam. "Someday, when they come here in concert and I have front-row tickets, our eyes will meet and he will point me out to his roadies so they can escort me backstage and he can meet me. It will be happily ever after."

"Okay, Esther, whatever you say. Now go find a movie." Audrey grinned and booted her toward the door.

Our Friday night plans didn't work out so well. There was no one home in the apartment Audrey had picked out, so she and Esther decided to go to a last-minute party and I went to the library. I could always stand to do a little more studying. It was easier to fill my head with knowledge than with thoughts of Liam.

Chapter Nineteen

"How did 'studying' go with Sam?" Audrey made imaginary quotation marks in the air when she said "studying." Almost a week had passed since our attempt at a movie night, and I thought she was gearing up for another attempt this weekend.

"It was okay," I answered. "It was just studying."

"Just okay?" She was disappointed. "Not awesome? Not amazing? Not anything better than okay?"

"We were studying biology. It's not all that awesome."

"I thought there was more to it than that," Audrey prodded.

Like romance? Like interested in being more than just study partners? "Nah, it's all studying."

"But he's cute," Audrey protested. "I've seen the way he watches you when he's over here 'studying.'" Again, she made the quotation marks in the air when she said "studying."

"Maybe, but there's nothing there," I replied.

"Maybe there would be if you would just give it a chance. He is very cute. I bet he would take you out to eat if you let him."

"He already offered," I admitted.

I could tell my roommate was frustrated with me before she even opened her mouth. "Did you go?"

I nodded yes.

"And you didn't tell me?" she demanded.

I scrunched my face up. "It was kind of embarrassing."

She stared at me. "What was embarrassing? Did you throw up during the meal? Burp?"

I shook my head. "He told me he was taking me to *his* place. Which was Sam's Club."

She coughed before squinting at me. "Sam's Club?"

"Yeah, I guess because his name is Sam and it's Sam's Club."

"Oh." Her eyes were wide with disbelief.

I motioned at her with my hand. "I know. Crazy, right? But it gets worse. We ate samples."

"For your meal? Are you sure he was considering that taking you out to eat?"

"Yeah. He said it'd be like a buffet. I was thinking Rodizio Grill."

Her lips parted, but no sound came out for a moment. "He really took you to Sam's Club to eat the samples?"

"Yes, he really did," I reassured her with a fervent head nod.

"He didn't buy anything after trying the samples to take home and cook for you?"

"Nope, not even a hot dog and pretzel at the little cafe."

"I see what you mean." She thought for a moment. "Maybe he was out of money but still wanted to go out with you."

"I'd rather he be up front about it if he is broke at the moment than go scrounging for samples at a food warehouse."

"Maybe next time he'll actually take you to someplace real to eat."

"There won't be a next time. What if the second time isn't any better than the first time? Would I be doomed to a marriage with a cheapskate?"

"Just because you date him doesn't mean you're going to marry him."

"I could totally date for fun, if it was actually fun," I said, although maybe I was lying to myself about that.

She bulged her eyes. "Camille, all I'm saying is that you're too picky. Everything you mentioned about this guy is fixable."

I didn't want to have to fix the guy. I wanted him to come already perfect. Maybe I did have too high of standards since nobody was perfect. But I didn't think that was necessarily bad; it was better than settling for less than what I wanted. I should love a guy for who he was, not who I wanted him to be.

"Isn't that the point of dating? To find someone you can live with the rest of your life?" Unlike my roommate, I didn't think I could marry a guy for his potential. I didn't want to have to be behind him every step of the way, pushing him toward the end goal. I wanted someone who was self-motivated. I wanted someone who knew what he wanted. Most of all, I wanted Liam the guy and not the famous rock star.

"Well, good luck finding your Prince Charming, because I don't think he exists."

I was beginning to wonder that too.

"If you didn't have this perfect fantasy guy, you would realize the real guys standing in front of you are perfectly fine."

"It's not that." I rubbed my forehead. This discussion/argument/lecture was starting to give me a headache.

"Are you sure? Because you seem to find some reason to shoot down any guy who even comes close to asking you out."

"Why waste time—his or mine—dating someone I'm not interested in?"

"Maybe you need to get to know them better. Give it more of a chance?"

After Liam, I was painfully aware of when things clicked and when they didn't. These days, things with guys tended to fall quickly into the "don't click" category. But I couldn't really explain to my roommate that I had briefly dated the lead singer of Gear and after him, guys just didn't seem to measure up.

"Oh my gosh!" Esther yelled from her bedroom. "Did you guys hear that?" I hadn't even realized she was home. I was glad she hadn't been out here with Audrey, ganging up on me about my dating problems.

"What's going on?" Audrey and I rushed to her room to see what was wrong.

"They just announced Gear is coming to Salt Lake in concert! They just added one more date as the final show on the tour. Ah!" She did a little dance around her bedroom and then grabbed my arms. "We totally have to go!"

I cleared my throat. "I probably can't go." I tried to say it casually, like it wasn't a big deal that Liam was going to be a mere forty-six miles away from me and it had been barely three months since he'd been anywhere close to me.

"Don't say you can't go!" Esther said. "You don't even know when it is."

"I totally want to go," Audrey said, jumping on the excitement wagon. "*Want?* You don't even have to ask. Of *course* I want to go."

They looked at me and silently peer-pressured me.

"Maybe," I conceded only to appease them. I didn't know if I could emotionally handle seeing Liam again. "When is it?" I asked, pulling up my calendar on my phone.

"It's the first weekend in November." Esther specified the date. "Tickets go on sale Saturday at midnight. That is totally worth staying up till midnight to get good seats. Going together could be a whole roommate bonding experience."

"That's my mom's birthday." I felt a whoosh of relief. Of course I wasn't too sad about it, but I didn't need to tell them. Besides, I justified it in my mind, we had already bonded as roommates. We didn't need to go to a concert to feel connected. I didn't want to buy tickets for a band I didn't want to see.

"Really?" Audrey demanded.

I held up the calendar app on my phone as proof.

"Let me see that." Audrey grabbed my phone from my hand to check my calendar. "Are you sure you're not making that up?"

"No, I'm not making it up." I was pleased that I really did have an excuse.

"C'mon," Esther begged. "It'll be awesome."

That didn't sway my decision. "I don't know," I hedged.

"Well, make up your mind by Friday night. The show is going to sell out quickly." She typed on her phone.

"I'm sure it will." The band had only increased in popularity since I'd met Liam. The new album had taken off. Not that I was checking or anything.

"Is it a money thing? We can put it on my credit card and you can pay me back. We can donate plasma or something to pay for it. We'll find a way." Esther turned her attention back to her phone.

"You don't need to find a way. I just won't go. I don't mind missing it." I didn't mind not opening my fresh scars again. I didn't need to voluntarily put myself in a painful position. "Besides, I'm sure my family will want to do something for my mom."

"Maybe you could celebrate early," Audrey suggested.

There wasn't an easy way of getting out of this. My sister would probably want to go once she found out. Unlike me, she didn't feel the same way about keeping the Liam secret. She told everyone and anyone about her short brush with fame. But she was still young and naive and thought love could find a way. Or at least thought we could fall in love and make it work. I think she even secretly thought there was a small chance that maybe Liam would fall in love with her and whisk her off to Happily Ever After.

I tried to think of a way out of this discussion or at least a way to pacify my roommates for a while. I needed more time to build a good argument for why I couldn't go.

"Don't think you're getting out of this," Esther said and pointed a warning finger at me.

Surely I could come up with a better excuse to get out of it. Avoiding being forced to buy tickets this Friday was easily the first step. And maybe if I just never mentioned it again, they would forget. Wishful thinking.

Chapter Twenty

I HATED WHEN IT RAINED a lot because then I had to go running at the inside track. I liked to run outside in nature and breathe in the fresh air. Somehow, it helped me think better. Especially now that Friday was coming and I had yet to think of a great excuse about why I shouldn't go to the concert with my roommates. And sometimes the indoor track smelled funky. Bad weather resulted in busy days at the track.

"Camille?" A guy running from behind caught up to me.

I stopped, which was not the best idea when other people were jogging behind me. "Riley?"

Someone bumped into me, and I quickly apologized for stopping suddenly.

A smile broke across Riley's face. "It is you."

I stepped off to the side, out of the lane of runners. I was so surprised it took me a few minutes to regulate my breathing. I hadn't seen Riley, well, since my senior year in high school. I hadn't talked to him since the night of senior prom when we went together but he ditched me because he had gotten back together with his ex-girlfriend. He went on his mission, then I went on mine, and any time before or after that, I hadn't gone searching for him.

"Hey, how are you?" I asked. I leaned forward, resting my hands on my knees, breathing heavily.

He held his arms out wide. "It's been . . . years."

"Prom senior year." I nodded, acknowledging the painful truth.

"How are you?" he asked. He went to hug me but then didn't.

"I'm good. What have you been up to?" I undid my hair and then immediately pulled it back up into a ponytail. Maybe if I was moving, even slightly, he wouldn't try to touch me. That would just be awkward.

"You know—mission, school."

"Okay." I wasn't sure what to say.

A moment of silence.

He motioned with his thumb over his shoulder. "I was going to grab a smoothie. Do you want to come get one? My treat?"

I hesitated. My first reaction was no. It had been two and a half years. I wasn't still angry with him, and I wasn't finished with my run. But I was curious. "Um, okay." Why not? I could stand to live a little.

We drove to a smoothie place close to campus. After our smoothies were made, we found a booth to sit in.

Once we were settled, Riley started asking questions. "How long have you been home?"

"Home?" He must have been referring to my mission. "You mean from my mission? How did you know?"

He shifted his eyes. "My mom followed your mom's blog about your mission. I went and checked it out."

Back in high school, he had been *the* quintessential guy for me. I would've died to know he had looked me up.

"Should I be worried that you cyberstalked me?" I smiled.

"Not exactly. I checked it once and then the blog was gone."

We took it down after the paparazzi incident. Too many people trying to find out about Liam through me. It was easier to close the account, and most of my social-media accounts, than deal with the harassment. I was called names, insulted, and hated, and I came to understand what it felt like to be a hiss and a byword. It didn't take too long to realize I preferred to be anonymous, and I understood what Liam meant when he said that.

He continued before I had a chance to respond. "I, uh . . . you know, I still feel bad about prom. Several times on my mission I wanted to write and apologize to you."

"Oh." What else could I say when he was apologizing for something that was long over and done with but had left a scar nonetheless?

"I didn't because I wanted to do it in person. I at least owed you that much. And it would make me face up to my actions and not take the easy way out."

"Okay."

"When I got home from my mission, I looked you up and found out you were on your mission. So I never actually had the chance to apologize." He let out a deep breath. "I'm sorry about all that. I was immature and stupid and didn't have enough brains in my head to think about being considerate of you."

"Well, you know—"

"I was going to call you and cancel because my girlfriend and I made up right before the dance, but my mom overheard me talking and basically threatened certain death if I reneged on our date. So we came up with the plan that I would still go with you but spend the dance with her."

"I was mad at you for a long time."

"Understandable." He dropped his head.

"But then after my first year here, I realized it was high school and . . ." There were a whole lot more fish in the sea. People weren't mean and nasty like in high school. And most guys weren't immature enough to ditch their dates at a dance. Living with roommates at college and having companions on the mission helped me understand everyone's life was hard in one way or the other.

"Can I make it up to you?" he asked.

"What were you thinking?"

"Taking you to the next formal dance and it can be our dance do-over."

I made a swiping motion. "You don't have to—"

"I want to. It would make me feel better if you let me. Sort of like recompense for ruining prom."

I raised an eyebrow. "So, you're RSVP-ing for a dance sometime in the future? Like homecoming?"

"Yeah, but I wouldn't mind seeing you before then."

This was strange. I actually wanted to go out with him.

The conversation lulled. I took the opportunity to take a long drink. It was a good way to use the silence. "This girl put way too much wheat grass in my smoothie." I made a gagging, coughing sound as I swallowed. It was really strong.

"She probably didn't realize it." Riley stirred his smoothie with his straw, then took a drink.

"I told her a tiny bit. She was more interested in you than measuring my wheat grass. She kept checking you out. Did you notice?" I teased and pointed an accusatory finger at him.

"No, I didn't notice. Maybe she was distracted. It's still early." He downplayed it. I couldn't tell if he really hadn't noticed or if he was just being nice.

"Yeah, she was distracted. By you. I might go ask for another drink."

"Aw, that might make her feel bad. What if it's her first day?"

I shrugged. "I guess it might not be bad if I drink it fast." Or just stopped drinking it at all. But I didn't want to be rude and throw most of the smoothie out in front of him. I settled on taking tiny sips and not really drinking the rest before we left.

* * *

"I had a blast from the past today," I said to Audrey, who was eating breakfast when I got home. I went to the sink, emptied the smoothie, and threw the cup in the trash.

"Oh yeah? What was it?"

I pulled my hair out of its band and shook it out. "I ran into the guy who ditched me at prom." Grabbing a water bottle from the fridge, I sat at the table with her.

She set her bagel on her plate. "You got ditched at prom? What happened?"

"High school for me was sort of like one of those awkward Drew Barrymore films. This guy, Riley, was my dream guy in high school. I watched him from afar for three years. He knew I liked him because my blabbermouth friend told him. She claimed that maybe if he knew, he would ask me out."

"Did he?" She resumed eating her bagel.

I took a long draw of water while nodding. "Eventually, and it was to prom. He had been dating the class president, who was this tiny, petite, peppy blonde, but then they broke up."

"And you finally caught his eye?"

"Kind of," I said. "He knew I liked him, and I think I became his backup plan for prom. Then plans changed because he and his girlfriend made up hours before it started, but he had committed to going with me. I still went as his date, but he left me sitting by myself all night while he danced with his girlfriend.

"It sounds terrible."

"At the time, it was. I felt humiliated the rest of my senior year; thankfully, it was almost over. It stopped being gossip pretty quick because graduation was coming up, but in my mind, I never lived down the embarrassment. Once we graduated, I didn't think about him again until I ran into him on campus today."

"And?" Audrey's eyes were wide, expectant.

"He apologized for senior prom."

Her hand went to her heart, and she sighed. "He apologized for senior prom? After all these years."

"Yeah. He said he felt really bad about it and was glad he ran into me so he could apologize in person."

She scraped the chair back across the faded tan linoleum floor and brought her plate to the sink. "Hmmm. Why was it so important to him?"

I shrugged. "I don't know. Maybe it was one of those things he always felt bad about. Then he asked me out."

"For real?" Audrey shrieked. She shut the water off just so she could rush over to hug me.

I patted her arm, not really sure why my news was hug-worthy. "Yeah," I admitted, nodding.

"Did you say yes?" She stepped back and put her hand on her hip. "Or did you find some reason to not like him? Like his eyebrows are too thick or something silly like that?"

"No." I playfully stuck my tongue out at her.

"So?"

"I gave him my number."

"You're so weird, Camille. The one guy who left you with baggage and you're giving him a chance. I don't get you."

Sometimes *I* didn't even get myself.

* * *

He called that night.

"You didn't wait two days or four days or whatever the rule of thumb is for not appearing too anxious," I said when I answered. A nervous excitement went through me.

"Oh. Should I have?" he asked. I didn't think he realized I was joking.

"No. I'm glad you didn't. I hate the waiting game." Maybe he had grown up and matured over the years and learned from his mistake in high school. Maybe this time I actually had a chance.

The conversation wasn't stilted or awkward. We talked about all the typical stuff: classes, majors, missions. We found out we were both taking Bio 100, and it was an easy excuse to get together. He finally got around to what I was hoping for and asked me out.

"What kinds of things do you like to do? Are you an inside girl or an outdoors girl?" he asked.

"I like both. I like hiking around the mountains; movies are great. Sometimes it's fun to play the games at Chuck E. Cheese's."

"Chuck E. Cheese's?" he repeated, sounding surprised. "That's for kids."

"But aren't we all kind of big kids?" Maybe Chuck E. Cheese's would have to be a one-time thing with Liam.

"Uh, sorry to disappoint you, but I probably won't be taking you there."

"That doesn't sound fun to you?"

"No." He was definitive in his answer.

"Okay. What should we do?" I left it up to him. I was up for anything.

"How about snowshoeing? Like hiking and playing in the snow all at once."

I hadn't been hiking since . . . I stopped since *Liam and I were supposed to go* was how I was going to finish the sentence, but I was trying not to think of him. "Snowshoeing works."

"Should we plan for Saturday morning?"

I was enthusiastic about the idea. "Great. Like eight?"

"That early?" he asked, sounding surprised yet again. He had been up early the other morning when I'd run into him. But maybe he wanted to sleep in on the weekend.

"Yeah, you know, get a jump on the day."

"I was thinking more like ten."

"Let's compromise and say nine? I have a lot of studying I need to do later in the afternoon." I was excited about the date but didn't want it to take up my whole day.

"That sounds good. I'm looking forward to it."

After I gave him my address and hung up, I looked at the clock. We had been talking for almost two hours.

Chapter Twenty-One

WE STOOD AT THE BASE of the trailhead to Stewart Falls. It instantly reminded me of Liam and the hike we never took.

"I thought we were going snowshoeing." I wasn't disappointed; this sounded fun too. I looked toward the top, squinting in the morning sun. Inhaling the cold morning air deeply, I felt positive, refreshed.

"Yeah, that sounded like too much work and it hasn't snowed enough yet." His tone of voice confirmed his lack of passion for it, and I wondered why he had suggested it. "Then I planned on going ice blocking only to find it has been banned in some places because it ruins the grass. I thought this would be a sufficient replacement activity." We started on the trail.

"This is good too. I thought you liked snowshoeing because you run. Outdoorsy stuff."

He walked beside me, his free hand hovering around my elbow. It was sweet that he was worried about me slipping. "I don't really love running either. I do it for exercise."

"Like a necessary evil?"

He laughed. "Yeah. Although I haven't seen you at the track lately."

"Only on days with bad weather."

"You only run on rainy days?"

My running would be very sporadic if I did. "No. I only run inside on days with bad weather. Otherwise, I run outdoors. I like it better." I thought for a moment. "I run in the summer, I run in the fall, hot days, cold days—I run them all."

He looked at me closely and squinted. "Is that a song I should know?"

"Nope, just making up a rhyme."

"Why?"

"No reason." Guess he didn't get it. "Sometimes I do it as I run. It helps me keep my rhythm."

"Oh, huh. So how far do you run? Do you do it every day?"

"I run every day but Sunday. Usually it's anywhere from three to five miles."

"Wow, you mean, sometimes you run more than a 5K for your daily jog?" His mouth hung open for a second. "I can't believe that."

"Yeah."

"Sounds like torture to me." He grinned but was completely serious.

"It's a great way to clear your head." I actually found it very relaxing. It helped take Liam off my mind.

"I don't have enough on my mind to want to jog five miles. One mile and some push-ups are enough for me."

I wondered how soft his six-pack was. If he had one at all.

"The runner's high definitely helps make the day better." I didn't feel I had to justify it to him. Simply put, running made me happy.

He looked at the trail, obviously ready to change the subject. "What do you say? Should we do this?"

"Yes. Let's do it." It looked like a lot of fun.

After thirty minutes of walking, he stopped and took a water bottle out of his backpack. "Mind if I take a quick break?"

"Sure."

He took a drink, then offered his water bottle to me. I shook my head in refusal, finding the thought of sharing a drink a little too intimate at this point.

"You're not a germophobe, are you?" he asked, taking the bottle back.

"A germophobe?" I laughed. "No. I just don't like sharing drinks. You know, in case of backwash. That's gross."

"That's a germophobe," Riley said.

I was not a germophobe. I changed the topic instead of arguing about the finer points of germophobia. It was like getting into a discussion with Liam about armpits. It could end only in awkwardness or possibly anger.

"You ready to get moving?" I asked.

"Sure thing," he said, putting his water bottle back in the side pocket.

After three more water breaks, we reached the falls. The return trip took less time, but we had been going for almost two hours. "I'm ready to warm up. Should we get some hot chocolate after?" I was thinking through places to suggest we go.

"A snack might be good," he said.

We walked to Riley's car, but instead of climbing in the driver's side, he opened the hatchback. I assumed he was putting the gear away, but he didn't. He put the seats down. Then he unzipped his backpack and pulled out a blanket that he spread out on the seats.

"What are you doing?" I asked as I watched his surprise unfold.

"I packed a picnic. I figured we'd be hungry by the time we finished."

I was a little bit hungry, but I had brought a couple of granola bars I was going to share because I thought we were snowshoeing. But I had to give Riley credit for planning. And creativity points for having a picnic in the backseat of his car.

He sat on the blanket and patted the spot beside him, signaling for me to sit. "This would have been way cooler if it were at night and by candlelight, but I didn't want to risk setting my car on fire."

"That was probably a good choice," I said, accepting his offering. Once I was in and settled, he closed the hatchback. From an insulated grocery bag, he began pulling out food. He had some crackers and a can of cheese spread, two bottles of water, some grapes, and a can of lime-and-chili almonds. Had he gone to the store and bought all this arbitrary food or just rummaged through his pantry? Maybe these were the hors d'oeuvres. Was there more food in his bag that would tie this meal together?

"If you had told me, I could've fixed some sandwiches," I said. "I do have two granola bars I can add to this, if you'd like."

He waved off my suggestion. "I was going to bring some sushi, but I didn't know if you liked it, and it needs to be kept cold."

"Sushi?" I thought that was an odd choice for a sledding/picnic outing. "Do you like sushi?"

"Yeah, I like it okay. I don't get it very often because it's expensive if you go out to a restaurant, and sometimes the stuff you get at the grocery store isn't that great. How about you?"

I would be hesitant to buy sushi at the grocery store, mostly because I wouldn't know how fresh it was. After being spoiled by Liam when he took me to that really expensive sushi bar, I was afraid to try anything other than that. "I've only had sushi once, and it was really good but very expensive. I think you were safe not buying sushi." I bumped him gently with my shoulder.

"I did get this sandwich, though, that we could share." From the bag, he pulled out a sub that he must have picked up at the grocery store. The final part of the meal that did (sort of) tie everything together.

"Great," I said. "Enough talk about food. Let's eat."

Granted, it was a little strange eating a picnic in the back of his car on a cold morning, but it had been a fun time, and all in all, I'd count the date as a success.

* * *

"You're very . . . intense," I said. It was the day after our first date, and Riley had invited me over for dinner. He was now walking me back to my apartment.

He looked at me. "Is that a bad thing?"

"No, I'm just not used to a guy being so . . . aggressive." Not a Mormon guy, at least. It wasn't a bad aggressive. It was more of a "let's spend all day together and what are you doing tomorrow" kind of dating style. Other guys I had gone out with seemed more content with just hanging out.

He took my hand. "I feel like I owe you. I dissed you in high school, and I don't want you to think I'm still that same jerk."

I laughed. "I think you've proven yourself."

"Good. Because I really was a jerk back then." He laughed with me. I had a good time on the date that night but not enough to kiss him, so when he leaned in, I thought about telling him I didn't feel it just yet. But I didn't want to make him feel bad, so I went along. The sparks weren't there . . . yet. But we still had time; it was only our second date. But it wasn't like kissing Liam.

* * *

He promised to text the next day, and he did. Being Monday, he invited me to his ward's FHE.

"Three dates in three days. He might be the guy," Esther said by way of greeting when I returned home that night.

"Let's not jump to conclusions," I replied. I wasn't anywhere near thinking that. I was going to take it one date at a time and see how or where it went.

After a couple of days, I texted him but never heard back. One week passed and still no call, no text. Then one week became two weeks.

"Has Riley texted?" Audrey asked. She was still hopeful.

"No, I don't think he's going to," I replied.

"You don't know that."

I chewed on my lip. "I think that's just how he is."

"Maybe he's busy," Audrey suggested. "You know, with classes and all."

It was a viable excuse, but still. "Too busy to send a text saying he's busy?" I hadn't realized how angry I was at him until now. "I don't think it's going to go anywhere."

"Maybe he ran out of minutes?"

I started laughing, glad she had lightened the mood. "Who has minutes anymore?"

She shrugged. "I don't know; a lot of people. Maybe he has a pay-as-you-go phone and he ran out of minutes and his phone got shut off?"

"Maybe. He could borrow one from his roommates though. Or stop by."

"I hate that he's doing this and now you have to not like him all over again."

"I like him, but he's sort of fallen off the face of the earth. I'm not going to keep playing the hoping-and-wishing game. I did that in high school, and when my dream finally came true, it was anything but a dream. I know better this time. Maybe he's too chicken to tell me he doesn't like me that way."

Audrey wrinkled her brow. "After he looked you up and personally apologized for the dance that happened in high school, I don't think he'd end things like this."

I wouldn't have thought so either, but his actions were telling me otherwise. "The ball is in his court, and he hasn't made a move. So my move is to move on."

"I'm really surprised. I thought you two would work out. Maybe he would even be *the one.*"

I started laughing and shaking my head. "I'm not so sure about that. He's nice and all. I think out of all the guys I've dated, I liked him the best. But something was missing."

"Like what?" She gave me a wary look. "You can't decide that after only three dates."

"There's no click." No finishing each other's sentences, laughing about the same thing at the same time.

"You sound like that song from Gear. You know, 'Click'?"

Yeah, I knew it. How could I not? It was the same conversation I'd had with Liam, driving back from Salt Lake. The same song he had sung to me before it had ever come out on their album.

Chapter Twenty-Two

"Camille!" someone called out. It was hard to hear over the hustle and bustle outside the entrance to the library, but I stopped and looked around. "Camille." I saw Riley raise a hand and motion for me to wait.

"Riley," I said, surprised. "I thought you had disappeared. I never heard back from you." I took in his appearance. He didn't seem to be missing any limbs or have any visible sign of personal injury that would've hampered his ability to call me. It had been over two weeks.

"I am sorry I didn't call. I got really busy. Papers, tests, a new job. I was really stressed out." He tried to catch his breath. He must've been trying pretty hard to catch up to me.

I clenched both hands on the straps of my backpack. "You could have texted and let me know. Or called. There are plenty of ways to let me know. Any way would have been acceptable." I didn't bother masking my disappointment. He should know he'd let me down.

He hung his head. "And I meant to. Every day. But I dropped my phone in the toilet—true story—and lost all my contacts." He held up his hands helplessly.

I chewed on my lip, deciding whether or not to believe him. I wanted to give him every benefit of the doubt, but I was finding that hard to do. "You know where I live. You could've stopped by."

"You're right. But every day seemed to get crazy busy, and by the time I thought of it, it was like eleven o'clock at night, or even midnight, and it was too late to stop by."

He did have a point. It wasn't the greatest excuse, but it was an understandable one.

I had considered texting or calling him, but then I always talked myself out of it. A couple of times, I even typed a text on my phone. I just never hit Send. If he wasn't interested, there was no sense in chasing him.

Riley continued. "But I thought about you." He gave me a weak smile and held up his phone. "I got a new phone. Maybe I can get your number again? Please?"

I could see he was sincere. I could hear it in his voice. "Sure."

"I'm glad I ran into you today. Maybe we can plan a time to get together? What do you say? Are you willing to give me a second chance?"

I forced myself not to start nibbling on my lip again; it was becoming raw. Was I just saying yes to disappointment again?

He ran his hand through his hair before leaning in close. "Camille, I got overwhelmed. I'm sorry."

"Okay," I said. "Let's just chalk up everything to school being busy. We can start fresh." I told him my phone number and watched as he programmed it into his contacts. Starting fresh. I liked that idea.

Riley broke out in a grin.

"But," I held up a finger, "I need to know right now if this is the way it's going to be. Because if being MIA is something you do a lot, that doesn't work for me." I sounded like a miserable cow, in Liam's words, but I didn't want to waste more emotional energy on Riley if this was who he was.

"I know, Camille, and I'm sorry. I dropped the ball. It won't happen again."

"Really?" I said softly. I wanted to believe him.

He nodded. "Yes. I promise. Can I make it up to you? How about Sunday night? We could go to a fireside my ward is hosting," Riley said.

I nodded, perking up. "Sunday night would be great." Perhaps our budding relationship just needed a jump-start.

"Definitely." He waved before we parted ways.

He surprised me by texting me later that day. *Let's not wait until Sunday. Study tonight?*

I smiled when I read his text. I had to give him credit—he was making up for lost time. It seemed once he was back on board, he acted immediately. I sent back, *Sure. 7 pm. @ Library.*

Maybe this was the restart of something good. Maybe I hadn't given things enough time to click.

And because I was desperate for something to distract me from the Gear concert, I asked him out that night when we were together. "What are you doing Saturday night? Maybe we can get together and hang out? Watch a movie?"

Riley shuffled a little, looked away for a minute, then looked back at me. "Um, I can't. I sort of have plans."

"Oh yeah?" I tried to sound upbeat. I didn't want him to hear the disappointment in my voice. "A date?"

"A girl I know invited me to go see Gear. Before I ran into you the first time. And I didn't mention it because I didn't think we were . . ."

I held my palm up to stop him. "That's okay. We're barely dating." We were barely anything.

"Are you going? To the concert, I mean?"

I shook my head. "No."

"Didn't get tickets? I heard it sold out in two minutes."

"No. I don't want to go."

"Oh. You don't like Gear?" He looked at me minutely closer. "Not your kind of music?"

"Something like that," I said mildly. I added a smile to convince him.

Chapter Twenty-Three

"YOU WENT FOR ANOTHER RUN?" Audrey asked as I came in the front door. She was on the couch with her legs crossed underneath her, reading a text book.

"Yeah." I went to the sink to refill my water bottle.

She set down the highlighter she was holding. "Is there a marathon coming up that I don't know about? Or is it about Riley?"

"No, I just needed to run again." I paced around the kitchen, catching my breath, shaking my legs out. The Gear concert was tomorrow night, and I was hyperaware of it.

"Are you stressed? Becoming obsessed with exercise?"

"No. I told you. I just wanted to run." I shrugged, then sat at the table. I knew her inquiry about my emotional state was well-intentioned.

"Yeah, but . . ."

I took a long drink of water and looked at her. "What?"

"You've been acting strange the last couple days. I want to know what's up."

I met her eyes. "Nothing's up." I kept my voice even so she wouldn't feel the need to inquire any further.

"I don't believe you."

"Believe what you want. There is nothing up." I rested my elbows on the table and then put my head in my hands. I rubbed my face and stretched my shoulders. Once this weekend was over, I wouldn't have thoughts of Liam floating around my head.

"Camille—"

I set my water bottle on the counter. "I'm going to take a shower." I walked toward my bedroom without waiting for Audrey to finish.

After the shower, Audrey continued where she had left off.

"I'm just worried. You're always—"

There was a knock at the door, interrupting Audrey's interrogation. She hopped up and went over to answer the door. I rolled my head to the side, listening for who was here.

"Hi?" she said.

"I'm looking for Camille. I was told she lives here."

With the front door opened, the kitchen was behind it, so I couldn't see who was there. But I recognized his voice immediately, though his accent was much more Americanized.

"She's right here," Audrey said, opening the door wider to let him in. She pointed to the kitchen to her left. "In there."

And there he was. Liam. Standing in front of me. He was wearing jeans, a hoodie, and a baseball hat, looking like any other average guy walking across campus. Except his jeans probably cost as much as tuition for one semester and he had a few days' growth of facial hair.

"You know, you look like the lead singer from Gear," Audrey said, looking at him with scrutiny. She stood close, staring at his face. Where were his fake glasses now?

He glanced at her before catching my eye. "Yeah, I get that a lot." He said it so casually there was no room for discussion.

I resisted the strong urge to hug him. My knees felt weak, as did my insides, and I needed to pull myself together. I grabbed my water bottle and took a long drink, hoping to buy more time while I tried to figure out what to say to him. I immediately regretted it. I swallowed too fast and started choking.

"Camille? You okay?" He crossed the room to me.

I coughed and sputtered until I was able to catch my breath. "Yes. I think so. Have a seat," I managed, pointing to a chair across from me.

Audrey sort of hovered in the kitchen, looking in the fridge, then in her cupboard. I'm not sure if she was genuinely hungry, didn't know what to do, or wanted to hang around to find out more about this guy.

"How are you?" I croaked out, then coughed a couple more times, my eyes watering.

"I'm doing well. How are you?"

I gave a thumbs-up. "Once I stop choking, I'll be well also."

"Good to hear."

"Yes." I coughed one more time, this time to clear my throat.

Audrey was still standing by the sink, hesitant. Finally, she moved. "I'm Audrey," she said as she stuck out her hand.

He took her hand. "Liam. Nice to meet you."

He was pulling off the American accent rather well.

"And you're friends with Camille?" Her question was loaded with all sorts of curiosity.

"Yes." He didn't offer any extra information.

"Do you go to BYU?"

"No. I'm just passing through, actually."

"Audrey," I said, sort of sing-songy. "He's already had the third-degree questions from my dad."

She looked between him and me. "He's met your family?"

I probably shouldn't have said that. "When we first met, yes."

She waited for a second. I think she thought I was going to give her more of an explanation. "I'm just wondering. You've never mentioned Liam before."

"Like me that much, do you?" Liam asked. This time it was him who looked from her to me.

"You're making it awkward," I said to Audrey through a fake smile and gritted teeth.

"I just want to know—" she protested.

I motioned with my head and widened my eyes. "Go," I whispered, as if instructing a small child.

Audrey made this pining look. "But . . ." she whined. Her hands fell to her side, and her shoulders slumped.

"We'll talk about him later," I offered since it was obvious she wanted to talk about him.

"What are you going to say about me?" Liam surprised me by asking. A grin crept across his face, and he leaned closer across the table.

"Oh, you know, all the things girls normally talk about when discussing boys." I spread my hands out in front of me on the table. They were trembling a little, so I quickly pulled them off the table again and folded them in my lap.

"But I don't know. I never had sisters. What do girls talk about when discussing boys?" His tone was playful; his left eyebrow was cocked. Only I knew he wasn't playing. It was part of his charming act he put on for the world. I couldn't decipher if the cause behind it was concern, anger, or just teasing.

Audrey hadn't moved. I stood to encourage her to leave.

"How do you know each other?" Audrey said quickly, squeezing in as much as she could say before I gently encouraged her to go to her room. "Did you date or know each other before her mission or on the mission or—?"

"Audrey." I shot her a warning look.

"Okay, I'm going, I'm going." She walked out of the room backward. "But don't think I'm not going to eavesdrop," she called before she shut her bedroom door.

"Nice to know we have some privacy," I murmured, turning back to Liam. I took my place at the table and looked at him. He was watching me with those intense blue eyes.

"How have you been?" he asked. My inside got all jiggly again.

"Just fine," I said tersely.

His voice dropped to a whisper. "I've missed you." His hand reached across the table for mine.

I couldn't address his admission. "Is this your attempt at being normal?" I asked, motioning to his clothes.

"I already proved to you I'm normal." He smiled and winked. "This is my attempt to look like everybody else." He leaned back in the chair, draping his arm over the back.

I nodded. I also listened carefully to detect any sort of sound that would signal Audrey had come out of her bedroom or even opened the door a crack.

"I stopped by and visited your parents."

I nodded again. "Is that how you found out where I live?" I sat ram-rod straight, trying to keep it together.

He looked me in the eye. "They like me, Camille. Why don't you? Usually, it's the other way around."

I took in a deep, cleansing breath and let it out slowly. "I like you. And that's the problem." Underneath the table, I was fiercely peeling the cuticle on my thumb.

"Why is it a problem?"

"Because sleeping with you isn't an option. Nothing has changed since I visited you."

"Can't we just pretend that never happened? I was a jerk and insensitive, and Twick—"

"Did she ever stop following you?"

He nodded at me. "Eventually. It took her awhile to accept we weren't getting back together."

I leaned toward him. "Oh yeah? What changed?" My voice was low, just in case somehow Audrey was listening.

"I met you," he said simply, without hesitation.

I snorted without meaning to. "C'mon, the charming stuff doesn't work on me." I realized I was contradicting myself. It did work on me. And that frustrated me. I didn't want his charm to work on me. I didn't want to react to him like so many other fangirls did. I put my head in my hand while trying to gather my thoughts. "I'm not one of your groupies," I whispered fiercely.

He leaned in and took my hand in his. "I don't want you to be one of my groupies. I want you to be you."

I was fighting the urge to give in and throw myself into his arms. But I stuck to my guns, clinging to practicality, because otherwise, my emotions would betray me. I slid my fingers out from under his. "But you're this star, and I'm . . . I'm nobody. It's like you're royalty and I'm a commoner." I sputtered along, trying to explain away my hesitation while also convincing myself I was right.

He sat back and folded his arms across his chest. "It worked for Kate Middleton and Prince William." It almost sounded like a challenge.

"You're not Prince William, and I am not Kate Middleton." I stabbed my finger at my chest.

"You agreed to think about it. Would you just please allow me a date? On your terms. Just a normal guy and a normal girl going on a normal date. Please?"

It sounded so tempting. So tempting. Did we deserve a second chance? Would things be different this time?

"Please," he whispered. "Please?"

"All right." I gave in all too easily, my resolve crumbling. "When?"

"Now," Liam said without hesitation.

It was Friday, and I was done with classes. I had run twice, thanks to Liam's band playing in Salt Lake tomorrow night, and I had no excuse to put the date off. "Now?" I gulped. I wished I had at least a couple hours to gather the courage to go through with it. "Let me, um, grab my coat."

"Great."

I hurried into my bedroom and shut the door, leaning against it.

Audrey was next to me in a heartbeat. "Who is he?" she demanded. "There was a lot of whispering going on. I want details."

"I, he—" How could I explain? "We met right after my mission, and we . . . he . . ."

"What?" My roommate stared at me, waiting, her eyebrows lifted expectantly. "Dated?"

"Oh! It's complicated." I threw my hands up. "It was nothing."

"Nothing serious?"

"Not even nothing casual. It was just nothing." I shrugged and tried to wave her away.

"You sure are flustered over nothing."

"Yeah. He seems to have that effect on people," I muttered. I went to my closet and stared at the clothes hanging there. They all seem to meld together into one big blob. How was I ever going to decide what to wear?

"Tell me about him," Audrey encouraged.

I continued to stare into the depths of the closet. "Maybe later. Right now, I need my jacket."

Her mouth fell open. "Are you two going out?"

"Not exactly," I said evenly, trying to downplay her excitement. But honestly, I didn't know what else to call what we were going to do.

* * *

Once we were outside, he reached for my hand.

"Not yet," I said out of the corner of my mouth. I didn't want to seem too cozy with him. "I'm pretty sure we have an audience right now."

His brows furrowed together. "What do you mean?"

"I bet my roommate is watching." I glanced back at the front window of my apartment, and sure enough, Audrey was standing there. I gave a casual wave. She gave me a huge smile and a double thumbs-up. "Yup. I was right."

Liam started to look back. "No. Just keep looking straight ahead."

"You really think she'll recognize me?" He sounded skeptical.

I chuckled. "It's not necessarily *who* I'm with, just the fact that I'm with *someone*."

"Seriously?"

"Yes," I said emphatically.

He led me to a black Escalade with black tinted windows.

I stopped before climbing into the vehicle. "If you're trying to be inconspicuous, you're failing," I said as he held the door and I got in.

He climbed in the driver's side and turned to face me. "You think the SUV is a bit much?"

I patted his hand. "Maybe just a bit," I said kindly.

"Now may I give you a proper kiss?" he asked.

"Still have an audience," I reminded him, pointing to the apartment window. Audrey was still standing there, gawking.

"Maddox won't mind."

"Who?" I asked, confused. Then my eye caught sight of someone in the back seat, and I jumped.

"You remember Maddox from when you visited me, right?"

"Maddox," I said, acknowledging the man sitting silently in the back seat. He was clothed in a dark suit and had sunglasses.

Maddox gave a slight nod. "Camille."

"You could've given me a heads-up that he was in here," I whispered fiercely to Liam. My heartbeat hadn't regulated itself yet. "And I wasn't referring to him, but Audrey."

"Ah, yes, the nosy flatmate."

"Not really nosy. Just curious, as she well should be. It's not every day I have a stranger show up out of the blue and whisk me away in a tinted-window Escalade."

"I was hoping you wouldn't mind my popping round on a whim. I thought about ringing you, but I was worried you wouldn't see me." He turned on the ignition.

"Instead, you pop round to my apartment where you could be easily recognized and cause all sorts of gossip?"

"Yes. You are worth the risk."

I splayed my hands. "This was just on a whim?"

"That's better than saying I was in the area and thought I'd come see you." He looked at me expectantly.

I took a deep breath. "And here we are."

"Yes. Here we are. Where shall we go?"

"You really don't have any plans?" I was surprised. I assumed he would've had it all laid out. I wondered what he thought would happen when he came to visit me.

"I wasn't sure you'd fancy a visit. I thought it better to wait and see if you'd even talk to me."

"Of course I'd talk to you."

"We could go to that fondue place again."

That would guarantee at least a couple hours with him. "I would love that."

It was silent again. I looked out the back window. "If you back out and take a left, we'll be on our way."

Liam did as instructed, and we headed north. We drove in silence for a while.

Liam finally spoke. "We're playing in Salt Lake tomorrow night."

I nodded my head but couldn't meet his eyes. I stared straight ahead and pressed my teeth into my lips. "I know," I eventually replied. "My room-mates are going."

"But not you?"

"No. Not me." What the heck. I might as well be straight up with him. What did I have to lose? "I was afraid to see you again."

"Afraid? Why?"

I turned my whole body toward him. "Because it's really hard to keep seeing someone I can't have. I can't very well move on with my life if I'm still hanging on to you."

"I can't very well move on when I can't get over you."

My heart thudded in my chest. "I can't keep doing this. I can't keep saying goodbye and then seeing you again and having to go through the heartache again."

"Then don't. Don't say goodbye."

I didn't respond. I didn't know what to say. How many times did I have to explain that my hesitation came from knowing there was no way anything between us could work out? "Liam, I want a man who can take me to the temple." I sighed as I said the words.

"Okay, let's go. Where is the temple?"

"What that means is I want a man I can marry in the temple."

"I wouldn't be opposed to getting married there if that's what you wanted. But I didn't think we were talking marriage here. I just want a date."

"I decided a long time ago, once I had a testimony of the gospel, that I would serve a mission and that I would get married in the temple. If you don't share the same beliefs, there is no way that can happen."

"Do you think I'm not capable of change?"

"I totally believe you are capable of change. Look at all you've accom-plished in your life since you lived with your great aunt. I've never experienced anything like that, ever. But I don't want you to change for me. I only want you to change if it's something you want to do."

"How about we don't think about the future? All I'm asking for is to take it one day at a time and that you give me another chance."

"What did you have in mind?" Wasn't that what this was? Weren't we trying to give things another chance right now?

"Come to my concert tomorrow night?"

"And?"

"See another side of me, the side you don't know. Maybe you'll like me."

"But that's the side that makes me think it won't work. The lifestyle. The parties," I said, adding silently to myself, the sex, drugs, and rock and roll. Seeing him in his element might make it all the easier to say no to him. Maybe I should go. Maybe seeing him in his element would make him less attractive. Maybe this would confirm it and I could finally get over him.

But what if it didn't? The thought came as a surprise.

"You keep assuming I have this lifestyle. Why?"

I squirmed. "Because you're a famous rock star."

"Aside from the 'misunderstanding'"—he made quotes in the air— "when you came to visit, there wasn't partying, drugs, or girls. What you saw—that's my life. That's me."

"I realize things are good when it's just the two of us."

"So why would it be any different if we were a couple? It'd still be just the two of us."

I considered his point while I chewed on my bottom lip. Would it ever be just the two of us?

"Besides, your parents said Kaela couldn't come unless you supervised."

I was a little surprised. "You've talked to my parents about the concert?"

"I asked their permission. I did promise your sister."

At least he was solid enough to make good on his promise. I considered his invitation for a moment. "Okay, I'll come. But, Liam, that doesn't change—"

He played with a strand of my hair. "I don't think you understand, Camille, how much I'd give up to have you."

"You make it sound like a conquest," I said. "I'm not a conquest."

"That's not it."

My voice softened. "I don't want you to quit everything you love."

"I can quit the drinking. I can quit the parties and the perceived life-style. But I can't quite quit you, Camille."

Huh.
I think that took my breath away.
Just a little.

Chapter Twenty-Four

"HEY, THERE'S STARBUCKS IF YOU haven't had your fix for the day." I pointed to the sign we were approaching.

He shook his head. "Actually, I'm good."

"That's not like you to pass up coffee." Something was up. I studied his profile for a moment, trying to decipher what it was he wasn't telling me. "You don't want to go to Starbucks?"

"Only if you want some lemon pound cake." Liam stared straight ahead. He gripped the wheel and concentrated with more energy than necessary.

A thought hit me suddenly. "Did you stop drinking coffee?"

His voice got quiet. "Trying to," he said.

"Trying to? But you love your coffee."

"But I like you more." His thumb tapped the top of the steering wheel.

My hand went to my chest. "Don't quit your coffee for me."

Liam looked at me with a serious expression. "Camille, I am not doing it for you. I am doing it because of you."

Oh. That was good, I guess. I mean, if he was doing it for himself.

"I met with your missionaries." He looked over at me briefly. Was he watching for my reaction?

I tried to keep my expression neutral. "Really?" He had just passed up Starbucks. "You met with missionaries?" Maybe the rumors Esther had heard were true.

"Yeah, really. Bird and Ekpale. Elder Bird was from Alaska; Elder Ekpale was from Ghana. We played basketball a few times at the church. Ekpale and I are more football—you know, soccer—fans, but it's kind of hard to play on a wood floor."

His lingo sounded sufficiently believable. "What did you think about what you heard?" I tried not to get too excited or read too much into it. Just because he really had talked to the missionaries, which Esther would be thrilled to know, didn't mean he believed them.

"It sounded like something I'd heard before."

My heart softened. "Like at The Melting Pot?"

"Precisely. The elders thought I was brilliant because I knew all the answers." He laughed.

"Really? You paid attention over fondue?"

"I didn't tell them I'd been told this stuff before. They were so impressed with me."

I smiled at him and rolled my eyes.

"Your smile is so beautiful." He reached out and took my hand.

I looked at my hand entwined with his and smiled some more. In fact, I may have looked like a smiling fool. I directed him into the restaurant's parking lot, and he shut off the engine and turned to me.

"And what came of your meetings?" I asked, continuing the missionary conversation.

"Well, I'm not baptized yet."

I couldn't help but notice the *yet*. It made my heart jump. Was there hope?

"Have you thought about us, Camille?"

I swallowed hard. "Every day," I answered. It was the truth. Unfortunately, what I had come up with for a solution involved either me giving up all my beliefs or him giving up his way of life. I didn't see either of them happening, so I still had little hope it could ever work out between us.

He rubbed his thumb over mine. "I couldn't get you off my mind. From past experiences, I've learned if I can't stop thinking about something, I need to write it down. So I wrote a song. Then one song turned into two, and pretty soon I had ten songs and I still couldn't stop thinking about you."

"There's your next song," I said.

"What?"

"I wrote you a song
To clear my head,
But one turned into ten.
If I gave you some time
To change your mind . . ."

Liam snapped his fingers. "That's actually pretty good. Have you got a finishing line?

I thought for a second, knowing what I really wanted to say but chose not to. "You won't stab me with a pen?"

He started laughing. "I don't think you're going to stab me with a pen."

"Attack you with a hen?" I suggested, then added quietly, "Maybe you'd love me then?"

He sang it back to me, coming up with his own tune.

"I wrote you a song
To clear my head,
But one turned into ten.
If I gave you some time
To change your mind
Maybe you'd love me then."

He looked over at me, his eyes alive. "That's brilliant! Where have you been all those times I've had writer's block?"

"See, there was a reason you met me. I can help you rhyme."

"It's much more than that, Camille."

I knew where that was going.

"You probably don't know this, but we only needed a couple more songs for our next album but weren't coming up with anything we liked enough to record. We took a break for a couple months, hoping to come back to work with some fresh material. It was during that time that I met you."

I shook my head, motioning that I hadn't known.

"After I came back from your house, I wrote so much stuff that we scrapped most of the other songs and used the new ones. I had met my muse."

I scowled and shifted in my seat, trying to get comfortable. But that was hard when my nerves were making me uncomfortable. "I'm not a muse."

"Oh, but you are."

"I think Twick is responsible for all of this. You know," I pursed my lips, "if she hadn't stolen all of your stuff, you never would have ended up on that highway and we never would have met."

A small smile crossed his face. "You have got a point."

"And there's the best revenge of all," I said.

"Meaning?"

I swirled my finger in a circle. "Does she realize she put all this in motion? It's like the opposite effect of what she wanted. She wanted to ruin you, and instead, she . . ." I trailed off.

"Made it possible for us to meet and provide a muse for me to write material for our best-selling album yet. That is way better than revenge. I should be thanking her."

"I don't know if I'd go that far," I said. "But I would love to be there to see it if you did."

Liam grinned. "That would burn her."

"Her plan backfired."

He began singing again to the same tune he had just used, but he added different lyrics.

"I could have put you in jail
And denied you bail
To make you pay for your crimes.
You'd be stuck
And out of luck
With nothing on your hands but time.
You'd be doing me a favor,
Serving hard labor,
Staying out of my life,
Then you couldn't find me
With your back-stabbing knife."

"Have you got a pen, maybe some paper?" he asked, his eyes bright. He became agitated, feeling his pockets and looking around. "I've got to write this down so I don't forget it."

I dug through my purse and found a crumpled receipt and a pink pen. I watched as he scribbled our rhymes. When he was done, he looked up at me, pleased. "You're absolutely brilliant."

His happiness was so pure it made my throat tighten. This was Liam, the real Liam, not the rock star. I watched him, taking in the moment. He truly loved creating music. *This* was the man I could love.

Or did love.

The realization hit me hard, leaving me stunned.

He was silent for a moment. "I can't explain how I feel around you. I feel like I'm home. I left your family and came back to my place, and I felt so empty."

"It's hard to come home to an empty house. It's lonely if it's constant."

"It was more than that. Like all my life I have been searching for something and I didn't know what it was. I always thought the next thing might make me happy: the recording deal, the next album, the next concert, the next girl, the next fix."

"Liam, I'm not sure your impressions were accurate. I mean, it was just a couple of days. It was a great couple of days, but like being on vacation, coming home to reality is hard. It's like crashing from a high."

"I know how I felt. Isn't that what your church teaches? To listen to those feelings?"

"I . . . uh . . ." I couldn't argue that point. It made me clamp my mouth shut. I needed to stop and listen to what he was telling me.

"Camille, I've never felt like I did being at your house. For the first time, I didn't feel like I was looking for the next thing or what tomorrow or the next day or the next week would bring. I liked being there. I liked being with your family. I didn't want to leave. I kept finding excuses to stay."

I remembered what my mom said. "Are you sure it's not your, I don't know, wishing for a family life?" It very well could have been that.

"Why are you trying to talk me out of this?"

His words reminded me that just seconds before I had told myself to stop arguing with what he was trying to tell me, and here I was doing it again. "I'm not saying you didn't feel what you felt. But maybe it looked ideal with the glimpse you had."

He kept fidgeting with his phone, tipping it from corner to corner to corner. "Do you know how it feels to never be alone but still feel lonely?"

His words sank deep. This was Liam baring his soul, and I had just caught a glimpse inside.

I shook my head. "I can't say I do."

"It's the most horrible feeling in the world. I feel like that all the time. It's like I can't be myself. I'm supposed to be the rock star when I'm with someone. It is never about myself but what my fans want. I have no personal life, and that's tough on a guy who's very private."

He placed his phone facedown in the console. "I was so happy when you accepted my invitation to come visit. I wanted to get rid of that emptiness. I was desperate to get rid of it and didn't know how to. I thought if you came to visit, I wouldn't feel bad anymore. But then I screwed everything up, and I realized how much I'd lost. Being with you makes me feel whole."

I wasn't sure how to respond to that. Or how to feel when I realized Maddox was still in the backseat.

* * *

Instead of going back to my apartment after we ate, I had Liam drop me off at my parents' house. After spending the afternoon with him, I was officially confused.

"Hey, honey," my mom said cheerfully. She was in the kitchen chopping vegetables. "Celery?" she asked, holding up a stalk.

"No, thanks. Liam took me out to eat." Just like the first time, I left The Melting Pot way too full.

She stopped chopping. "So he did go see you."

"Yes. Obviously, he saw you too."

"We visited for a while. He seems well. I told him Amanda's family was in Disneyland this week in case he was going to stop by."

"He didn't say much about that other than that you gave him my address." I sat on a chair and rested my head on my hands on the table. "I'm so confused," I moaned.

"What happened? Is it Liam? Did you guys get in a fight?"

I lifted my head and brushed my hair out of my face. "No. We got along just fine, too fine. I just feel like I would be compromising everything I believe if I were in a relationship with him."

She wiped her hands on a towel and joined me at the table. "If he weren't a rock star, would you date him?"

"That and a member of the Church. I think we could have a better chance at making the relationship work."

"Why?"

"If we had the gospel in common, we'd have a similar foundation for our family. We'd have common goals and values." I started picking at my fingernail. "Right now, it seems everything is at his disposal. I've said it before, but he can have anyone he wants. Why does he want me?"

"Because you're beautiful, amazing, and kind—"

I rolled my eyes. "And you're my mom." I laughed.

"So you feel like you don't measure up to him? That you're not as good as him?"

"If he were just a normal, everyday guy, I would love to date him. We clicked."

"Clicked? That's a good thing." Her voice perked up as if she took encouragement from my words.

I sighed. "It is, but now any guy I meet, I'm comparing him to Liam."

"Well, when you meet someone you really get along with, it's hard not to compare."

"But I'm comparing these other guys to a guy I won't date because of his lifestyle. It's sort of ironic."

My mom nodded.

I stood up to get a drink. "And then there's Riley. He's a great guy . . ." I poured myself a glass of water and returned to the table. I forced myself to sit because otherwise I would start pacing.

"But?" my mom filled in.

"But he doesn't make me feel like Liam does. He runs hot and cold, and it is all or nothing with him. And I don't get all jittery and nervous and butterflies when he kisses me." He was everything I thought I *should* want in a man.

"You've kissed Liam?" my mom asked, sounding like one of my roommates instead of my mother.

I flushed. "Yeah, and now I compare every guy to him." I took a long gulp of water.

"I see your dilemma."

I swallowed hard. "And Riley would be a great guy to date. He has everything going for him. If only I felt something for him."

"You feel nothing?"

"Nope—as much as I want to—and I try to convince myself that I don't feel the way I feel with Liam when I am with Riley."

"Then you need to go with that." She got out of her chair and hugged me.

Because you can't fake the click, I thought.

Chapter Twenty-Five

THE NEXT DAY, WE WERE in Salt Lake, enjoying a VIP experience that few would ever have.

Liam took my hand and started toward the stage. Kaela and her friend Tori followed behind, whispering and giggling to themselves. He showed us their set onstage, explained how the special effects worked, and gave us a tour backstage. He introduced me to their manager, Simon, who was having a discussion with two of the band members: Beck, the bassist, and Nigel, the drummer.

"Tread and Cybil are around here somewhere," Liam told me as we headed back to the first room. There was a whole buffet set out on tables running along the wall.

"Are you hungry?" Liam asked.

"Yeah," I said, then looked at Kaela and Tori. "You girls hungry?" They nodded.

"Go on; help yourself. But no underage drinking," Liam said, then laughed at his own joke as he wagged a finger at them. He went over to the buffet.

The door to the room opened. I looked over, wondering if it was Tread and Cybil, but it was the drummer, Nigel. I only recognized him because of his jet-black hair and pale skin. I remembered him from my online research of the band and had always thought he looked a little like Severus Snape with a haircut. "So, Camille, is it?" Nigel said as he approached. "You're the chick Liam's gaga over?" He reclined on the couch, throwing one leg over the armrest.

I blushed. Was that a question I was supposed to answer? "Um, I guess." I sat on a boxy leather seat perpendicular from him. The way he was looking at me with such a hard expression made me uncomfortable.

He lit a cigarette and took a long drag before exhaling. "You guess? You got Liam wound up so tight playing hard to get."

"What?" I asked. Liam thought I was playing hard to get?

"Yeah," he sat up and leaned forward, his expression still set. "You messing with Liam's head—that ain't right." He pointed at me with the cigarette between two fingers.

"I wasn't . . ." I trailed off, watching Nigel lean back.

"What's going on?" Liam asked, sitting down with a plate full of food.

I shook my head quickly. "Nothing."

"It wasn't nothing," Nigel said, inhaling and then lazily blowing out some smoke. The smoke was making my eyes burn. "I was telling her to quit messing with your head. We need your head in the game." He tapped his temple.

A flash of anger crossed Liam's face. His fist tightened in a ball. "You're crossing a line, Nigel. That's none of your business."

"It is my business," Nigel said with a satisfied expression on his face, "when you're pining over her and it gets in the way of what's good for the band."

Liam clenched his jaw. "What's good for the band is you being sober. No one likes you when you're drunk, so why don't you do us all a favor and stop drinking before you get completely smashed. We have a show in a couple of hours, and we need your head in the game."

He pointed his hand, still holding his cigarette, at Liam. "You shouldn't worry about me, ol' boy. I can handle my liquor. You're the lightweight now."

Liam put his hand on my elbow and led me away. I looked back at Kaela and Tori and told them to follow. We went to another room that I assumed was Liam's dressing room. It had a huge mirror, lots of bright lights, and a couple of couches.

"Sorry about that. Nigel gets a bit nasty when he's drunk, and nobody likes to be around him. I didn't realize he was so smashed."

"Um, sure," I said, looking around the room.

"Go ahead and sit anywhere. I'll get someone to get us some drinks and stuff." Liam opened the door, spoke to someone out in the hall, and came back in. "We'll have it brought in straight away."

There was a knock at the door. "Come in," Liam called.

It was Tread and Cybil. Once again, my cyber-stalking paid off, enabling me to know who they were.

"This is the lovely Camille, the muse for our album?" Tread shook my hand.

Cybil smiled, then hugged me. "I feel like I already know you." Cybil was different from Twick. Instead of being tall, stick thin, glamorous, and intimidating, Cybil was pretty and friendly, almost maternal in a touchy-feely way. Softer and more rounded than sharp and angles.

I gave a timid smile and shrugged, not really knowing what to say with Tread calling me a muse.

"D'ya mind if we join ya?" Tread asked. "Nigel is being his typical jerk self and getting mad."

"Have a seat. I was having some of the food brought in here," Liam said.

"Brilliant. Don't know if I could stand being around Nigel. He's looking for a fight," Tread said.

"Is he always so confrontational?" I asked.

"More times than not. When he's been drinking a lot, which is quite often, he's like that."

"Why do you put up with it? Can't you find another drummer?" I wondered.

"He always says he's going to back off, but he never does. Things get very intense on tour, and that's how he deals with it. Then we finish, take a break from each other for a while, and by the time we start working on the next album, we aren't so sick of each other. Usually by then, he's back to being somewhat likeable, or at least able to work with. I don't know. We've never discussed when enough is enough."

"I've never liked him," Cybil said. "He's quite mean at times."

"Maybe once we finish this tour, we'll sit him down and discuss his attitude. We just tolerated him because he's always like that."

"But who wants to be around someone like that? Doesn't it just make you feel mean and nasty? Sort of like it was with Twick?" I said.

"Twick was difficult in a different way," Tread said, then laughed.

I wasn't sure what he was laughing about.

"Twick was a drama queen. She just needed attention and a lot of it," Cybil added. "But sometimes she was just a miserable cow." Then Cybil, Tread, and Liam shared a laugh.

"It sounds awful having to spend so much time with such unpleasant people," I said.

He threw his arm around my shoulder. "That's what I like about you. You're honest. Painfully honest."

There was a knock at the door, then it opened and a guy stuck his head in. "Twenty minutes until sound check,"

"Okay," Liam and Tread said in unison.

"You're staying for the show, right?" Liam looked at me.

"Of course."

My sister elbowed me in the side. "Make sure we get their autographs," she whispered without moving her lips.

"And autographs," I piped up. "The girls here need autographs and pictures. Bragging rights." They had mentioned this several times, in no uncertain terms, on the way up here.

"Of course. If you can handle a few more minutes with Nigel, we can get a band picture and get you girls all set up." Liam opened the door and gave instructions to some guy who looked like a roadie. We shuffled back into the first room, where the rest of the band was. Nigel was still in the corner, looking smug and pleased with himself.

The roadie came back with a few T-shirts. We put on our shirts and stood with the band while someone snapped pictures with the band's camera, then with Kaela's and Tori's phones.

"Girls, do you want to watch the concert backstage, or do you want to be in the seats?" Liam asked.

Kaela and Tori looked at each other and then at me. "What are you going to do?"

"I'm going to stay backstage, if you don't mind," I said.

"We'd rather be in our seats," Kaela said.

"So where should we meet after?" I asked.

Liam slipped an arm around my waist. "You are staying for the after-party, right?"

"Yes. But I need to make sure the girls get where they need to be first."

Tori sighed. "My mom is meeting us outside as soon as the concert is over." She rolled her eyes. "You know, tomorrow morning is church and all."

I looked to my sister. "So are you staying with me or going home with Tori?"

Kaela's lips turned downward. "Mom and Dad said I had to come home with Tori."

Oh, the struggles of being sixteen. "Okay. Text me when you meet up with Tori's mom so I know you're safe and not in trouble or anything."

Kaela eyed Liam briefly. "And you text me to make sure you're not in any trouble." Her words were heavy with insinuation.

"Ha ha," I replied sarcastically.

Liam was waiting patiently as we hashed out the details. "We're going to do sound check, and then we need to get ready for the show," he explained.

"Can we watch?" I asked. I liked the idea more than being left in a room alone with Cybil. She seemed really nice, but I wasn't sure I'd know how to make small talk with her.

Tread stood and stretched. "Right, then. I'm just going to take something for this headache. I'll see you out there."

Cybil's eyebrows furrowed for a brief second. "Another headache? What's going on with you, Tread?"

"You know how it is, babe. Touring always screws me up." He walked up to her and kissed her on her cheek. "Don't worry, it's really just a headache."

She cocked her head. I got the impression she didn't believe him. There seemed to be a short, quiet power struggle. "I'll come with you. Make sure you're taking the right stuff."

Tread shoved his hands in his back pocket and followed Cybil out.

"What's up with that?" I asked.

Liam frowned. "Tread's been taking sleeping pills off and on this tour. Problem is it starts with a sleeping pill. Then add a few drinks, and before you know it—"

"He's hooked again," I filled in.

"Precisely. Cybil is on high alert, as well she probably should be. Tread's not good with self-medicating. He tends to overdo it."

"That's . . . cause for alarm." I hadn't ever been around an addict before.

"I already talked to him once about it, but Cybil's keeping a close eye on him. Once we stop touring, he'll be more reasonable, go to his NA meetings, and get back to normal. Touring gets brutal toward the end."

"Does that tempt you?"

He looked me straight in the eyes. "No. I've seen too much with my mum and brother to want to go there." Liam put his arm around me and pulled me into him. "But enough of that. Let's get you girls situated."

The show was basically what we saw for sound check, except for one huge difference. The second encore. It was a ballad, which I found a strange choice. Wasn't the point of an encore, especially a second encore, to keep the energy of the crowd high? What did I know though? I wasn't an expert on concerts.

But even stranger was the black-and-white picture that appeared on the jumbotron while Liam crooned a chorus of "I can't quite quit this girl." It was a candid picture of me and Liam from this afternoon. The picture was amazing. I was laughing, and Liam was gazing at me with an expression I could describe only as affection. It was like the camera caught the perfect moment.

I was pretty sure the song was Liam's declaration.

I had seen the photographer taking pictures, but it was very informal and kind of random. Liam had explained they did this to compile shots for videos.

And then suddenly, I was on the screen, somehow discovered from where I stood in the wings of the stage. A camera was focused right on me.

I sucked in my breath as I looked up to see my surprised expression. Liam had told me there would also be someone filming the concert. I thought nothing of it.

Until that moment.

But something seemed off. Showing a picture of me didn't seem like something he would do since he went to such great lengths to protect his privacy.

One look at Liam's face, and I knew the pictures being shown on the jumbotron weren't his doing.

* * *

Liam started yelling the moment he was offstage, demanding to know who was responsible. Cybil kindly led me to the after-party room, telling me it was better to let the boys fight it out. The way she said it made me wonder how much of this kind of thing she had dealt with. She also mentioned they would shower before joining the party.

I stayed in the hallway for a minute, texting Kaela to make sure the girls were together and okay. She texted back that they were with Tori's mom. Once I knew they were where they needed to be, I used my pass to get to the room where the after-party was.

The room was crowded, many of the girls wearing way more suggestive outfits than my skinny jeans and T-shirt—not quite as risqué as something Twick would wear but not something one would wear to church either. I was uncomfortable. I was not this kind of girl, throwing myself at a musician, being willing to cheapen myself in an attempt for his attention. Maybe I felt out of place because I didn't want to face this. I mean, what would happen after tonight? Where did we go from here?

It was about thirty minutes later when the members of Gear walked out. As soon as they did, the crowd converged on them. I slowly walked backward, letting myself be pushed to the edge of the room. I stood back, watching and finally understood what Liam meant when he told me he was never alone but lonely. These strangers pawing at him, hugging him, going crazy over him, wanting something from him. They didn't know him. And it seemed exhausting.

Nigel stumbled his way over to me. It seemed like a difficult feat with so many people packed into the room. "Miss Muse," he started. His breath smelled like liquor. He leaned in so closed I thought he was going fall into me and pin me against the wall.

I put my hand out and pressed it against his chest, feeling claustrophobic. "I think you're drunk." I didn't want to get into another conversation with him like earlier in the day.

"I'm coming to apologize," he managed, putting a hand on my shoulder.

I ducked out from under it. "Consider it done." I was able to sidestep so I was no longer in front of him against the wall.

"Don't go." He once again moved closer to me.

I stepped again to the side. "I'm sure there are plenty of other girls in this room who would love to spend some quality time with you."

He pointed a finger at me. "I want to see what's so special about you. You got our Liam in quite a tizzy. All Liam can talk about is Camille. All he writes about is Camille. Camille, Camille, Camille."

I looked around, trying to locate Liam. Or even Tread or Cybil, for that matter. Someone I could signal, who could help get Nigel away from me. Liam was on the opposite side of the room, a group of fans converged around him. He was smiling for pictures, signing autographs, and completely unaware that his drunken bandmate was coming on to me like a creep. Tread was in a similar situation, completely involved with the crowd.

I worried it was too loud in the room for me to yell to him and have him hear me.

"Watching you two today inspired me to share your love with the world. What do you think of the slide show?"

My mouth gaped as realization dawned on me. "You did that?"

A smug grin emerged, and he leaned in close. "I'm the one who made it happen."

Nigel had completely betrayed Liam.

"I thought everyone should know who Camille was. Maybe you can inspire me."

He leaned so close I panicked. My chest tightened, and I wondered what he was planning on doing. I shifted my position, causing him to lose his balance and stagger into the wall. When he straightened, he had a stunned expression on his face.

Nigel was suddenly yanked back away from me.

"What are you doing?" Liam yelled through the din of voices.

Nigel stumbled back into the crowd, lost his balance when they tried to move out of the way, and landed backward on the floor. He quickly sat up, throwing both his arms in the air as if he were blameless. "Just talking to her, mate. You left her all alone."

Liam took a step back, and I thought for a moment that he was going to hit Nigel. His eyes were narrow, his lips tight, his fists curled, and he looked like he was ready to swing. Nigel scooted back, trying to stand from a crab position. He was immediately surrounded by people offering to help him up.

Liam wrapped his hand around my forearm and pulled me into his shoulder. I straightened and held on tight, thankful for being rescued while shaking from the adrenaline surge. "Are you all right?" he whispered in my ear.

"Can you take me out of here?" I asked, feeling a little wobbly.

Liam pointed a finger inches away from Nigel's face. "Don't ever do that to her again."

Nigel brushed himself off but said nothing.

Liam spun around and stalked out of the room, taking me with him. Once outside the room, Liam fired questions at me. "Are you okay? He didn't hurt you? Did he?" he asked.

I shook my head.

"He didn't . . . force you to . . ."

"No. He kept talking about me being your muse, and I couldn't get away from him. I've never been around someone so drunk before."

"But you're okay?"

I rested my head on his shoulder, fighting the tears threatening to come. "He just scared me . . ." I trailed off as I choked up.

"I'm sorry, Camille. I should have been there with you. I shouldn't have left you alone." He led me into his dressing room. "I'll grab my bag, and we can get out of here. Do you want to see the tour bus?" he asked.

"Um, sure. As long as you don't expect anything to happen in it." I hoped I sounded light but firm. I didn't want a repeat of what just happened with Nigel hitting on me. And I definitely wanted to think about something else.

Getting from the backstage area to the tour bus was unlike anything I had ever experienced, topping the time at the fund-raiser. There was a crowd of people the bodyguards literally had to push through. As soon as the way was cleared in the front, the rear would swell back in on us. It was a crushing pressure. So many people pushing and reaching out to even touch Liam. Cameras were flashing, and people were calling out, screaming, and it was only once I stepped on the bus and the doors snapped shut behind us that I felt like I could breathe.

"How can you do this? This is crazy." Adrenaline kicked in, and I started to react to what had just happened. I was trembling all over, even inside.

Liam lifted a shoulder and shook his head. "I don't know. You get used to it. At first, it was really exciting to be in the moment of the mob. Now it's just sort of old."

"I could see how it'd get old quickly." I took in the front part of the bus. "At least you get to travel in luxury." It was nice, set up like a small living room with a couch and a couple arm chairs. There was a large TV mounted to the wall that separated the kitchenette area.

"Yeah." Liam rolled his eyes and looked tired. "Hours on the bus with the same company can get old too, if you catch my drift."

I was sure he was referring to Nigel.

Liam showed me their kitchenette and his bedroom. I sat on the edge of the bed, with Liam right beside me.

He lifted my chin and pressed his lips to mine.

I gently pushed against his chest, needing space. "Um, that last song you sang . . ."

"Did you like it?" Liam asked slowly.

Of course I liked it. I loved it. He was singing to me. What girl in her right mind would not like that? "Yes. But that kind of puts it out there to the world that we're . . ." I trailed off once again, not knowing how to finish the sentence. Were we dating? A couple? Or what I always defaulted to: a passing interest?

Liam laced his fingers with mine. "I just wanted to tell you how I feel."

I knew how he felt. I knew how I felt. I just didn't have the courage to admit it to myself or him yet.

"I'm still trying to figure out why you were on the screen though. I didn't tell anyone to do that."

I debated whether to tell Liam it was Nigel's fault. He'd eventually find out either way. I just worried that the fall-out from Nigel's stunt would be worse now that he had hit on me. "Nigel planned it."

Liam's body went rigid, and I could see his hand tighten into a fist. "I'm done with him." His anger was almost palpable.

"What are you going to do?" My heart raced, and I worried what would happen the next time Liam saw Nigel.

"I—"

"You know what? Never mind. Let's talk about something else that's not so provocative."

Liam bobbed his head slightly. "Provocative," he repeated as if considering the word.

I realized maybe I should've chosen a different way to say that. I scooted back and cleared my throat. "Were you going to stop by and say hi to Amanda while you were in town?" That was safe, common ground. Maybe they were back from Disneyland by now. "I think she's finally in remission."

"I meant to." He inched his way toward me again.

My list of fears came into my head. Did we really matter to him? "When you left after her fund-raiser, you said the experience had changed your life and inspired you. Were you just saying that?"

He murmured as he brushed my hair off my shoulder. "Visiting Amanda is not really what I want to talk about right now."

"Because it isn't a priority?"

"I ran out of time. It doesn't reflect my commitment to her." He shrugged it off.

"What is your commitment to her?"

"I wanted to help, that's all."

"What'd you do? Pay for her trip to Disneyland? Introduce her to the band?"

He sat up straight and stopped trying to engage me. His eyes were hard. "I just tried to help out. Can't you let it alone?"

I looked at him but didn't say anything. I was ashamed of myself for being so judgmental, but I was disappointed. I was under the impression that he really cared about her . . . and me. I had believed him, but when I'd first met him, he hadn't been completely forthcoming. Why would this time be any different? Was I just falling for his charm again, or should I give him the benefit of the doubt that he was being honest with me?

I stood, feeling upset. I wasn't sure if it was adrenaline from being combative or sorrow for hating myself for being so insecure. "I guess I want to know she matters to you."

"Is this really about her? Or you? Why won't you give me any credit? You're not the only one with good intentions. Just because sometimes I use my fame or my money instead of showing up and volunteering or organizing a fund-raiser doesn't make me a bad person. It doesn't make my intentions bad."

I opened my mouth to say something, but he cut me off.

"Have you even considered that everything I did, everything I've done, was for your benefit? To help your fund-raiser? Protect you from the paparazzi? Doesn't that make me a good person? But because I'm not your religion, I'm not good enough?"

I took a step back. His words stung. "I—" I really had no defense, no excuse.

There was a knock on the door. "Dude? Is someone in there?"

Liam opened the door to an even more drunken Nigel, who was stumbling around with a very skinny groupie.

"Go somewhere else, Nigel. I already want to hit you," he growled and shut the door. It sounded like they banged into a wall while retreating, but we could hear giggling and laughing on their side of the door. Then more people boarded the bus, and there was more laughter and what sounded like clinking glass.

Although I disliked Nigel, I was grateful for the interruption. It gave me a breather from the intensity of the situation and time to regroup. "Sounds like a party out there. Don't you want to join?"

His eyes were hard as he looked intently at me. "We still have a conversation to finish in here."

Suddenly there was loud banging, a crash, and yelling and screaming. "What is going on out there?" Liam stood and yanked open the door. He was immediately pulled from the doorway. "Outside now!" The flashlight shone in my eyes. "You too. Now!"

We were basically manhandled out of the bus and around to the backside, away from the fans, though the fans screamed and pushed toward us when they saw us exit but were held off by a wall of police officers.

"What is going on?" I whispered to Liam, my heart pounding wildly in my chest.

"I'm not quite sure," he said back.

"Quiet!"

We were lined up and instructed to spread our legs and have our hands above our heads. They proceeded to cuff everybody. Then the police went down the line, searching everybody.

"How old are you?" barked the policeman to the girl who had been with the Nigel.

"Fifteen," she mumbled.

"Have you been drinking?" he asked, although it was quite obvious by her unsteady stance that she had.

"Just a sip." She giggled. Why did she find it funny? She was being questioned by a police officer.

"Who gave it to you?"

"I had some with my friends before the concert. Then I had some with him on the bus." She pointed at Nigel. "But it was just a little bit."

I watched in horror as the officer took her and handed her off to another policeman. Granted, I hadn't been drinking, but was I going to get arrested just for being on the bus? Was I somehow guilty by association?

Liam was next. He was completely silent while being searched. I held my breath, hoping and praying they weren't going to find some reason to arrest him. The officer seemed satisfied with his search, having found nothing, then he moved on to me.

I was the last person.

He shined the flashlight right in my eyes. "What's your name?"

I squinted and turned my face away. "Camille Weston." My voice was shaky, I felt sick inside, and I was afraid I was going to wet my pants.

"How old are you, Camille?"

"Twenty-one."

"Were you doing any drinking on the bus tonight?"

"She wasn't doing anything," Liam said.

The cop pointed his flashlight at Liam. "I did not ask you."

Liam's chin lifted, and his lips became a thin, tight line.

I shook my head. "I don't drink."

"That's not what I asked you."

"No. I was not drinking on the bus tonight." Why was he so mean? I wasn't doing anything wrong.

"Drugs?"

"No."

"What were you doing on the bus?"

"Talking."

He raised an eyebrow and shone the flashlight right into my eyes. I squinted and looked away. "Talking?" he challenged.

"Yeah."

"Is this your purse?" He pointed to my purse in front of me on the ground, where I had been instructed to leave it.

"Yes."

"Got any drugs in there? Anything sharp in there?"

"No."

"Mind if I take a look?"

Without waiting for a response, he dumped it out on the ground. I found it humiliating and degrading at the same time. That was my personal stuff he was dumping out without any respect for what was inside. Receipts, change, my wallet, makeup, and a tampon lay scattered on the ground. My cheeks burned with anger and embarrassment.

He pulled on a pair of rubber gloves and searched through it. He looked through my wallet, checked my identification, and looked over at me, then rifled through the rest. When he didn't find anything, he motioned to the stuff. "You can pick it up now. But stay where you are. I'm not done asking questions."

He undid the cuffs, and I scrambled to gather it all, feeling tears burn in my eyes. The officer had been so mean, so gruff, treating me like I had committed a crime when I hadn't done anything. I rubbed my wrists.

Next, he undid Liam's cuffs. "You can go," the cop said.

"Simon," I heard Liam say. I looked at Liam to see that he was looking at the backstage door.

Simon stalked out to the bus. "What's going on here?" he demanded.

One cop stepped forward. "We had reports of illegal drugs and underage drinking going on in the bus."

"Do you have a warrant to search the bus?" Simon yelled.

The cop seemed unfazed. "No. We have probable cause."

"Which was?" Simon took a step closer to the cop. Although he was angry, he didn't intimidate the officer, who didn't back up.

"A witness."

Simon looked unconvinced. "A witness?"

"Sir, we need to ask you to step aside."

He stood his ground. "Why?"

"Because we are taking some of these people into custody."

I looked down the line. Nigel, the giggly girl with him, a roadie, another girl, and some guy I didn't know were all in cuffs.

"C'mon," the policeman said, and he lead the ones in cuffs toward separate police cars.

Simon was on the phone, yelling instructions to someone, and I took in the scene of chaos as I stood there shocked.

"Camille, I'm sorry," Liam said, looking apologetic. "I didn't know any of that was going to happen, or I wouldn't have taken you on the bus." He put his hand on my arm.

I shook it off. "Don't!" I said through gritted teeth. "What if Kaela had been with me?" I demanded, a tear rolling down my cheek. I swiped at it and motioned wildly at the police. "What . . . I can't . . ." I couldn't make sense of what had just happened, of what I wanted to say. "That was the scariest thing that has ever happened to me! I just . . . want to go home," I managed before turning from him. It took me a second to orient myself as to what direction I should be headed.

"Camille, wait." He hurried to grab my arm. "That's not how I live my life; you know that," he said in a low voice.

I shook his hand off me. My hands were shaking. "I wish I did, Liam, but I don't know that for sure. I don't know anything for sure," I said, wiping the tears off my cheeks. "I should go."

"It won't always be like this."

"Like what? Being hit on by a drunk Nigel or being manhandled by the police?"

"I'm sorry. Maybe inviting you here tonight was a mistake."

"You're right; it was a mistake. Every time I've just about convinced myself I'm over you, you show up again. And I convince myself to give it one more shot, and then I get beat down with reality—our worlds don't mesh."

"That's not what I meant. I never feel like seeing you or spending time with you is a mistake. But maybe having you spend time with me at a concert is a mistake."

"But that's your world, your life. How could you and I ever work?" I spread my arms wide.

"Aren't you at least willing to give it a go?"

"You fulfilled your obligation to my sister, so let's call it good." I shook my head. "I'm trying to be preemptive to save our feelings. It's the logical thing to do."

He scowled and gave an unexpected laugh. "Logical? Who are you? Spock?"

I gritted my teeth and swallowed back my retort.

He pointed his finger at me. "It was so much more than an obligation, and you know it."

My throat ached. Instead of saying anything, I put a hand on one side of his face and kissed the other side. "I wish . . ." I started. "I'm sorry, Liam." And then I walked away.

Liam didn't chase after me. I knew no matter how many reassurances he gave me, what happened tonight was a very real part of his life. My head was going to win out over my heart this time. Telling him goodbye was for the best. Or at least I kept telling myself that. Repeatedly.

Chapter Twenty-Six

ESTHER WOKE ME UP THE next morning. "You know Gear?"

I opened my eyes to see her face inches from mine. She was dressed up, and her hair was done. Why was she ready for church so early? "What?" I mumbled. "You woke me up to ask me that?" I thought we had an unspoken rule to never interrupt anyone's sleep unless it was absolutely necessary. "Absolutely necessary" being defined as "death" or "fire."

"No. I woke you up to tell you Riley's here. But you owe me an explanation about Gear."

I pulled my head off the pillow and glanced at the clock. It was 9:30 a.m. How could I have slept so long? Why was he here? The fireside wasn't until tonight. My arms were stiff. Why did I feel like I had been hit by a truck? "Um," I mumbled. "Can you tell him I'm still asleep?" I rubbed my eyes before resting my head back on my warm pillow.

"He seems upset. I think you should come talk to him."

I let out a groan as I sat up in bed. Wasn't he supposed to be at church or something?

I stumbled out to the living room in sweats and a new Gear T-shirt, still trying to wake up. "Riley." I blinked a few times and yawned. "What's going on?"

He was dressed in a suit and tie, pacing by our front door. I guess he was on his way to church. Couldn't he have just texted or called? "Can we talk?" His voice was so brusque I snapped to attention.

"Um, okay," I looked around and saw Esther in the kitchen. "Let's go out in the hall," I suggested. The hallway might give us more privacy and seemed as good a place as any.

Riley started talking as soon as I shut the door. "You were at the Gear concert last night."

"Yeah," I said weakly. As if the T-shirt I was wearing didn't give me away. I rubbed my eyes, not feeling completely awake.

"So that was you on the huge screen when they introduced a song *not* on the album called 'Can't Quite Quit This Girl.' Then showing pictures of a girl who looks just like you looking pretty cozy with William Jones. I thought it was too much of a coincidence."

"Yeah. That was me," I admitted. I rubbed my hands over my face, trying to feel more awake.

"Where did the pictures come from?"

"There was a photographer taking pictures, and I didn't realize it."

"Taking pictures when?" He widened his stance and folded his arms.

"Yesterday."

His eyes narrowed. "You said you weren't going."

"I wasn't going. Then my parents told my sister she could go but I had to go with her." I noticed a blood vessel bulging in his temple. If he was that worked up about our conversation now, he was not going to like what I had to say next. "We . . . know the lead singer," I managed.

His arms dropped to his side, and he stepped toward me. "You know William Jones?" He sounded a little incredulous. "Of course you must know him, or else you wouldn't have been in the pictures."

I started picking at my thumbnail. "Yeah." It was weird saying it out loud, admitting it. It made it that much more real. Knowing Liam and being a small part of last night wasn't just my own experience and something I could keep to myself anymore. Suddenly, I was sharing it with a lot more people. I pulled my hair away from my face and pushed it over my shoulder, then leaned against the wall. "I guess that's how I'd put it."

Riley ran his hand over his mouth, paced a couple of steps, and let out a small laugh. "You never mentioned him."

I shrugged. "There was no need. It was something from before. It's over now." It sounded so simple, and yet it was so complicated.

"Not for him," Riley muttered. "You don't write a song like that about someone you're over."

"He wrote that song awhile ago." Actually, I wasn't sure how long ago it was. But it didn't matter now. None of it mattered. I had to be through with Liam Jones. I shrugged a shoulder. "I didn't think it was a big deal."

Riley let out a couple huffs of air that sounded like he was trying to talk but no sound was coming out. "What part of knowing William Jones and having him write songs about you and having your picture up on the jumbotron is not a big deal?"

I didn't have an answer for him.

"Are you guys dating?"

I gave him a questioning look. "No." I shook my head to reiterate the point.

He cocked his head to the side, looking at me closely. "Are you sure?"

I spread my hands wide. "Yes, I'm sure. Besides, you and I, we're not really dating. And you were on a date yourself."

"That I committed to *before* I started dating you," he said pointedly.

"And that's how it is with Liam."

"Liam?"

"William, Liam. Same guy." I waved my hand in the air. I was tired and didn't feel like arguing.

"You have a nickname for him?" Riley's head dropped.

"Riley, he's from the past. I've moved on."

"Have you? Because, again, I don't think he has. Now I don't even think we should try dating. I can't compete with a guy like that. I just wish you had been straight up with me."

I opened my mouth to deny the accusation but stopped. "You know what? You're right." I had my list of "shoulds," all the things about a guy that made it so I should date him. Riley had many of those things on the list: he was of the same faith, he was a returned missionary, we had many of the same values, he came from a good family, he was a good guy. But the one thing missing was the click.

"You were dating him at the same time?"

"Not dating him but thinking about him. Because with him, things just clicked. And with you, I kept waiting for things to click and hoping they would click and wanting them to click because you're a nice guy."

He groaned and looked down. "Don't say it."

I held my palms up. "I tried, Riley. I really did. But the click just wasn't there."

"You're breaking up with me for the lead singer of Gear and using one of their songs as the reason?"

"I'm not breaking up with you for him."

"Wow, do I feel like a loser."

"I'm sorry." I tried to reach out to him, but he stepped aside. "That wasn't my intention."

Now I didn't have anyone. I broke up with Riley because of my feelings for Liam, and despite my feelings for Liam, I resisted all his advances. What was wrong with me?

Chapter Twenty-Seven

"WHAT IS WRONG WITH YOU?" Audrey asked. "You broke up with Riley?"

"Well, technically, we were never a couple." I sank into the couch and covered my face with a throw pillow. But yes, I had broken up with Riley.

"And you're dating William Jones and never told me?" Esther asked. "What is wrong with you?"

"I'm not dating Liam!" I said forcefully, but I kept the pillow on my face to avoid looking at them, and it muffled my words too much to really drive the point home.

"I can't believe he was in our apartment, sitting right there, and I didn't know who he was!" Audrey added.

"And that I wasn't here to meet him!" Esther moaned loudly. "My future husband, and my roommate doesn't tell me she knows him?"

I pulled the pillow off my face. "Girls, really. I don't need a guilt trip right now."

"Well, I'm going to guilt you. How could you keep a secret like that from us?" Esther put her hand to her chest and glared at me. "Especially when you know how much he means to me."

"That's just it. It's nice to dream about what could be, but in reality, it could never work. The sooner I accept that, the easier it would be." I covered my face again.

"You keep telling yourself that and you will never get married," Audrey warned.

This was turning into the argument about always finding something wrong with the guys I dated. "I'm twenty-one. I'm not in any danger of being an old maid." It sounded muffled from under the pillow.

"If you find something wrong with every guy, it *will* make you an old maid, one excuse at a time."

Under the pillow, I rolled my eyes. "That is the least of my worries right now."

"So how did you meet him in the first place?" Esther asked. She sat on the edge of the couch and tapped my feet to make me move them.

I shifted, although I didn't want her to get too comfy. "I ran into him in the middle of Nowhere, Utah. He needed a ride."

"You gave him a ride? How romantic," Esther exclaimed, her voice whimsical.

I dragged the pillow away from my head, knowing I would have to face them some time. "And he helped me do my fund-raiser by being the draw for the crowd."

Esther snapped her fingers. "I remember that. It was on the news. I was so mad I missed my chance to meet him."

I nodded. "It was my fund-raiser."

"I can't believe you've been living with me all these months and know how much I love him and still didn't tell me."

I pursed my lips, trying to figure out what to say and what to leave out. "It just didn't make sense. I really didn't think he'd actually do what he promised."

"What did he promise?" Audrey asked carefully.

I sighed. "He promised my sister and me tickets when Gear came through in concert."

"There has to be more, Camille. He wrote a song about you," Audrey said.

"He wrote a lot more than one," I said. I rested my head on the back of the couch and stared at the ceiling. What a mess this was becoming.

"What?" Esther screeched.

"Yeah," I said. "'Click,' 'Tattoo Kind of Girl'—" I counted them off on my fingers.

"That's you?" Audrey's eyes opened wide. "You're the tattoo girl?"

I dropped my head. "Yes."

"Again, how come you never mentioned this?" Esther said.

I looked back and forth between Audrey and Esther. How did I justify that? It was personal and hard to wrap up in a neat explanation. "It's kind of a farfetched story to begin with. My giving a rock star a ride and not knowing who he was—"

"You didn't know who he was?" Esther's head dropped, and her mouth hung open with shock.

I picked at my cuticles, fidgeting. "I had just gotten home from my mission. I had no idea who Gear was or that Liam was the singer."

"Why wasn't I the one who gave him the ride? I deserve that privilege, being such a big fan." Esther let her body go limp, and she slid off the couch like she was a pile of goo.

"Well, I was just trying to be a good Samaritan and didn't know who he was for a few days."

"And last night? What was that all about?" Audrey wondered.

"Yeah, you were on the big screen." Esther found some strength and was able to sit up against the couch.

"I had no idea they were going to do that. I had never even heard that song before." I held my hands out helplessly.

"It was so weird looking up and seeing you," Audrey said.

"Did you go backstage?" Esther was hungry for details.

"I did. And I almost got arrested."

"What?" Esther and Audrey said in unison.

"Yeah. There was a small raid on the tour bus." I pressed my hand against my temple. I could feel the beginnings of a headache coming on. I wasn't sure if it was from going to bed so late, getting up after only a few hours of sleep, or the curious but concerned interrogation by my roommates. Stress. Whatever the cause, I was sure it was going to become worse if my day continued going the way the morning had.

"What were you doing on the tour bus?" Audrey asked. There was a cautionary tone to her voice. I almost wondered if she thought something inappropriate was going on between us.

"I read about that on the internet. So it was true," Esther said.

I nodded. "It sure was. The drummer is kind of a jerk. He was on the bus with underaged girls, and they were drinking and partying, and apparently, there were some drugs involved somehow. It was scary."

"I can't believe our roommate knows Gear," Esther said to no one in particular.

"Not Gear. Just Liam," I clarified. "Last night was the first time I met the rest of the band. The whole night was completely unbelievable. Being backstage, being sung to, and almost being arrested. I'm exhausted."

"So Riley was there?" Audrey made a vague motion to the door.

"Yup. With another girl, I might add."

"And he saw your picture on the big screen," Audrey said.

I nodded. "He sure did. Thus, the reason for the early-morning visit."

"That's gotta be a little intimidating, being in competition with William Jones for the attention of a girl."

"Try being in competition with Twick Openshaw," I muttered.

Esther's eyes got huge. She snapped her fingers and pointed at me, her eyes blinking quickly as realization dawned on her. "You're the reason they broke up. Oh. My. Gosh. How have I not put this together?" Her hands went to her head in a mind-blown gesture.

"Well, no, I don't know if I was the reason. Twick does a pretty good job all by herself for giving Liam reasons to break up with her. They don't exactly get along."

"You know Twick too?" Audrey asked.

"No, not really. I mean, I met her—kinda—once and then saw her one other time."

"What's she like?" Esther questioned.

"She's not very nice to me."

"You have met all these famous people and not said one word of it to anyone. I don't even know what to say." Esther shook her head. She made no effort to hide her disappointment with me.

I took a deep, tired breath, then swallowed hard. "It's not . . . a big deal."

"Maybe to you it's not, but to me, it is." Esther's voice was sad. "I don't have the lead singer of my dream band writing songs about me."

I rested my head in my hand. "But he's a rock star, and I'm nobody, and I don't see how it will ever work out."

"Oh ye of little faith," Esther chided.

I peeked out from my hands. "I'll admit it, I have no faith that anything will ever come of it. We are too different."

"You're too different? He seems to write an awful lot of songs about you. There must be something there," Audrey said.

I let out a long, drawn-out sigh. "What is the point of discussing it any further? I understand your curiosity, but discussing it is not going to change the facts: Liam is a rock star. I am not. And unless that changes for either one of us, I don't see a way our relationship can work."

"The Lord works in mysterious ways," Esther said, completely solemn.

Her words irritated me a little. I was trying to make good choices in my life. And as attracted as I was to Liam, I just couldn't ever believe that choosing to have a romantic relationship with him was a good choice. "It probably would have to take an act of God to make it work."

"You never know what's going to happen," Audrey chimed in.

They were just being silly, deluded fangirls. I needed to accept the reality of the situation, accept my sadness, and move on.

Chapter Twenty-Eight

I ABANDONED MY ROOMMATES BY going to church with my parents at my home ward. Actually, I was trying to escape. Several people from the ward stopped by to ask me about Liam before church, and my phone blew up with texts. I wasn't sure if they knew about it from being at the concert or just from what was trending on social media, but whatever it was, I was getting a lot of unwanted attention. It seemed the nature of my relationship with Liam was traveling far and wide, and I was fielding many questions. It was kind of ironic, because as of that moment, there was no longer a relationship.

Unfortunately, I'd forgotten it was fast Sunday. My mom reminded me as soon as I took the first bite of an apple I picked up from the fruit basket in the kitchen.

Amanda's mom, Tessa, was the first one to stand up to bear her testimony in sacrament meeting. "Amanda is in remission. We would like to thank everyone who has helped us all along the way with love and support, meals, money. I have never felt as loved as I did when everyone was supporting us. I know the Lord sends us angels to help along the way, when we think we can no longer make it through another day. We had one of those angels who came to us as quite a surprise, and we thank the Lord every day for the help we received."

"Liam," I heard loud and clear. I looked around, wondering who had said it. My mom, dad, and Kaela were all looking straight ahead, listening to Tessa. It reminded me of the day I'd first met Liam when I'd heard "Stop." A shiver went down my spine, and a warmth spread through my chest. I missed much of the rest of the meeting, lost in thought. If her angel was indeed Liam, I had things to deal with.

I went up to Tessa afterward and gave her a hug.

"Thank you, Camille. I appreciate everything you have done for us, done for Amanda. You have been a huge help."

"I wish I could have done more." My measly little fund-raiser had been just that: measly without the help of Liam.

"But you did so much. You organized that fund-raiser. You introduced us to Liam, who has proved to be such an angel."

"Liam?" In my mind, I tried to make the connection to what I was missing. But it was his name that came into my head . Why was I doubting?

"He did so much for Amanda."

"You mean like paid for her trip to Disneyland?" Was there more to this than I knew?

"Well, yes, there was that too. But he paid for her treatment here. He paid for her to go to UCLA Medical Center for her bone-marrow transplant because we couldn't pay for it ourselves and we were about to lose the house and it was our only hope."

My mouth hung open. I stared at her, trying to process all that she had told me. "He paid for the bone-marrow transplant?" I finally managed.

"He not only paid for the transplant, but he also had his own marrow tested to see if it might be a match and donated blood to her bank, paid off our house, and paid for our trip to Disneyland. We didn't know he was going to do all this stuff; he just did it." Her eyes teared up. "She wouldn't be here with us today if she hadn't had those treatments."

He hadn't forgotten them at all. Instead, he had made them a part of his life. He cared enough to buy their family more time. And here I had been accusing him and judging him of far less.

I choked up, my eyes filling with tears. "I had no idea he did so much," I said. I wiped away the tears with the palm of my hand, mentally berating myself.

"He never told you?" She seemed surprised.

I shook my head. "No. We haven't been in touch all that much."

Tessa looked at me. "He's a sweetheart, Camille."

How did she know I needed to hear that?

"I've been wrong about him," I said more to myself than to anyone else.

"Sorry?" Tessa said.

"Nothing. Just having a realization."

She put her arm on my shoulder. "Well, just know how much we appreciate everything you did to help us."

* * *

I left church immediately after talking to Amanda's mom. I was overwhelmed, feeling conflicted and confused.

When my parents and sister returned home, I was just sitting down to have a chocolate mint brownie I had made to distract me from my nervous energy and jumbled thoughts.

"Yum," Kaela said, checking out the brownies and inhaling deeply. "Can I have one?"

"Of course," I said. "I certainly don't want to eat these all myself." I managed a weak smile.

My dad patted his belly and straightened. "A brownie would hit the spot."

I pulled out the chair beside me so he could sit. My mom grabbed some glasses and retrieved the gallon of milk from the fridge and joined us at the table.

"What's this?" Kaela asked. "Impromptu family meeting?" She sat slowly, as if she were hesitant.

"More like a let's-pray-and-break-our-fast-so-we-can-eat-brownies-and-solve-Camille's-conflicts," I suggested.

"Oh." Kaela nodded.

Once Dad offered the prayer, Mom looked at me. "What's up?"

"Liam," I said.

Kaela perked up. "Did he call you?"

I shook my head. "I just need to figure out what to do about him. I didn't know he had done all that stuff for Amanda's family. He's a better guy than I've been giving him credit for. I keep telling him this will never work out because I keep equating him with his lifestyle. I don't want it to be that way, but it's the truth."

"But I've been the good brother." Kaela snickered.

That stopped me. "What?" My parents and I looked over at her.

She froze midbite. "What?"

"What do you mean by 'but I've been the good brother'?"

Kaela chewed and swallowed and chased it down with some milk. "Okay, so in Sunday School today, our teacher showed us this really old church movie from like the nineties."

My dad made a big production of clearing his throat. "Hey, careful. I was alive in the nineties."

My sister waved her hand in the air. "All right, maybe not *really* old. Just old. Anyway, it was about the prodigal son. In the movie, the brother who hadn't messed up, who had always done the right thing was angry that everyone was making such a big deal about his brother's return and changing his life around. That's what he said: 'But I've been the good brother.' Then he realized maybe he needed to change since he was guilty of wrongdoing."

I held my breath for a moment.

"I remember that movie from my mission," my dad said.

"Yeah," Kaela continued. "The guy's wife said something like, just because he didn't do the same bad things, it didn't mean he didn't do different bad things."

"What? You've thoroughly confused me."

"The brother was sinning because he was judging his repentant brother," mom said. She leaned over and rubbed my arm. "So with Liam, maybe instead of seeing how he has to change, maybe you need to see how you need to change. Instead of all the things he isn't, look at all the things he is."

Kaela licked her fingers, interrupting the profundity of my mom's wisdom as it settled in. "It's on YouTube. You should watch it." She stood.

"What is?" I asked.

"That movie we watched at church."

I nodded. I had briefly forgotten about the movie because I was too busy thinking about Liam. And how profound my little sister was.

"So can this count as family home evening for the week?" Kaela looked hopeful and waited for my parents' response.

My mom and dad both laughed.

"Yes, I suppose it could," Mom answered.

"Good. Can I go upstairs now?" She scooted her chair away from the table. "And maybe take one more brownie with me?" She didn't wait for an answer as she snatched a brownie from the plate.

There was a moment of silence.

"But you like him, right?"

"I actually think I love him." I had come to realize he was, as he had once said about me, pretty much perfect.

Mom's eyes widened. "You do?"

"Yeah." I felt like I was just getting used to the admission myself.

"Remember Grandma was a convert?" Mom said.

I nodded.

"And Grandpa married her because he loved her and knew she was a good person."

"I know."

"She didn't get baptized right away."

"I just never thought I would ever consider dating someone who couldn't take me to the temple."

"Maybe he will be able to take you to the temple, but you just haven't given him that opportunity."

That definitely gave me reason to pause.

"Does he respect you?"

I thought back to the situations where I'd had to clarify my beliefs. Once he had understood I lived by them, then yes, he had respected them. I nodded.

"And if his fame bothers you, you'll have to be willing to learn how to deal with it like he has."

Maybe I had some things I needed to change. Or a lot of things to change. I definitely had some things I needed to change about how I handled my relationship with Liam.

* * *

I knew what I needed to do. Just thinking about it made my heart pound in my chest. I went to my bedroom and shut the door, hoping the quiet, contained space would still my nerves. I inhaled deeply. Learning of Liam's generosity at church had left a heavy weight on my heart. I'd had no idea how involved or instrumental he had been with Amanda. I had been unaware of his kindness, and something seemingly insignificant to his bank account had been extremely significant to Amanda's family. Talking with my family had given me some much-needed perspective about my relationship with him.

I took my sister's advice and pulled up YouTube. Watching that movie had driven a simple truth home to me. Liam was capable of change. Maybe he wasn't the bad boy I thought he was. Now I needed to change. This whole time I thought he needed to change when all along it was me.

I debated whether I should call him or procrastinate the day of my repentance a little longer. I didn't have to debate long, like less than a second, because I already knew the answer. I was wrong about him, and I should apologize. But I lacked the courage. Would he even want to talk to me? One thing I did know, acceptance or no acceptance, I still needed to apologize. Silently, I prayed before picking up my phone and calling his private number.

Was he home yet? I kind of hoped he wasn't and that he was on the bus and going through some area with no reception and not get my call. Although, this wasn't a conversation I wanted him to have in front of his bandmates. I really wanted to take the easy way out and text him, but sometimes the easy way was not the best way. This was something I needed to do in person—at least over-the-phone in person and not just a message or text. I wanted him to know I was sincere and have him hear my heartfelt apology. But that still didn't make it any easier.

I was relieved when his voice mail picked up. "It's Liam. You know what to do." At least that was better than nothing.

"Hey, Liam, it's Camille." I took a deep breath. "I owe you an apology. I was wrong. I was wrong about you, and I realize that now. I judged you, and I wasn't fair. I know I made it clear that I wasn't willing to give you a chance, but I found out I didn't know you like I thought I did, and I'm very proud of you. I'm proud of what you did, and I'm proud to be your friend. I don't know if you consider me your friend, and I understand if you don't, but I hope that someday we might be friends again."

"I'd like to be more than friends," Liam's voice suddenly said on the phone.

"Liam?" I asked, shocked and scared at the same time. "Have you been listening this whole time?" My heart thudded.

"You didn't give me a chance to speak." He sounded amused. "Besides, I wanted to hear what you had to say."

"I thought I got your voice mail."

"No, it's me."

"Where are you?" I blurted out.

"Home. Why? Where else would I be?"

I was momentarily confused and scrambled to regain my footing in the conversation. "I don't know. On the bus?" Did they hang out last night to get Nigel out of jail? Or did they just leave him in jail to figure his own way out of the situation?

"Well, no. Not at the moment. We got home last night."

"Okay, well, then," I stammered. Great. No time like the present. I fell back onto my bed, wishing it would swallow me like a sinkhole. "What do you think about what I said?"

"I'm curious, luv. What changed your mind?"

I cringed with the shame I felt over what I was going to say. "I talked to Amanda's mom at church today."

"Ah, Amanda's mum. And what did she tell you?"

I gulped. I felt like I was swallowing a large, dry piece of humble pie. "How much you've helped them. How you paid for Amanda's treatments, which made it possible for her to live."

"So now I'm a respectable bloke?"

I deserved that. "It made me realize I've been wrong. I haven't been fair to you. You're a better person than the one I was accusing you of being. And I'm sorry."

"It changed? Just like that?" His voice was heavy with disbelief.

"Everything you did for Amanda's family was more than a passing commitment, and you never told me."

"I didn't want you to think I was doing it for your sake."

"I've been so unfair to you, and I'm sorry. That's really all I can say—I'm sorry." I chewed on my lip.

"What do you want, Camille?"

Emotion was thick in my throat. "Your forgiveness. To know that you don't hate me for treating you so badly."

"I could never hate you. Meeting you has changed my life."

Tears sprang to my eyes. I felt better knowing he was willing to forgive me, but I was still ashamed of my behavior. "How? By being a lesson in patience?" I was choked up but managed a laugh.

"Well, that too." He laughed. "I've become a better person."

"Well, I've learned that I can completely misjudge a person." I sat up and swiped my free hand across my eyes.

"Uh-huh?"

"And I overreacted last night. I was shaken and angry—"

"I shouldn't have brought you into that whole thing. I'm sorry for that."

"And I'm sorry about all the mean things I said last night."

"So where do we go from here?" he asked, then waited. There was complete silence on his end.

The ball was in my court. Here was my chance, take it or leave it. I took a deep breath and exhaled slowly. "If the offer is still there, I would like to see you again."

"I would like that very much. Just say the word."

"But—"

"No buts this time."

"This is an important *but*," I said, happy to feel like our conversation was no longer strained.

"Buts ruin things."

"I have to clarify; the standards are still there."

"I can respect that," he said quietly.

Liam was a good person, and maybe we could have a relationship without his lifestyle getting in the way. Maybe now that I was more open to the idea, there was a chance it would or could work.

Chapter Twenty-Nine

I WAS POURING A BOWL of cereal, humming to myself. It was a crazy time, this push right before the end of the semester, and I had so many other things I should have been concentrating on. But instead, I was daydreaming. It had been almost a week since I had sorted things out with Liam, and I had talked to him on the phone every night. Tonight, we were going to make plans for him to come visit for Thanksgiving.

I went to the fridge to get the milk when Esther gasped. "What? Oh my gosh." Her voice sort of faded out.

"What?" I turned to where she was sitting at the kitchen table, staring at her phone. "What's the matter?"

She was white as a sheet. "Tread Ingleston is dead."

"Tread? As in Tread from Gear?" I asked, dread growing in my chest as a wave of fear washed over me.

"Yeah. Oh. My. Gosh," she whispered.

"What happened?" My heart was racing, my first thought being, *Is Liam okay?* I leaned over her shoulder to look at her screen. Had there been an accident? Was it just Tread, or was it others in the band also?

She scrolled down. "They found him this morning in his home. Possibly an accidental overdose."

"Liam," I said to no one in particular.

"What?" My roommate looked up at me, confused.

But I didn't take the time to explain. Instead, I searched for my phone, dumping out my purse, then my backpack, then moving to my bed and ripping all the blankets off. It fell out among the tangle of sheets.

I shook the phone after I punched in the number like that could make it connect any faster. As the phone started to ring, I swallowed hard, not knowing what I was going to say.

238 SALLY JOHNSON

"Camille?" Liam answered, his voice so hoarse I barely recognized it.

"Liam? Are you okay?" My eyes teared up in relief. I was so glad he answered.

I think he started crying. "Did you hear about Tread?"

"I did," I said, my voice gentle. "That's why I'm calling."

"Cybil called a couple hours ago from the hospital. I can't believe he's gone. I can't believe it."

"It's true?" I managed, my throat tight. It hurt to swallow.

"Yeah," he said. I could hardly hear him.

I didn't know what to say, so I said the first thing that came to my mind. "What can I do?"

It was quiet on his end, but I could hear him breathing. "Liam?" I waited. "I need to know you're okay."

When he finally answered, he seemed disconnected. "I don't know what to do. I don't know what to do."

Right then, I knew. "Liam, I can go there. Do you want me to?"

"Yes," he said.

"I'm coming," I said, sliding off my bed, rooting around my closet for a carry-on bag. "I'll grab a flight and get there as soon as I can. I'll call when I land."

"Hurry," he said and hung up.

I flung clothes into my bag, grabbing some from the top of my dirty laundry pile. I went online and found a Southwest flight to LAX leaving in just over three hours. I charged it on my emergency credit card, figuring this qualified as an emergency. I checked in online and hurried out the door. If I drove quickly, I could make the flight.

I sped the whole way to the airport, praying I wouldn't get pulled over. I had only a carry-on, so I went straight to security. Once I was at the gate, I finally caught my breath. I called my mom and left a message on her phone, called work, and emailed my teachers to tell them I had an emergency and I had to go out of town unexpectedly. Hopefully that would get me through the next couple of days, and I would have to get caught up on Monday. If I lost my job, I'd just have to find another. Liam was more important. I also reserved a rental car and googled directions to Liam's house. It was all fast-paced and frenzied, but I needed to make sure Liam was okay. And the only way I could do that was to see to him myself.

My mom called just as I was boarding the plane. "What's wrong, Camille? I got your message. What happened to Liam?"

"Not Liam. His bandmate, Tread, was found dead. They don't know why. I called Liam, and he sounds a mess. I am getting on a plane right now to go down there. I don't think he should be alone."

"Camille, be careful. Call me when you get there."

"Okay, I will. Thanks, Mom," I said and hung up. I sat back, closed my eyes, and prayed as I took off into the unknown.

* * *

I didn't know what I was expecting, but when Lupe let me in the house and led me to Liam's bedroom, I realized I was not prepared. All the blinds were closed, and he was sitting on the floor, leaning against the frame of his bed. His legs were pulled up tight to his chest.

"Liam?" I asked, worried about disturbing the silence. I walked carefully as my eyes adjusted to the dark. Was he asleep? I accidentally kicked an empty glass bottle left on the floor, and it careened across the wood floor, eventually coming to a stop. But not before jarring Liam to attention.

"You're here," he said, reaching out to take my hand. I sat next to him, and he hugged me. He smelled of alcohol.

We sat there so long we eventually fell asleep. I woke up stiff and achy, prompted by Liam's waking.

"I thought I was dreaming," Liam said, looking at me intently, then looking around the room. The daylight peeked through some gaps in the blinds, making me squint. "You really came." He rubbed his eyes and pressed his hand against his temple. I could see several empty bottles strewn about the floor. I bet he had a massive hangover.

Liam looked terrible. His eyes were swollen and red-rimmed. His face was scruffy, his hair flat against his head. He was wearing baggy sweatpants and a stretched-out T-shirt. How long had he been sitting there before I'd come?

"Could you find me some water and something to take for this headache?" he asked, cradling his head in his hand.

I stood and stretched, then looked around. "Where should I look?"

"My bathroom mirror should have some pills, and there's a fridge over by the TV." He motioned with his hand slightly in the direction of the huge TV. I located the minifridge and grabbed a chilled bottle of water on my way to the bathroom. There was a bottle of Advil behind the mirror that I brought out with me.

"Here," I handed him the water, then opened the bottle and shook out two pills.

Once he swallowed, he leaned his head back. "Thank you."

There was silence for a minute before I went ahead and started the dreaded conversation. "I'm so sorry, Liam. It's such terrible news. Do you think . . . ?" I drifted off, unable to come out and say what I was thinking.

"He killed himself? I don't know." He shook his head, wiping his eyes with the palm of his hand. "I want to believe he didn't, that he wouldn't, but he hasn't been in a good place lately. We've been fighting with Nigel as a band, telling him he needs to go into rehab or quit the band. Cybil and Tread have been fighting because Tread was partying a lot on this tour. She thought he needed to get professional help. It's been bad."

I felt young and inexperienced and didn't have the eloquence to say the right thing. I listened to him and let him talk, and when he was eventually all talked out, I encouraged him to take a shower and promised not to go far.

Once he had showered and changed his clothes, he lay on his bed and fell asleep.

I wandered out of his bedroom, squinting at the daylight. I felt like I'd stepped out of an alternate universe.

"Mister William?" Lupe came up to me, looking worried.

"Asleep." I nodded. I went to the kitchen, searching for something to eat. I was starving. The last thing I'd eaten was the pretzels on the plane. And I needed to call my parents to let them know what was going on.

Gwen was there. She didn't bat an eye as I walked in, as if it was perfectly normal that I was there. I helped myself to his fridge, having a small moment of happiness when I found Uncrustables in the freezer. It brought back memories of my summer visit.

Liam stayed in bed the rest of Friday and all day Saturday, sleeping or just staring out the window. He wouldn't eat anything, no matter what I suggested. By Sunday I was worried. I had a flight out that night, but I couldn't leave Liam in that condition. He had staff and people around, and it was their job to take care of him, but that was just it: it was their job.

I called my mother in tears. My stomach was tied up in knots. I had to leave, but I didn't think it was a good idea. "Mom?"

"Honey, how is Liam?"

I swallowed hard. "That's why I'm calling," I said, trying to clear my throat. "I'm really worried," I managed.

"Oh, Camille." My mom had this way of being so comforting just through her tone of voice.

"I don't know what to do. He's not eating; he stays in bed all day. I'm really worried." I didn't feel it was the time to share my thoughts on death just yet. Although I believed in life after death, unless he believed the same, I didn't know how much of a comfort it would be to him. But I hoped once the emotion of the situation calmed down, he'd be open to talking about it.

"He's upset, honey. His best friend just died. You can't change that. You just need to be there for him."

"But I can't be here for him. I have school and other commitments, which aren't necessarily more important than him, but I can't neglect them either. But I can't leave him like this."

"What if you bring him home with you?" my mom suggested. "He can stay with us."

I was relieved. "You don't mind?"

"No, of course not. Why would I mind? In fact, I would feel a whole lot better having him here with us than being there alone."

I cried even harder. Like my mother, I would feel much better knowing Liam was with us than wondering if he was okay in LA. "I'll ask him and let you know what he says."

When I passed the idea by Liam, he didn't argue or protest. "I would like that." When I threw some stuff in a bag for him, I noticed he still had the dad jeans I had bought. I really wished he'd make a joke about not packing them, but he didn't say much at all as I packed and as we made our way to the airport.

When we got to my parents' house, my mom took him into the guest room and put him to bed.

* * *

"Camille, where have you been?" Audrey demanded when I let myself into the apartment. I was expecting nothing less than my roommates being all twenty questions.

"I had to . . . I went . . ." I felt like I was moving in zombie mode and couldn't quite shake off the heaviness I carried. I felt much better having him under my mother's watchful eye but still worried about how he would deal with Tread's death.

"We have been texting you and calling you, and we didn't know where you were. Did you go to see Liam?" she guessed.

"I did. I'm sorry I didn't text you back. Liam was in really bad shape." I hadn't spent much time paying attention to my phone while I'd been with him.

"He's really upset?" Audrey asked.

"Yeah. It was like he was comatose. How's Esther taking the news?"

"She's pretty upset, but it's not like you, where you know them personally."

"Just Liam. I only met Tread once."

"Do they have any more information about how he died?"

I frowned. "No. They have to perform an autopsy, of course." I didn't think anyone was going to be surprised if the cause came back as an accidental drug overdose. Of course, I hoped it wouldn't be, but I figured it would be better than an intentional one.

"Do you think it was accidental?"

I chewed on my already-raw bottom lip. "I don't know, and I really can't guess. I hate to speculate. You just never know what really went on."

"Are you going back to see Liam?" Audrey asked.

"As soon as I can. I feel better being around him. It makes me feel like I'm actually doing something." I didn't want to tell her everything, especially that Liam was one town over, sleeping in our guest room. I didn't want to cause a mass hysteria at my parents' front door or another visit from the paparazzi. "If I hear anything, I'll tell you guys."

"Esther would appreciate it."

This was the worst possible time to have something like this happen. I mean, I knew death was never convenient. I wanted to be at my parents' house, spending time with Liam, instead of finishing semester projects and papers and studying for finals. I forced myself to concentrate just a little bit longer at school to get my work done before I rushed home.

My mom had somehow worked her magic when I went to my parents' house that night to check on Liam. He still looked like he had just rolled out of bed, but at least he was *out* of bed. And best of all, he was at the table, picking at the food on his plate. At his house, he had refused to eat.

I rushed over to him and hugged him. Hard. "How are you?"

"You do know you have an amazing mother?" he responded.

I put my arm around her and gave her a squeeze. "Yeah, she's pretty great."

"Well, I hope you appreciate her."

"Of course I do." I smiled, then tried to discreetly pull her aside. "What did you do?"

My mother shrugged. "Nothing, really. We talked, I gave him a shoulder to cry on, and I reassured him. I'm sure it's nothing different from what you did."

"But he's much better."

"The shock has worn off. Reality will set in, and it'll get hard again. Then there will be the funeral and the finality will become real. He's going to have a rough time in the next couple of weeks. I offered to let him stay as long as he would like."

"As long as he doesn't go out in public, we should all be safe." I made a halfhearted joke.

"Then we'll keep him inside at all costs." My mom gave me a wink and went back to the kitchen. She didn't seem to have any problem having a rock star stay in her house.

* * *

I returned home as often as possible, which was not as often or for as long as I would have liked. My roommates made comments about how it felt like I didn't live there anymore. Thanksgiving arrived, and although my family and I had many things to be thankful for, having Liam with us made it a little more subdued. But despite his sadness, he was still very much a part of our family time. We did all the traditions, things I had missed on my mission, particularly Thanksgiving dinner and setting up the Christmas tree the next day.

The long weekend was too short, and soon enough, I was back at school.

Liam was in a funk when I arrived home after school on Monday. Going home as soon as I was done with classes had become the new norm, and today was no different. The door to the guest room was ajar just enough for me to see him lying on the bed, staring out the window. I knocked and waited until I heard a quiet "Come in" before I entered.

He was lying on top of the bed on his side, staring off at nothing. I consoled myself with the thought that at least he wasn't in the near-comatose state he'd been in at his house.

"What's wrong?" I asked him.

"I just got word on the funeral arrangements."

"You okay?" I sat down beside him.

He sat up, his hands on either side of him gripping the edge of the bed. "It just makes it so real, so final."

"Liam, I am sorry. I've never had anyone close to me die before. I had a great-grandma die, but she was like a hundred years old, and she was ready, and I was eight. It really didn't affect me. But Tread . . ." This whole dealing-with-death situation was so unfamiliar to me. I didn't know how to navigate it. I had taught people on my mission about our beliefs on death, but this was the first time I had ever dealt with it firsthand. Seeing Liam in pain made my heart hurt.

"I miss him." He pinched the bridge of his nose, then rubbed his forehead.

My heart swelled. I reached out and pulled him into my shoulder, patting the back of his head. "Of course you do. He was like a brother to you."

"He was my family."

"I know." I continued to play with his hair because I didn't know what else to do.

"I keep thinking back to something the missionaries said."

"What's that?"

"That death isn't the end."

"Yeah."

He looked up at me. "Is that true? Do you really believe that?"

"I do. I really do believe that."

"So Tread isn't dead forever?"

I shook my head adamantly. "No, his spirit is up in heaven."

"And when I die and I'm up in heaven, I'll see him again."

"Yes, absolutely. But that doesn't mean you're going to do anything, right?"

A confused expression crossed his face. "Do anything? Like suicide? Absolutely not. I'm sad, not suicidal. I miss him and just need to know that someday I'll see him again."

"I truly believe you will."

"How do you know that?"

"I feel it. I feel that it makes sense and that it's right."

"Somehow, that makes me feel better."

"It at least provides comfort," I said softly. "But it doesn't mean you're not going to hurt."

"I need to call Cybil but don't want to."

"To find out the results of the autopsy?" The full toxicology report was still looming. Although the preliminary autopsy concluded drug overdose, I knew once the full details were known, it was going to be hard on Liam.

"Yes. No. That and funeral arrangements."

"Is Cybil taking care of that?" I wondered if I should offer to call her. But maybe Liam felt an obligation to be the one to do it since he was Tread's best friend. I couldn't say that I felt completely comfortable doing it since I really didn't know Cybil. But if it would ease Liam's burden, I would do it.

"Cybil is doing it, but our manager is helping."

"I'm sure she must be overwhelmed," I said.

He looked away. "I feel like I can't handle her grief and mine."

"What can I do? Do you want me to call Cybil and check on her?" Again, I was willing. I worried it would be awkward, but this was one of those situations where I had to think a little bigger than my own personal hesitations.

"You would do that?"

"Of course," I said. "Whatever you need."

Liam looked back to me and met my gaze. "I've got a favor to ask of you," he said.

"Okay." I waited.

"You've agreed even before you know what it is?"

I nodded. "What is it?"

He put his hand on mine and squeezed. "I wanted to ask you to come to the funeral with me."

I let out a relieved breath. That request wasn't so hard. "Of course. You don't even need to ask. I was planning on it."

"But that means we are going public, and that changes everything."

"Going public?"

"Announcing that we are a couple. Even if we weren't a couple, we'd be made out to be a couple." He splayed his hands.

I laughed. "I thought we kind of did that already on the big screen at the concert."

"I mean the *public* public. It'll be a lot more intense. The world, the fans, the internet, and worst of all, the paparazzi."

"So basically the paparazzi?"

"Yes."

"They'll be there?"

"They're like germs—they're everywhere." Liam managed a small laugh after his joke.

"Okay."

"It's your call though. I understand if you don't want to."

I put my hand on his knee. "Liam, what I don't want is for you to have to go alone."

"Thank you."

Chapter Thirty

THE FIRST THING I SAW as we approached the church where the funeral was being held was the tall, blonde, ever-beautiful Twick Openshaw talking to the cameras. She was dressed all in black, with a huge black hat complete with netting and what looked like ostrich feathers, and big, black Audrey-Hepburn-style sunglasses. She was carrying a dainty black clutch and a white handkerchief.

"Twick's here," I announced. I didn't know if I should be alarmed or worried. Would she cause a scene about me being there with Liam? Suddenly, I started having second thoughts about agreeing to accompany Liam to the funeral. It was so much easier being supportive in the comfort of my own home. But returning to California with Liam for the funeral was what he needed, so that was what I was doing.

Liam let out a sigh. "I'm surprised, and at the same time, not surprised. I don't know if I can deal with her drama today." He had been concerned enough about drama that he had hired a car to take us to the funeral and had his security team accompany us.

"Maybe she won't cause any drama," I said, hopeful.

"Maybe if she weren't Twick Openshaw. But she is, and drama is what she does best. It's like her middle name. So don't be surprised if she starts with me or you or Cybil or anyone who happens to be round her." Liam grabbed my hand and headed to the entrance of the church. I ducked my head, hoping to avoid Twick, the paparazzi, and the whole media circus going on.

I could hear Twick talking as we approached. "Tread was like a brother to me. We spent so much time together. It was always the four of us: him, Cybil, William, and me. I'm devastated."

Liam snorted. I hoped he didn't confront her about what she was saying. We didn't need a scene before the funeral even started. Emotions were running high, and it would be too easy for things to get out of hand.

"William! William! William!" The paparazzi swarmed once they caught sight of him. I was surprised it had taken so long.

He put his hand to his temple, shading his eyes, and hurried me into the church. "Twick is unbelievable!" he said, sounding disgusted. "She makes it all about her. She can't think about anyone else but herself."

I rubbed my thumb over his hand, hoping to soothe him. "I'm sorry."

We were ushered to the front, where there were rows marked "Reserved." I assumed Cybil and the rest of the band would be sitting with us. "Is Tread's family coming?"

"They are. Then they're going to take the body back to London and have a private family ceremony there before they bury him."

I wondered if Liam would return to London for that. I assumed Cybil would. "Poor Cybil. I'm sure she wishes he could be buried closer."

"Tread loved Cybil, but she can't deny his family that right."

As the chapel began to fill, I could hear Liam's breathing become quicker and quicker. He kept folding and unfolding a piece of paper. I put my hand on his to calm the fidgeting. "Are you okay?"

Liam gave a bitter laugh. "I sing in front of hundreds of thousands of people, and it doesn't bother me a bit. Ask me to get up in front of a room full of people to say a proper goodbye to my best friend and I'm panicking."

"This is understandably harder."

His voice became quiet. "I can't cry in front of all these people. I don't know if I am going to get through the eulogy." Liam smoothed the crumpled piece of paper slowly and with great care. "Would you read it over to make sure it sounds okay?" He passed the paper to me.

"You don't have to say a lot of words; just a few significant thoughts will mean more than pages of stuff."

Tread was my best friend. But at the same time, he was more than that. He was my brother, and I loved him like a brother. For years, he was the only family I had. I'm going to miss him a lot. There is a place in my heart that will always be empty. I look forward to when I see you again, my brother.

"Do you think I need to say more?" Liam looked anxious.

"This is all you need to say. You loved him. That's enough."

There were a lot of tearful goodbyes. Liam made it through his short talk but not without stopping and pinching his eyes to fight the tears several times. I found myself holding my breath the whole time he was standing up at the microphone, praying he would get through it. I brushed some tears from my own eyes, not able to stop hurting for Liam.

Cybil's tearful goodbye was difficult to get through. By the time she finished expressing her love and appreciation for Tread, I didn't think there was a dry eye in the overflowing church.

Tread's parents each stood and expressed the pain of losing a child so young and how a parent should never have to bury a child.

The priest said a few closing remarks, which I hoped provided some comfort to those attending. I found his words a bit hollow. I felt sad that he could only tell Tread's loved ones he was now with the Lord but wasn't able to reassure them that they'd all be together eventually in heaven.

The four remaining members of Gear, Tread's dad, and his brother were the pallbearers. It broke my heart seeing Liam carrying the coffin, tears flowing freely. He was biting his bottom lip and avoiding eye contact with everyone, even me. I filtered out of the church along with my row, taking in the solemn sadness all around and the intense grieving. Cries were stifled, tears were wiped away, handkerchiefs clutched. I stepped back, feeling I didn't belong to the immediate circle of family and friends watching as the casket was placed in the hearse. I hadn't been to many funerals in my life, but the few I had attended, two while on my mission, had been very different. The funerals for the members of the Church had been celebrations of life, with a hope for the future.

The bodyguards led the way back to the safety of the car. I was able to breathe easier once the doors were shut and I was out of the crowd. I observed what was going on outside while I waited for Liam to join me.

When Liam got in the car, I waited before speaking. I wasn't sure where his emotions were at the moment and was afraid to say the wrong thing.

"There's a reception after. Lunch, open house, I am not sure what. I can't say I much feel like going," he told me, staring straight ahead.

"Then don't," I said.

"I feel like I should. Out of respect. It's the proper thing to do."

"Is it at a restaurant or a bar or someone's house?"

"It's not really proper to go to a bar to celebrate his life when he was trying to be sober. Especially since alcohol was the thing that finally killed him anyway. I can't celebrate his demons."

"Then hopefully it's at someone's house."

"Cybil and Tread's. It just makes it that much harder to be someplace where everything there reminds me of him."

"Let's be quick, then."

* * *

People were already milling about when we arrived. The driveway gates were crowded by media and the paparazzi. Their being there felt very disrespectful.

Liam declined when I suggested we get something to eat. "I just want to talk to Cybil, and maybe then it will be okay to go."

Nigel was with Cybil when we finally located her. I found it odd to see him with her. It looked wrong. It should have been Tread, not Nigel the Instigator.

Nigel handed Cybil something. "Thought you might want this."

"His phone? How did you have that?"

Nigel looked down and shuffled his feet. "He left it."

"He left it? At your flat? Is that where he went?"

"He did come over—"

"Why would he ever go to your flat?" Cybil cut him off. "No one likes you." Her voice rose higher and higher.

"I called him. I owed him money, and he said he'd stop by to pick it up."

"And the rest was history?" Cybil spat out.

"Cybil," Liam went over to her and put his arm around her shoulders. "Come away. You don't need to do this right now." He gently tried to pull her from the situation.

She shook off his grasp. "Don't!" A tear rolled down her face. "I need to know what happened. I need to know why he did it. Why he chose to drink that night." She stepped closer to Nigel. "I need to know why he did it!" she screamed.

Nigel's face seemed to crumble. "I loved him too! I didn't know. I didn't know. I thought he knew what he was doing. I thought he could handle it." Nigel looked tragic.

Cybil's eyes narrowed. "It *was* you. It's all your fault . . ."

"Cybil, don't." Liam took her arm.

Nigel took a step back. "He could make choices without you being round, telling him what to do all the time."

"Fabulous choice he made, huh, Nigel? Fabulous choice!" She was getting hysterical. A girlfriend, or possibly a sister, came over and led her away. She collapsed not far off on a sofa, sobbing.

"Liam." Nigel reached out.

Liam shook his head slowly, holding his arms up, out of Nigel's reach. "Sorry, man, I just can't . . . I can't even look at you right now. What were you thinking? You knew better." Liam turned and started walking away.

He made one last plea. "Wait."

Liam's expression was a mixture of sadness and hatred. The muscle in his jaw twitched. His hand balled into a fist before unclenching. "I don't care if I ever see you again. As far as I'm concerned, without Tread, there is no Gear. Especially one with you in it." He didn't wait for a response. He took off walking, holding my hand so tightly it hurt.

"Liam," I said, shaking my hand from his grasp.

"You're not going to say calm down, are you? Because I'm not sure I can."

"No, actually, I was afraid my fingers were going to fall off from lack of circulation."

He looked at my hand, and a small smile appeared momentarily. "Sorry. I didn't realize . . ."

"I know." I pulled him into a hug, listening to his breathing as it slowed.

"William?" came a voice from behind us. We separated, coming face-to-face with Twick.

"Twick," Liam said with no emotion. He let out a deep breath.

She was staring at me with an accusatory look, so I said, "Hello, Twick."

It must have surprised her, because she flicked her eyes over to Liam, then smirked. "You're still around?"

I could feel Liam tense up beside me. "If you're here to cause—" he started in a low voice.

"Liam, I am not here to cause anything or start anything," she cut in. "I just want to tell you I am so sorry. I am truly sorry." She leaned in, hugging Liam. It was very heartfelt, even for Twick.

She stepped back, scowling at me, then turned her attention back to Liam and rubbed his arm. "Take care of yourself," she said. Twick's ostrich feather had brushed up against my nose, and I almost sneezed as she walked off.

Liam looked around, taking in the crowd. "I need to go. I can't stay here any longer."

Chapter Thirty-One

LIAM WAS QUIET AS WE walked to the car. Not that I was surprised or shocked. I sort of expected it to be that way. But he was more withdrawn than he had been before the funeral.

"You okay?" I asked, taking his hand.

"No."

"What are you thinking about? Tread?"

"I'm thinking about going home. And I can't. I can't go back to my empty house where nothing means anything and I don't care about anything. I don't want to be alone. There's cold comfort in stuff."

"I'll go back with you."

"I know you would, but you can't stay forever, can you?"

"Right. But I can stay today." I rubbed his arm.

"I can't stay there. I don't want to stay there."

"It's totally understandable."

He stopped and turned to me. "I have a favor to ask." His expression was so intense.

I laughed. "It never stops at just one with you," I joked, thankful for the chance to lighten the mood. Even if it was just a little bit, it was welcome.

"Can I come home with you?"

"I've heard that before." My memory flashed back to the first day I met him. "Didn't my mom already say you can?"

"It's not your mom who matters here, luv. I need to know you want me there."

There was no hesitation, no second thought, no doubt. "Of course I want you there. I would always want you there," I said.

"Let's go home, then."

* * *

"Liam heard about the autopsy and toxicology report today," Mom said by way of greeting as I came in through the garage. It had been two weeks since the funeral, and Liam had some good days and some bad days. Today seemed to be the latter.

"He texted me that he just heard," I said. "It wasn't great news, was it?" The coroner's office said it would take four to six weeks to get the full report back. Every day I wondered if that day was the day and how knowing the details would affect Liam.

"No. Cause of death: CDI—Combined Drug Intoxication."

I hung my keys up and slung my purse on the back of a kitchen chair. "So it was more than just one thing?" I asked. It didn't come as a surprise, but I think we were all hoping for something different, something better.

"Yes. Sleeping pills, cold medicine, and alcohol, combined with lithium and valium. Liam's pretty upset." Mom motioned toward the hall with her head.

I nodded and walked slowly to the guest room. Liam was lying on the bed. It was a familiar sight, although since about a week after the funeral, it had been less frequent.

"Hey," I said, sitting on the other side of the bed. "I heard the bad news."

"Yeah."

I took his hand. "Want to talk about it?"

He continued staring at the wall, with his back toward me. "What's to talk about?" he said in a dull voice. "He drank way too much, took double the sleeping pills he should have, chased it down with more pills, and now he's gone. I can't imagine what Cybil must be feeling right now. She worked so hard to keep him sober."

"She's probably feeling exactly how you're feeling right now."

He rolled over and put his head on my lap. "He didn't have to die."

I stroked his hair. "At least he wasn't trying to die. It's not much comfort, but it's some."

"I can't say it makes me feel better."

I kissed his head. "I know. I guess it will just take time." Not for the first time since Tread's death, I didn't know what to do for Liam. "How can I help, Liam?"

He thought for a minute and then shrugged.

"Maybe you need a change of pace."

"I can't say I'm up for it, luv."

I considered it for a moment. It wasn't exactly ideal timing, with it being so close to the end of the semester, and I didn't have anything planned. "What about a quick bite to eat?"

"I'm not exactly hungry either."

"This is what we're going to do. Let's plan a date for this Friday night. Finals end Wednesday, I won't be stressed. Let's go do something. We can go out to dinner, go to Temple Square and see the lights, do some Christmas shopping—whatever you like. Plan?"

"Plan," he agreed. His reluctance didn't escape me.

"Or we could keep it local and give it an hour tonight and go to downtown Provo. We could check out a club and find some music to listen to."

"I don't know. I can't say I feel like doing that."

"C'mon," I coaxed, pulling on his arm. "You can put on your old disguise. You already have the beard. Pull on the hat, pull on the sunglasses, pull on the hoodie, and find you some old-man jeans. I bet no one will recognize you."

The mention of the old-man jeans brought a small smile to his face.

"I realize I don't know exactly what you're going through. But I do think it'd do you some good to get out of the house and get some fresh air. What do you say?"

Liam grunted but didn't move.

I let go of his arm and put my hand on my hip. "I won't even hold you to an hour. Let's just drive there and see what's happening."

He finally caved. "All right, but no promises."

We went to the same restaurant we ate at the night of the outdoor concert last summer. Although it was inside this time, there was a live band. I figured it was dark in there and he was already in his recognition-avoiding clothes. Maybe hearing some music would make him feel better. Or worse. I hoped for better.

I didn't realize until we were there that it was possibly inspiration to go to that club. Liam came alive. His eyes brightened, he leaned forward in his seat, he tapped his foot, and his head bobbed with the music. For a short time, I had a glimpse of the old Liam, and it was a relief to know he was still in there.

At the end of the set, Liam stood. "I'll be right back."

I didn't know where he was going, and I watched as he approached a guy by the edge of the stage. They exchanged a few words, and then the man led him backstage.

When Liam returned about fifteen minutes later, looking even more like the old Liam. The light was in his eyes, he had purpose in his stride, and he seemed to have renewed energy.

"What was that all about?" I asked.

"I had a great idea while listening to those guys."

A feeling of overwhelming happiness flowed through me. "Oh yeah? What was it?"

He motioned toward the stage. "I like those guys. I see a lot of potential in their music. I went up there and told them I wanted to work with them."

I blinked back my surprise. I hadn't seen this amount of enthusiasm from Liam in weeks. "Okay. I bet you just made their"—I grasped for the appropriate word—"lives."

Liam chuckled.

It was so nice to see him happy. It made me happy that he was happy.

"And so?" I asked.

He stood. "I told them I'll be in touch." He motioned to the door with his head. "What do you say we call it a night? I don't want to overstay my welcome here. Spending too much time in one place might bring the fangirls running." He winked at me and threw his arm over my shoulder.

"Yeah," I said dryly. "I don't want to have to fight the fangirls for you."

He made a *pfff* sound. "You don't need to worry about them."

I cocked my head and looked at him. "I don't? Why not?"

"Because you're the only girl I need."

And this time I believed him.

* * *

I had promised my roommates, and Liam had consented, that they could come meet Liam once we were through with finals. Because I finished my last test before them, I went to my parents' house ahead of time. I was hoping Liam was having a good day because I never knew from one day to the next what it was going to be. And I didn't want Audrey and Esther over if it was a bad day.

He was showered, dressed, and watching TV with my mom when I walked in.

"Hey, honey, how are you?" Mom asked.

I sank into the sofa beside Liam, exhausted but relieved. "Finals are over. Christmas break is official. I'm excited. What have you two been up to?" I rested my hand on his knee.

Liam sat up and angled himself so he was facing me, sitting almost on the edge of the couch. "We've been doing some shopping," he said, visibly excited.

His excitement made me hesitant. "Oh . . . yeah?"

He looked back and forth between me and my mother. "Yeah."

"What kind of shopping?" I asked slowly.

"Yeah, what kind of shopping?" Kaela asked as she walked through the room into the kitchen.

Mom let out a tiny squeal.

"The kind of shopping that reflects what's been on my mind lately."

My pulse quickened, knowing it must be some sort of big announcement but not knowing exactly what.

Kaela returned with a package of Oreos, already opened, a cookie in her hand. "What's been on your mind lately, Liam? Inquiring minds, like mine, *really* want to know." She winked at him and then turned to me. "Oreo?"

Her insinuation didn't get past me.

"I love you like a sister, Kaela, but this gift is for Camille."

Kaela made a big show of pouting as her shoulders drooped. Liam didn't give into her play at emotional manipulation. He turned to me. "Care to go for a drive, luv?"

The intrigue was killing me. "Yes, let's."

Liam gave me vague directions to Provo Canyon and then programmed an address into my GPS for me to follow.

"You went shopping in Heber?" I was fishing for clues, wondering what he was up to. "Or did you go farther to Park City?" Park City seemed more his kind of shopping, but I had learned, especially in the last few months, that nothing about my preconceived notions of Liam were to be relied on. Time and time again, he proved to be so much more, so much better than my assumptions of him. "Or are we going skiing?" Maybe he bought a ski pass for the two of us.

"Nothing like that. But I will be staying with you for Christmas and thought it was the perfect timing."

"I'm still not understanding." If it was some sort of Christmas gift, I couldn't imagine what it could be. Which led me to more concerns that if it was extravagant, where did that leave me in the gift exchange? What did one buy for the man who seemed to have everything?

"Let's just wait and see."

I followed the GPS into Sundance and finally pulled into a secluded driveway. Way back when I first met him, I probably would've made a snarky comment about him attacking me, but now I knew better.

Although it wasn't a snowy day, it was still a cold, crisp day with snow all around because of how high up in the mountains we were. He took my gloved hand and led me up the driveway until we came to a clearing. There was a large cabin with tall glass windows running along the east side of the house. I could imagine how amazing it would be to watch the sun rise with that kind of view.

"I realize I can't live in your guest room forever. So I've been thinking about the future, trying to come up with a plan I'm keen on."

"Okay."

"I put an offer on this house today."

He was moving here?

At least he wasn't showing me something he'd bought for me. It let me off the hook for coming up with some amazing Christmas gift for him. "Tell me about it," I said, taking in the massive structure before me.

"It's five thousand square feet, private. I can build a recording studio in there. Although I'd like to take a break from the music scene, and there is no Gear without Tread, I'm thinking eventually I'd like to try my hand at producing. Once I'm ready, of course. But for now, I'd like to be a bit closer to you, and I thought this just might be the place. The views are amazing, and I really think it will be a great place to clear my head."

"Would you be living there year-round?"

"I was thinking it'd be a nice summer cabin but also perfect in the winter for skiing."

"I bet it must be beautiful inside. How soon would things be happening?"

"If everything goes well, it'll close in the next four to six weeks."

"What will you be doing in the meantime?"

"I think I'll head back to California after Christmas."

I had to admit I was a little crestfallen.

"But before I sign the paperwork, I want to make sure you're good with this."

"Of course I'm good with it." How would I not be good with it? Sundance was closer than LA.

He took both of my hands in his and faced me, his eyes meeting mine. "I know I need to keep meeting with the missionaries and get baptized in the temple before we could even think about getting serious."

I gave a slight chuckle at his confusion, but I wasn't going to correct his innocent misunderstanding about baptism. "Almost but not really. Yes, I would hope you would keep meeting with the missionaries, but I would only want you to get baptized when you have your own testimony." And in Mormon terms of relationships, we were as good as serious. In my terms of the relationship, we were as good as serious as well.

"You don't mind if I hang about for a bit? Maybe, like, forever? Being around you . . . I haven't found any other person who makes me feel the way I do when I'm round you. Being with you is the only time I have ever felt at home."

Despite it being freezing outside, it was getting pretty toasty inside my winter coat as Liam's words warmed my heart.

"I have one more thing."

"Uh-oh, there's more?" As with the last few times he'd asked, I was thankful that it was now a joke between us. "You know you can ask anything."

"Let's make this official. You and me." His eyes sparkled. His lips were slightly parted as if he was waiting to kiss me.

I took advantage of the moment and threw myself into his arms and kissed him. "Yes. I think it will work out."

He stopped and made a show of what I had just said. "Wait. Did I hear you properly?"

My heart pitter-patted double-time. "Yes."

About the Author

Sally Johnson grew up in Massachusetts and received her bachelor's degree in English from Brigham Young University. She and her husband, Steve, have four children and currently live in Las Vegas (but sadly not in a hotel). She has always had an overactive imagination and has finally found a way to put it to good use.